HARVEST
Moon

Center Point
Large Print

Also by Denise Hunter and available from
Center Point Large Print:

Sweetbriar Cottage
Blue Ridge Sunrise
Honeysuckle Dreams
On Magnolia Lane
Summer by the Tides
Lake Season
Carolina Breeze
Autumn Skies
Bookshop by the Sea
Riverbend Gap
Mulberry Hollow

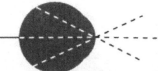

HARVEST

Moon

A RIVERBEND ROMANCE

Denise Hunter

CENTER POINT LARGE PRINT
THORNDIKE, MAINE

ISBN: 978-1-63808-481-5

The Library of Congress has cataloged this record
under Library of Congress Control Number: 2022940809

One

It was not the sort of day when bad things happened. Eighty degrees. September breeze. Sky expanding, wide and blue, above a canopy of trees. Air thick with the fresh smell of pine and the loamy scent of earth. It was a perfect Saturday.

Gavin Robinson had reached the summit of Roan Mountain just after noon, enjoyed a sandwich, and was now trekking back down the trail. After months of setting up Robinson Construction, LLC, he finally had a free weekend. The late-afternoon sun had fallen behind the mountain hours ago, and evening was quickly approaching when his phone vibrated in his pocket. It was a miracle he had a signal this far from civilization.

He fished the phone from his pants pocket. His brother's face lit up the screen. Gavin stopped midpath and swiped at the sweat trickling down his temple. "Hey, Coop. What's up?"

"Where are you?"

Cooper's tense tone put him on instant alert. Had their stepdad suffered another heart attack? "Heading back from Roan. What's wrong?"

"We got a call from Dispatch earlier. Someone

reported a small plane going down. A subsequent call reported a definite crash south of Marshall. Gavin . . . it was a yellow plane."

His breath stuttered in his lungs. Mike, his best friend, was a proud owner of a Cessna Skyhawk—the only yellow plane kept at the local airfield. Had Mike taken Mallory and Emma for a joyride today? He pictured the young family as he'd seen them last weekend, working their apple orchard, Mallory steadying a ladder for Mike while two-year-old Emma toddled barefoot around the grassy property chasing butterflies.

Please, God, let them be all right.

"He's a good pilot," Gavin said.

"I know."

Gavin heard what Cooper hadn't said: a dozen things could go wrong, despite a pilot's expertise.

"Took me a while to reach you—I'm almost to the crash site now. The medevac arrived minutes ago. I gotta go. I'll have details soon, and I'll call you back when I know more."

Gavin disconnected, turned on his ringer, and set off at a fast pace. He was glad his brother was sheriff—he'd get answers quickly. But Gavin had a gut feeling the downed plane was Mike's. Only one question remained: Had the crash been survivable?

He refused to believe otherwise. Instead, he

made a plan as he rushed down the trail. He would head straight to Mission Hospital, where they would transport the Claytons. He would use Mike's phone to access his parents' number and call them with the bad news. Mallory's mom was her only living relative, but they were estranged.

Emma. He remembered the girl's blonde curls bouncing as she'd played hide-and-seek with him in the orchard last weekend. *" 'Ere are you, Gabin?"*

His traitorous mind conjured up the image of her tiny body sprawled in the plane seat: unconscious, pale skinned, blood oozing from her gashed head.

No. He couldn't think about that. He had to remain positive.

A while later he glanced at his watch. It seemed as if hours had passed since the call. He'd made good progress though. He was almost to his car now, but the hospital was more than an hour away. He said yet another prayer for the Claytons, his throat thickening as he begged God for mercy.

His phone pealed, breaking through the sounds of nature. Cooper. He accepted the call. "Tell me you have good news."

A beat of silence. "I'm sorry, man. Mike didn't make it."

Gavin's chest squeezed tight. His feet faltered to a stop. He struggled to draw a breath.

Mike.

"Mallory's being airlifted to Mission. But it doesn't look good, Gavin. They think she has life-threatening injuries."

God, please . . . no. He could hardly process it all. His best friend . . . gone, just like that. And Mallory barely hanging on. "Emma?"

"She wasn't on board. Thank God for that. The plane is . . . It's a wonder Mallory survived the crash, buddy."

Gavin pressed a palm into his eye socket, thinking of Emma. Her father was dead, and her mother's life was hanging in the balance. He swallowed against the lump in his throat and forced his feet into motion. "I'm almost to my car. I'll head to the hospital now."

"Wait. Do you know where Emma is?"

"I assume she's home with a sitter—they use the Bauer girl sometimes."

"It's going on seven o'clock, and the sitter will need to go home. Why don't you head over there instead and relieve her?"

"Mallory shouldn't be alone at the hospital. Mike wouldn't want that."

"She'd want Laurel with her, wouldn't she?"

Laurel. Of course. And his ex-wife would want to be with her best friend. "Not thinking straight. I'll call her. I still have her number—

unless she's changed it." Or blocked him. He hadn't talked to her since their divorce finalized three years ago.

"Sure, but maybe it would be better if I called her."

"Right. Yeah." They hadn't exactly parted on friendly terms. Regret and despair over the last year of their marriage threatened to swamp him. But he resolutely shoved it down. "Just a second and I'll get you the number."

He put the call on Speaker, found Laurel's number, and relayed it to Cooper. Somehow he'd never been able to bring himself to delete it.

"I'll call her right now," Coop said.

"Thanks, Brother. Will you let me know you got hold of her?"

"Sure thing."

Gavin disconnected and thought of Laurel, soon to be receiving this horrific news. His high school sweetheart had been friends with Mallory since elementary school. When Mallory had started dating Mike in their early twenties, he and Gavin hit it off. They became couple-friends. Even after Laurel and Gavin had moved to Asheville, they remained close, meeting up for supper and taking weekend hiking trips together.

The divorce had put a stop to all that, of course. But somehow, against all odds, Mike and Mallory maintained their friendships with each of them. And if the weight of it strained their own relationship, Gavin had never noticed. *They are special people.*

He broke through the woods and came out at the gravel parking lot where he'd left his Denali. He retrieved his keys from his pocket and made a beeline toward it.

He'd just thought of his friends in present tense—but Mike was gone.

Gone.

It didn't feel real. And yet, right this minute Gavin was heading to their house to stay with a little girl who'd just lost her father.

Laurel Robinson was this close to having the position of her dreams—and the best thing about it? Her friends and coworkers were rooting for her.

Ruby, the fiftysomething supervisor of The Dining Room, raised her glass. "To the next Walled Garden Manager."

"And let's not forget, the youngest one in the history of the Biltmore Estate," Kayla said.

Ruby winked at Laurel, her blue eyeshadow shimmering under the pendant light. "Also the first woman."

"Hear, hear."

Unable to suppress a modest smile, Laurel clinked her glass with theirs, the sounds fading into the cacophony at the Charlotte Street Grill &

Pub. "Lovely toast, ladies, but let's not get ahead of ourselves."

Ruby waved away her caution. "Please. Eddington's retiring the first of the year. Who else would they choose but his assistant?"

"They could always bring someone else in."

Kayla tucked her short brown hair behind her ear. "Why would they do that when they have the best horticulturist in North Carolina right on the grounds?"

"Someone who's spent her entire career busting her butt there."

"I appreciate your enthusiasm. I do. But I'm trying to manage my expectations." She glanced at Kayla. "You remember what happened at the stables."

"They only went outside because Ludwig didn't recommend Russo," Kayla said. "Of course they hired from the outside. But Eddington loves you. He's groomed you for the position and recommended you for it."

Laurel hoped and prayed they were right. Manager of the Walled Garden tended to be a long-term position—Richard Eddington had held it for more than twenty years. This might be her only chance. And where else would she go? The Biltmore Garden was a horticulturist's dream. She'd been enamored with the gorgeous estate since she first toured it in seventh grade. Scoring a job here shortly after she'd graduated with her master's had been a huge win. She'd slowly moved up the ranks, and now another dream was about to come true—and with it, the kind of pay that would buy her the security she craved.

The server came and took their orders, and as she scurried away, Laurel's phone buzzed in her pocket. Probably her mom. She tended to call on Saturday evenings to make sure Laurel wasn't working.

She checked the screen and frowned at the unfamiliar number, which bore her hometown area code.

Her stomach sank like a lead weight. Had something happened to her mom? Her stepdad?

"I have to get this," she announced, then headed toward the door for the relative quiet outside. She answered the call as she went.

"Laurel?" a man said.

It was so noisy in here. "Yes?"

He said something else, but someone's boisterous laughter drowned out the words.

Laurel pushed through the door, navigating around a group on their way in. As the door swung shut the noise level dropped considerably. "I'm sorry, I couldn't hear you. Go ahead."

"This is Cooper Robinson. I'm afraid I have some bad news. There was a plane crash near Marshall early this evening, and I was called to the scene. It was Mike Clayton's plane, Laurel. I'm sorry to tell you that he didn't make it."

A sudden coldness hit her core. Traveled outward, all the way to her fingertips, numbing them. Mike was dead? No, that couldn't be right.

"Mallory was with him. She survived the crash, but she's in real bad shape. She's being airlifted to Mission right now."

Laurel opened her mouth but nothing came out. Was this even real? How could this be happening? She'd just FaceTimed with Mike and Mallory on Wednesday. They were happy. They were *alive.* "What about Emma?"

"She wasn't on the plane. She's home with a sitter."

Mike is gone. Kind, generous Mike. He'd been so patient, lending his wife to Laurel for days at a time when she went through the divorce. Mallory propped her up and kept her going through the worst of it. And even though Gavin was Mike's best friend, even though he surely sided with him, Mike never seemed to hold a grudge against her.

"Laurel? Did you hear me?"

She tried to clear the boulder from her throat. "I—yes. I should—Mission Hospital you said?"

"She's probably arriving about now. They said something about internal injuries and—I'm gonna be honest, Laurel—it didn't sound good."

Dear God in heaven. "I'll head there now. Thank you for calling, Cooper."

She disconnected, unable to process that she'd

just spoken with her former brother-in-law for the first time in three years. Much less the fact that Mike was dead and Mallory was in critical condition.

She pocketed her phone and headed back inside for her purse. She had to get it together. Because her dear friend would need her now more than ever before.

What seemed like an interminable time later, Laurel parked her Civic in the ER lot and rushed toward the doors. Mallory would be fine. She had to be. She had a beautiful little girl to raise.

Was she conscious? Did she know Mike was gone? Would Laurel have to tell her? *Please, no.* The two of them . . . they were what marriage was meant to be.

The double doors split open, emitting a rush of cold air. Laurel headed to the front desk where a middle-aged woman greeted her with a placid smile. "Can I help you?"

"I'm here for Mallory Clayton? She was just airlifted in from a plane crash."

"Are you a relative, dear?"

"I'm her best friend. She doesn't have any family except her husband, but he died in the crash." Her voice broke on the last word. "I'm her emergency contact."

The woman's face softened. "Let me see what

I can find. Just a moment." She clacked on her keyboard while Laurel waited.

Seconds passed. Minutes. What was taking so long?

Finally the woman looked up from the screen. "She's in surgery right now."

Still alive. That was good news. "Can you tell me what's wrong with her?"

"Someone in that department might be able to help you. I can give you directions to the waiting room. A doctor will come out when it's over and give you an update."

"Thank you."

Laurel hadn't been able to get any information. She waited in the room with several others, too anxious to sit. She paced from one window to the next, pouring her heart out in prayer. For the umpteenth time she glanced at the utilitarian clock. Almost an hour had passed since her arrival.

She had no idea if the surgery would take one hour or ten. Why wasn't someone here to answer questions? Didn't they know being uninformed, feeling so helpless, was torture?

A tall woman in blue scrubs entered the waiting room, and all eyes swung her way. "Mallory Clayton?"

Laurel rushed over on quaking legs. She didn't like the solemn expression on the doctor's face. "Is she okay?"

"Hello, I'm Dr. Mertz. Are you a relative?"

"I'm Laurel Robinson. Mallory doesn't have any relatives. I'm her best friend and emergency contact. Is she all right?"

Dr. Mertz's eyes turned down at the corners in sync with her lips. "Why don't we go somewhere more private, Laurel."

Two

Gavin couldn't help himself. He went upstairs and down the hall to the nursery. He peeked into the room and found Emma sound asleep in her crib. It was just now getting dark outside, but Mike had installed blackout shades, and the room was lit only by a princess night-light.

His heart clutched at the sight of the child's sweet face. The slight rise and fall of her chest. She was fine. She would be fine. When Mallory woke from surgery, he'd take Emma to see her. It would be good for both of them. They were in this together now. Gavin would be there for them in whatever way they needed. He'd help keep Mike's memory alive for Emma, telling her stories about her dad—he had plenty of them.

Feeling somewhat reassured, he pulled the door closed and headed back downstairs. He'd arrived just after Chloe put Emma down. They'd seen each other before in passing, so the babysitter knew he was a close friend of the family. He'd simply told her the Claytons had been delayed and that he'd been sent to relieve her. He didn't want word of Mike's death spreading prematurely. Only when she stood awkwardly at the door did he realize she hadn't been paid.

Apologizing, he grabbed cash from his wallet and handed it over.

Gavin's body felt heavy as he took the steps. He was profoundly glad Emma was already down for the night. He needed time to process what had happened before he answered the toddler's questions about where her parents were. She was very verbal for a two-and-a-half-year-old, already stringing three and four words together. But what was he supposed to tell her? How could she possibly understand that her dad was gone forever when Gavin could barely process it?

He'd called his mom on the drive here and broken the news to her. She was informing the rest of the Robinson family. Praying for Mallory's recovery. Shock had faded enough that he'd shed his first tears as they talked.

Gavin blinked. How long had he been standing at the bottom of the stairs, staring into the living room? Toys cluttered the space. He moved automatically toward the pile of magnetic blocks and began cleaning up. Sunny, the Claytons' golden retriever, watched from her favorite spot near the hearth, head tilted, ears perked.

He was almost finished putting away the toys when his phone vibrated in his pocket. Cooper. He tapped the Accept button. "Hey, any news yet?"

"I just talked to someone at the hospital." A beat of silence ushered in the bad news. "I'm sorry. Mallory didn't make it."

A chill swept through him. His legs gave way, and he sank onto the sofa. It couldn't be true. Mike and Mallory just . . . gone? He would never see them again? His gaze swung upstairs, where Emma slept unaware that her world had just fallen apart.

"She didn't make it through surgery," Coop said. "The internal injuries were too extensive."

"This can't be happening."

"I know, Gav. It's awful."

Poor Laurel. She'd never been one to open up easily. Had always kept her circle small. So small Gavin wasn't sure there would be anyone left in it now.

"Is Emma all right?" Cooper asked.

"She's sleeping." He palmed the top of his head. "What am I going to tell her, Coop? What's even going to happen to her?"

"Do you know if they had a plan? A will?"

"I—yes. I think Mike mentioned something about that a long time ago." Gavin was executor, if he remembered right. But surely that was more than two years ago—before Emma was born.

"Is there a relative who might . . . ?"

"Mike's parents. They're older—they had him in their forties. But maybe they'd step in. Mallory's got a mother, but they haven't seen each other in years."

"Siblings?"

"They're both only children." *Were* only

19

children. Gavin scrubbed a hand over his face.

"Well . . . let's hope they named a guardian then."

"What'll happen to Emma if they didn't?" Dread swelled inside during the silence that followed.

"Child Protective Services will have to be notified in the morning—and Emma will become a ward of the state."

"*What?* No. That can't happen. They would never want that." Who would?

"I'm afraid that's the way it works when there's no plan. Family will have the chance to petition for guardianship. But if no one steps forward, she'll be put in foster care until a permanent home can be found. Hopefully it won't come to that. Why don't you go through their files and see what you can find?"

"I'm on it." After Gavin disconnected the call, he headed to the home office, his mind whirling. What if they hadn't named a guardian? What if Emma ended up with strangers? Shuffled through foster care the way Cooper's wife, Katie, had been? No. Surely Mike and Mallory had a plan in place. He just had to find the papers.

Fifteen minutes later he was forced to acknowledge that organization had not been Mallory's or Mike's strong suit. The file drawers weren't full of files at all, but rather stacks of papers, ranging from car titles to business contracts. How had they run Harvest Moon Orchards this way?

He sorted through the first drawer and was just getting started on the second when a knock sounded at the door. Probably Mom or Cooper. Thank God they hadn't rung the bell and woken Emma. He hurried to the door and swept it open.

He froze at the sight of his ex-wife, standing beneath the glow of the porch light.

Her brown eyes widened. She blinked. "Gavin."

She must've missed his Denali parked in the shadows at the side of the house. Grief was etched in the planes of her face, evident in the sag of her slender shoulders.

His heart squeezed tight. Her best friend had just died. And so had his. He reached out automatically, wanting to offer comfort.

Her shoulders stiffened and she crossed her arms. Full self-protection mode. It was a stance he'd seen a lot that last year.

He hadn't thought his mood could sink any lower tonight, but he'd been wrong. He dropped his arms to his sides. It was a sign of just how bad things were between them that the tragic loss of their best friends hadn't removed a single stone from that high wall of hers. Three years and a mountain of regret crouched between them.

"Where's Emma?" she asked.

"She's fine. She's sleeping. What are you doing here?" He hadn't meant to sound combative.

Her eyes flashed. "Same thing you are—making sure Emma's okay."

"She's fine for now."

Sunny brushed past him and crashed into Laurel's side, tail wagging.

Laurel's long brown hair tumbled over her shoulders as she bent down to rub the dog's ears affectionately. Laurel had come to Riverbend Gap occasionally since the divorce. Her mom lived here, after all. But she always managed to avoid Gavin. No accident, he was certain.

She straightened, meeting his gaze. "Mallory . . . she didn't make it." There were no tears. But she was probably in shock. Also, she didn't cry easily.

Although Gavin had managed to reduce her to a pile of tears in the middle of their king-size bed. He gave the memory a firm shove. "I know."

"What's going to happen to Emma?"

"Do you know if they had a plan in place?"

Something flickered in her eyes before they dropped to the dog. "I'm, uh, not sure."

He didn't know what that look was about, but he didn't have the emotional reserves to decipher his ex-wife right now. "Maybe you can help me search. I just started going through their files. It's a bit of a mess."

"All right."

He opened the door wider and let her inside. Seeing her so wrecked, he couldn't quite bring himself to tell her what Cooper had said about CPS. Hopefully they'd find the papers and everything would sort itself out.

Three

As Laurel brushed past Gavin, a whiff of pine and woodsmoke took her back years, to happier days. But the sight of the stairs, leading to Emma's room, yanked her right back to the present. Her gaze caught on the family photos stairstepping up the wall: Mallory and Mike on their wedding day, Mike holding a newborn Emma, Mallory tending the apple orchard that first year, her face glowing with hope and pride. She'd been such a good mother, despite the terrible example she'd had—maybe even because of it.

Laurel's throat thickened with tears she would not allow to fall. At the hospital, shock had held her in its grips. On the forty-five-minute drive from Asheville, worry for Emma had taken precedence. But now, with her ex-husband nearby, was definitely not the time to give in to grief. She mentally locked her heart in a safe and threw away the key.

Sunny sidled up to Laurel, and she ruffled the dog's ears. Poor girl. She wouldn't understand what was happening either.

Laurel headed for the office, Sunny on her heels. She would find that will. It was true that Mallory hadn't been the most organized woman, but she'd loved her daughter with a fierce love. She would've made sure there was a plan in place, though Laurel didn't know what that would be. Mallory was estranged from her mother and only had an aunt left now. Mike's parents? Laurel had never met them as they lived in Colorado, but she seemed to recall that they were older. Surely not too old to raise a child though.

"Do you know if they had a safe?" Gavin entered the room behind her.

The low timbre of his voice, so familiar, so missed, sent a shiver down her arms. "Not that I know of. If we can't find anything, we can check with Darius Walker—that's the attorney they used." Her heart gave a hard squeeze at her use of past tense.

"I've already searched through the file cabinet." Gavin knelt by an open desk drawer, its contents piled on the wood floor beside it. "The attorney's office won't be open tomorrow."

"No." Which meant what? That they might be on their own until Monday? She would stay with Emma until then. If she had to miss a day or two of work, it wouldn't be the end of the world.

Her gaze flittered to the bookshelves with their row of cabinets beneath. "I'll start there. Was Emma awake when you got here?"

"No, thank God."

In the morning the child would awaken, expecting her parents to be home. Mallory and

Mike had gone away overnight only once since she'd been born. Laurel had stayed with Emma while they'd celebrated their seventh anniversary. Mike traveled a bit with his job, but Mallory and Emma had been attached at the hip.

When Mallory had worked the orchard, Emma had been right there with her. At first in a stroller or worn in a sling around Mallory's body. Then in a playpen situated in the shade. This year had been more challenging as Emma was more independent and wanted her freedom.

How could Emma understand her parents were never coming home? Laurel couldn't even think about that right now.

The first cabinet turned up Mallory's old memorabilia from high school. There would be photos of her and Laurel in those boxes, and she didn't dare let herself go there tonight. She moved on to the second cabinet and found everything from old greeting cards to office supplies.

All the while Laurel sorted, she was aware of Gavin, only a few feet behind her. Her heart hadn't settled into a normal rhythm since Cooper's phone call, and the sight of Gavin at the door had done nothing to rectify that.

He looked so tired, those bright-blue eyes of his gone dull, the corners tugging down in that tragic way of his. His black hair had grown, falling in choppy waves around his face. He wore several days' bristle on his jaw. He'd always been meticulously clean-shaven, had kept a standing monthly barber appointment. She used to tease him about it because his fastidious grooming habits were ironic when he was really such a man's man.

But that was then. She didn't know him any-more.

Her mind skipped to the night ahead. Was he planning to stay here? The thought played out in her head—the one spare bedroom. He'd insist she take it. He'd sleep on the sofa. No, that wouldn't do at all. She'd send him home. She could stay with Emma. She would be the one to somehow answer the child's questions.

She made a note to google that later. *How to tell a toddler her parents are dead.* Her skin broke out in a cold sweat. She squeezed her eyes shut.

"Found it." Gavin's voice jerked her from her thoughts.

She dropped a stack of yearbooks and scooted closer, edging around Sunny, who wasn't budging. "A will?"

"Yeah."

Thank God they'd planned for Emma.

Gavin sat back on his haunches and flipped through the pages of a stapled document. She couldn't read from this distance and wasn't about to get closer.

He stopped and locked in on a page, reading.

Laurel could hardly stand the tension. "What does it say?"

Gavin skimmed through the legalese, searching for the information he needed. As a contractor he'd dealt with his share of documents. But wills were a little different, he was finding. And with Laurel hovering over his shoulder, her familiar scent wafting around him, he was having trouble focusing.

Finally he came across the section he'd been searching for. His eyes zeroed in on the words. *We, Mike and Mallory Clayton, residing at blah, blah, blah.* He skipped down to the lines below.

To the names.

A flush of adrenaline tingled through his body. His breath quickened. His heart tried to keep pace. How could this be? Why would they—?

"Did you find it? What does it say?"

His eyes swept across the names once more, just to be certain he wasn't seeing things. Nope. There they were, just as he'd read the first time. He closed the document as if doing so could make him unsee it.

"What? What's wrong? Didn't they name a guardian? Just tell me, for heaven's sake."

He cleared his throat. "No, they did."

"Thank God. Who is it? Not her mom."

Gavin looked up at her. "No."

"Then who?" she fairly snapped. "Who did they name?"

He swallowed hard. No way to soften this blow. "Us," he said finally. "They named *us* as Emma's guardians."

Four

It had not been love at first sight for Laurel and Gavin.

She'd noticed him right away when she entered biology class her first day of sophomore year at Riverbend Gap High School. She'd attended Hopewell Academy till now, but she'd seen Gavin before, knew of him. Everyone knew of the well-liked Robinson family.

Gavin was sitting at the desk closest to the teacher. He had short dark hair, and a pale-blue T-shirt clung to his lean, muscular frame. She was surprised he wasn't sitting in the back where the other jocks would no doubt gather.

He sized her up as she took the empty desk beside him. She'd been something of a science and math whiz at her academically rigorous school. She'd hated the idea of transferring—a public school wouldn't be as impressive on her college applications. But at least the classes would be easier—she planned to rise straight to the top. And not having to be the poor kid on scholarship was a bonus.

"You're new here," he said a full three minutes later.

"That's right."

The teacher started class, leaving no room for further conversation. He went over class rules, then instructed them to open their textbooks to chapter 1.

"Who can tell me what the basic unit of life is?" Mr. Morton asked.

Her school had covered this in seventh grade. She slipped her hand up, and the teacher called on her. "Cells," she said.

"Very good. Every living thing is made of these basic building blocks. Some organisms are made up of only one cell. Can anyone give me an example?"

Someone whispered behind her. A phone buzzed. Gavin raised his hand.

The teacher smiled at him. "Mr. Robinson."

"Protozoa."

"Excellent."

Laurel raised her hand. "Bacteria," she said when called upon.

"Very good."

Later that day Laurel found that Gavin also shared her algebra class. This time she took care to keep her distance.

On the second day of biology, she entered the room to find him at the same desk. As much as she wanted to sit elsewhere, there was no way she would allow him to think he intimidated her.

And so it went.

Week after week they competed to answer the

teachers' questions correctly. When Laurel got back a test, she made sure to leave it on her desk where he'd see the 97 or 98 percent written in red ink. Sometimes when she glanced over at his test, his grade was a point or two higher. Sometimes a point or two lower.

So he wasn't a stereotypical jock. But she knew she was the better student and intended to prove it daily. Whereas everyone in the entire school seemed to love him, he had nothing for Laurel but dark scowls and tolerant looks. That was okay. She wasn't here to make friends.

If sometimes, when she was studying at home, the memory of that scowl made something flutter in her chest, she wasn't about to admit it even to herself. If she took an extra-deep whiff when he passed her desk, it was only because she loved the smell of pine. And if she sometimes stole glances at him across the cafeteria, it was only because she was perplexed about what the other students saw in him.

Sophomore year passed slowly, and she made a couple of good friends to sit with at lunch. Her best friend, Mallory, still attended the private school Laurel's mom could no longer afford since the voucher program got canceled.

"He is so hot," Bethany said one day when she caught Laurel staring at Gavin across the cafeteria.

"Who?"

Bethany elbowed her. "Right. Like you don't gawk at him every single day."

"I do not!"

"Okay, whatever, don't tell me about your secret crush on the cutest boy in our class. Whatever."

"I don't have a crush on him. He's not even cute."

Bethany snorted.

Okay, maybe she'd gone overboard with that one. But her strange fascination with him was embarrassing. He could have any girl he wanted—and he sure didn't want her. "I'm keeping an eye on my competition, that's all. I intend to be valedictorian of this class, and he's ahead of me by 0.7 points. Plus, he's kind of a jerk."

Bethany's hazel eyes widened. "Gavin? He's the nicest jock in the whole school. He let me borrow his pencil in ninth grade. And he said hi once when we ran into his family at the Trailhead."

Laurel rolled her eyes. "Whatever." Maybe it was just Laurel he disliked. Was it because she'd come along and given him a little competition? Oh well. She glanced at him again to find him giving her another flinty look.

"Smokin'. Hot." Bethany propped her chin on her hand and heaved a breathy sigh. "I'll just sit here and pretend he's staring at me like that."

"He's glaring at me."

Bethany laughed. "Oh, girl. You are clueless."

Maybe Laurel didn't quite understand boys. After all, she didn't have any brothers, and her dad had left without so much as a farewell when she was five.

Sophomore year passed quickly and before she knew it, summer arrived. She got a job at Owen's Nursery, where she worked long days. But that was all right, because she also learned a lot about plants and trees and flowers. She planned to attend Clemson University on scholarship (fingers crossed) and become a horticulturist. Someday she would tend the grounds of the Biltmore Estate. Plus, her mom had her hours cut, and Laurel needed to pitch in.

Summer seemed to pass in a blink, and then it was junior year. Gavin was in her earth science and English classes, but she made a point of sitting far away from him and his disturbing scowls.

She was delighted to learn English wasn't his strong suit. Whenever she took a test to the teacher's desk to dispute the one or two questions she'd missed, she made a point of passing Gavin's desk, test score in plain sight, of course.

In the halls the looks he gave her alternated between the glower and the one that screamed "You bore me to death."

Junior year was more challenging than last year, and Laurel poured her heart into her classes.

Gavin seemed to skate by with much less effort. She wasn't sure how he balanced schoolwork with his rigorous sports schedule.

Laurel participated in concert band (violin) and did well. If her mom didn't always make the recitals, that was okay. She had to take whatever hours she could at the deli she managed. Sometimes Mallory came to support her, and Laurel returned the favor by attending her friend's art fairs. Mallory's mother always showed her face at these events, but privately she caused her daughter a lot of grief.

Laurel also attended school baseball games because Riverbend had a championship team and all the students went. The Robinson clan was always there in full force to support Gavin. The guy seemed to have it all. Academics, check. Athletics, check. Big loving family, check, check.

But by the time May arrived Laurel's and Gavin's GPAs were neck and neck.

For the English final the students would be randomly paired for a month-long Shakespeare project. It was her best shot to pull ahead. She was brainstorming a list of possible projects as the teacher read aloud the pairings.

"Hope Benford and Janae Curtis . . . Gavin Robinson and Laurel Jenkins . . ."

Laurel's gaze flew straight to Gavin. His spine lengthened, then he glanced over his shoulder at her and smirked.

Jerk. Idiot, she telegraphed. But if anything his expression grew even more impertinent.

Mr. Foster shoved his wire-rimmed glasses up on his nose. "Be sure and get with your partner this week. I'll need a paragraph-length description of your proposed project by Monday."

Laurel huffed. If she and Gavin worked together, they would receive the same grade—and she needed to score higher than him if she was going to pull ahead by the end of the year. Plus . . . a whole month of working with Gavin? No way.

She could dispute the pairing. But she wasn't exactly Mr. Foster's favorite student. He didn't seem to appreciate that she sometimes challenged his grading. But she would simply explain that she and Gavin had irreconcilable differences.

Or better yet . . . maybe Gavin would ask for another partner—of course he would. He hated her. And Mr. Foster *loved* Gavin.

When the bell rang she gathered her books, peering at Gavin from beneath her lashes, silently begging him to approach Mr. Foster's desk. Instead he exited the room with his gaggle of jocks, seemingly unperturbed by the pairing.

Great. Now it was all up to her. Heart in her throat, she shuffled toward Mr. Foster, who was wiping the dry-erase board clean.

"No, Ms. Jenkins, you may not switch partners."

Laurel blinked. He hadn't even turned around. "But what if—?"

"It's not about the cards you're dealt, but how you play the hand."

He was always quoting someone. Laurel barely stopped an eyeroll—he'd probably see that too.

"Do you know who said that, Ms. Jenkins?" he asked as he continued erasing.

"No, sir."

"Randy Pausch, a notable educator who died of pancreatic cancer. If he managed the cards he was dealt, I think you can manage yours. He authored a book entitled *The Last Lecture*. You should avail yourself of it. I think you'd find it most inspiring."

"Yes, sir." He definitely wasn't going to let her out of this. As she left the room Laurel's hopes deflated like an old balloon.

Maybe she could talk Gavin into asking him. But no way could she let Gavin know just how much this matchup bothered her. No, she was stuck with him.

Two days passed. Then three. Then it was Friday. The project proposal was due Monday, and they hadn't even spoken about it. In fact they hadn't spoken in three weeks, since he found her blocking the path to his locker. *"Outta my way, Short Stuff."*

She squirmed through English class. In two hours school would be over. Why hadn't he approached her yet? She couldn't call him—she didn't even have his number. And besides, just the thought of calling Gavin Robinson made her itchy all over. If he didn't come see her after class, she would have to approach him, an idea that ranked somewhere between water torture and death by firing squad.

But of course when the bell rang, he gathered his things and made a beeline for the door with his baseball buddies.

Drat! Why hadn't he approached her? She knew he cared about his grades. He was probably just trying to get under her skin—and it was working!

Laurel quickly gathered her things and caught up with his group just outside the door. "Gavin."

The whole group turned, staring down at her as if they'd never seen her before. *(Who are you? Do you even go here?)*

Gavin faced her, disinterest lining those cold blue eyes.

Her cheeks flamed. "I—we haven't discussed our project yet."

"So?"

"So, the proposal is due Monday."

He stared at her until she was sure her face was crimson. Finally, without tearing his gaze from her, he said, "See you guys after school."

The rest of the group melded into the crowd, flowing down the hallway, leaving the two of them in the open space between the door and wall of lockers.

He cocked a brow, giving her his supreme look of boredom. "Mr. Foster wouldn't let you switch partners, huh?"

She pressed her lips together. "When would you like to meet up and discuss the project? I have some ideas."

"I'm sure you do."

She blinked up at him, unable to think of a good retort. Why was she so tongue-tied around him? How tall was he anyway? And when had his shoulders gotten so broad? "How about Saturday night at the library?"

"I have plans."

Stupid. Now he knows how lame your life is. Why not just go ahead and tell him she stayed home and watched rom-coms on weekend nights? Her cheeks were probably nuclear by now. "Fine, what works for you?"

"Sunday night at eight."

That was pushing it. The form was due Monday, and what if they couldn't agree? A distinct possibility. "The, uh, library isn't open on Sundays."

He shrugged. "So come to my house. Come at seven—you can grab a meal with us first. See you then."

She definitely didn't want to face him on his turf. And *grab a meal?* But he was already walking away and anyway, what would she say? The coffee shop was closed on Sunday evenings, and she sure wasn't inviting him to her pathetic house on the poor side of town. *"Here, have a seat on our secondhand sofa. Don't mind the ripped cushion."*

She sweated it out all weekend. Finally Sunday night rolled around, and she changed outfits three times, cursing herself with each swap for caring one whit what Gavin thought of her.

The Robinsons lived in a charming white clapboard farmhouse on a beautiful property. When the door swept open, Lisa Robinson, a pretty blonde, welcomed her inside, and before Laurel could blink, she was seated beside Gavin at the table. She met his dad, and his younger brother and sister. They were all so nice—and talkative. They included her without putting her on the spot. There wasn't a moment's silence during the meal.

It was a drastic change from her own family suppers, which was often just her. And when her mother was there, they usually talked quietly about what had happened that day, then ran out of things to say.

Even Gavin seemed pleasant enough as he joked with his siblings, giving as good as he got. It was over an hour later when his brother and sister rushed off. Laurel offered to help Lisa and Jeff with the dishes, but the woman shooed her from the kitchen. "Oh, honey, you and Gavin should get started on your assignment."

Gavin ushered her out back to a picnic table sitting on a curved patio beneath twinkle lights. The sun had already dropped behind the mountains, ushering in twilight. She set down her folder and purse and took a seat.

Gavin lowered himself beside her. His body seemed to take up half the bench.

She'd sat in the middle, expecting him to sit across from her. She inched her thigh away from his as she opened her folder, then pulled out her notes. "Okay, I've been working on some ideas. The one I like best focuses on the play's use of symbols. I can write an essay and you could give a presentation. I'm particularly intrigued by the use of weather in the—"

"Or . . . we could do something a little more original."

She blinked. "Okay . . ." She scanned her list for a more creative idea. "We could focus on Macbeth's evolving character. There's a lot to work with there."

"What else ya got?"

She pursed her lips. "You're being awfully difficult for someone without any ideas at all."

"Keep them coming. I'm sure you can do better."

She glared at him before dropping her gaze once again to her notes. "We could translate the play into modern vernacular. I guess we could do the translation together, then act out a scene for the class."

"Everybody's going to act out a scene. We should do something different."

She snapped her folder shut. "Fine. Let's hear all your great ideas."

He leaned his elbows onto the table, his shoulder brushing hers. "I could build a model of the Globe Theatre."

She opened her mouth, then shut it again. Okay, not bad. "That sounds like a big commitment. We only have a month and all our other finals to worry about, not to mention extracurriculars."

"No problem. I'm good at building stuff. It won't take me long."

"And what would I do?"

"The Globe has an interesting history. Did you know Shakespeare was part owner? That they hung daily flags to represent what genre they were performing that day? Or that it burned down after some cannons were fired during a performance of *Henry the Eighth*?"

It irked her that she'd known only one of those things. Still, it was a decent idea. "So you're suggesting I write a paper on the Globe and you build the model?"

He lifted one of those broad shoulders. "What do you think?"

"I guess it would work . . ."

But what if he botched the model? Sure, academics came easily to him—sometimes she swore he had a photographic memory. She never saw him studying, not even in study hall.

But she couldn't afford a bad grade on this project. Alicia Wallace and her 4.22 GPA were on both their heels. "What if we worked on both of them together—the model and the essay? We'd have to coordinate our schedules, but I'm sure we could make it work."

She studied him in the waning light. They were closer than she'd realized. Dusk had darkened his eyes to stormy blue, and the twinkle lights highlighted his cheekbones, carving shadows beneath them.

No boy had the right to look that handsome. She was suddenly aware that his leg rested against hers and that their arms touched on the tabletop.

He lifted an impertinent eyebrow. "So you want to work together?"

"Of course I don't *want* to work together."

"But Mr. Foster wouldn't let you switch."

"He doesn't like me." *Drat.* She as much as admitted she'd asked. She clamped her mouth shut.

His lips twitched.

"Fine, I asked him. But you didn't want to work with me either."

"I never said that."

Laurel snorted. "You didn't have to. I know you hate me."

That brow again. Amusement flickered in his eyes.

Frustration crackled inside, building up until it released. The way he singled her out and somehow ignored her at the same time. The scowly looks. The condescension. She'd had enough. "What did I ever do to you anyway, Gavin Robinson? Just because I challenge your spot at the head of the class doesn't mean you have to be mean. You never even—"

And then his lips were on hers.

The shock of it made her freeze for what seemed like an interminable moment. Then her lips responded. They began moving against his long before her brain shifted into gear.

He's kissing me.

Gavin Robinson is kissing me.

He doesn't *hate me.*

Bethany was right.

Stop thinking!

Laurel melted into the kiss because how could she not? His mouth was soft and coaxing and so, so sexy, moving against hers like he wanted to thoroughly taste her. The kiss was confident and somehow reverent too. She wanted to curl up in his arms and purr.

She wasn't a complete novice; she'd been kissed a time or two.

But have you really?

She'd certainly never experienced anything like this. Not even close. Her chest squeezed so tight she could hardly breathe, and her heart seemed to have melted into a warm, oozing puddle.

When he pulled away she practically fell into his lap. Face heating, she opened her eyes. She couldn't tear her gaze from that beautiful face.

Gavin had kissed her. In the space of a few seconds, he'd turned her whole world upside down. He was inches away, his breath falling over her lips, giving her that familiar dark scowl.

Only . . .

It didn't seem quite so dark just now. And maybe it wasn't a scowl at all.

Then his lips tipped up just a tiny bit at the corner.

Oh.

Five

Gavin frowned at the document in his hands. Why would Mike and Mallory have made a divorced couple Emma's guardians?

He thought back over the timing. Yes, they'd definitely been going through the divorce when Mallory got pregnant with Emma. Mike had told Gavin the happy news after he moved back to Riverbend. They were at the Trailhead, and while Gavin kept his lips lifted in a simulated smile, all he could think about was his own son, gone much too soon.

He shook away the memory. "This makes no sense. We were going through the divorce when she got pregnant with Emma."

Laurel shifted away. "This is their old will. I'm sure they've updated it."

He did a double take. "Wait. You knew about this?"

Her chin tilted upward, and her lips pursed in a way he used to find adorable. Before the accident. Before the divorce. A lifetime ago.

"We both knew about it, Gavin. When they were pregnant the first time they made us guardians, remember?"

"What? I knew nothing about this."

She snorted. "Yes, you did. I talked to you about it that one time we ate at the Corner Kitchen."

He gave his head a shake. Maybe some marble would shake loose and he'd suddenly remember. Nope. "I remember Mallory having the miscarriage, but I have no recollection of that conversation, Laurel."

Her eyes sparked. "Maybe because all you cared about at the time was the McCafferty job."

"It was a 3.2-million-dollar build, Laurel. I was under a lot of pressure."

"That doesn't matter anymore. I'm telling you that you agreed to guardianship. We both did."

"And you didn't think to mention this when you got here?"

"I assumed they would've changed it after the divorce."

He jabbed the document in the air. "Well, apparently they didn't."

"That's not necessarily true. There's probably an updated version of that will around here somewhere. We just have to find it."

"You better believe we do." Because there was no way he and Laurel could co-parent this child.

Over three hours later they'd not only combed through every square inch of the office, but they'd also gone through the kitchen, living room, and bedroom. They were currently searching the couple's walk-in closet. Being in this space, going through their things, was dredging up memories for Gavin. There was no time to mourn right now. He shoved his feelings to the back burner, which, if he was honest, was already a little crowded.

His throat ached as he replaced the top on a shoebox and set it back on the top shelf.

This wasn't good. He'd hoped to have this settled before morning. So he could look that child in the eyes and tell her everything would be okay. But how could he promise her that when her future was so unsettled?

He checked his watch. "It's after one, Laurel." Even Sunny had checked out of all the excitement and found her spot at the foot of the bed.

Laurel was digging through the contents of a box. "Well, we haven't found it yet, so we need to keep searching."

He scrubbed a hand over his face. "We've checked everywhere in the house, and we don't even know if it actually exists."

"We haven't looked in the attic yet."

"Why would they keep an important document in the attic? Come on. We need to get some sleep. Tomorrow's going to be a long day, and Emma will be up early."

She stopped sorting through the box, her slim shoulders hunching a little. "I guess we could call Darius in the morning if we can track down his cell number. Find out if they updated their will."

"That's what I was thinking. If they did revise it, he'll have a copy." And what would they do if there wasn't an updated will? He didn't even want to say it aloud.

It had been a long day. His best friends were dead, their daughter's future was uncertain, and he was apparently stuck for the time being with the woman he'd failed in every possible way. "It's too late to drive back to Asheville tonight. You can have the spare room. I'll take the couch."

"No, that's okay. You can go home. I've got this."

"I'm going to be here for Emma when she wakes up."

She opened her mouth as if to argue, then shut it again.

"Mike's parents are flying in tomorrow." He'd been texting with Cooper all night. The couple was devastated and worried about their grand-daughter. They were relieved Gavin and Laurel were here with her.

"It'll be good for Emma to have them here," she said.

"Good for the Claytons too."

Laurel shoved the box back under the shelf. "I wonder if they might be able to . . ."

"I wondered the same thing. I never met them. Mike mentioned some health problems, but maybe. You can head back to Asheville tomorrow. You've got work Monday, and I can stick around until this gets sorted out."

"I'm not going anywhere—I'm more familiar with Emma's routines than you. And you do realize there'll be two funerals in a matter of days. I should help with Laurel's at least. Has anyone reached her aunt?"

"Cooper said they haven't had any luck with that yet." A wave of exhaustion washed over him. He couldn't think about all this right now. "The good news is, the will we found will buy us a little time since we're listed as guardians. But one thing at a time. Let's get some sleep. Did you bring some things from home?"

"They're in the car."

"I'll get them." He left before she could argue. As he took the steps, the day's events settled on his shoulders like a thousand-pound boulder. The realization that Laurel was here hit him fresh again. Life could change in the blink of an eye. Nobody knew it better than them.

He had to figure out this guardian situation. He couldn't stand the thought of letting Laurel down again. Couldn't stand the thought of letting Mike and Mallory down. Not to mention Emma . . .

Once outside he retrieved Laurel's bag from the Civic. The car was new—or new to him—and so was the duffel bag. He knew little about her life now, and somehow that seemed so wrong.

This wasn't the way it was supposed to work out between them. They were going to be married forever. They were going to raise a family and grow old together.

He headed back inside, up the stairs. The door to the spare room was pushed closed. He knocked softly, and a moment later she swept it open.

Even with her brown hair mussed and her makeup faded, she was the most beautiful woman he'd ever met. Her smile—when it finally came out to play—was a thing to behold. It was nowhere in sight now. He handed her the bag.

But once the exchange was made she didn't close the door or even step back. "Should we take her to church in the morning—try to keep to her routine?"

"Word about Mike and Mallory will have spread. Do you think it's a good idea?"

"Plus the Claytons will be arriving."

"And we have to get hold of Darius."

"True." She shifted uneasily. "We should talk about what we're going to tell Emma in the morning. She'll want to know where her mom and dad are."

His mind spun with possible explanations for why her mommy and daddy weren't home. Nothing sounded like something a two-year-old would comprehend.

Laurel cradled her arms over her stomach. "We

have to be on the same page so we don't confuse her."

"Should we just say they're . . . gone? Or that they're . . . I don't know, Laurel. How do you make a toddler understand her parents aren't coming back?"

"I did a quick internet search. It said to keep things direct and simple. Something like, 'Your mom and dad had an accident, and they won't be coming home.'"

They stared at each other in miserable silence. Those weren't words any child should have to hear. And he sure didn't want to be the one delivering them to sweet little Emma. But someone had to.

"It's not something she's going to understand at first," Laurel said. "She has no concept of death. She'll come to realize the truth over time."

His stomach twisted at the thought. He'd give anything if she never had to realize that truth at all.

Laurel was clearly feeling everything he was. Her eyes held so much sadness.

He resisted the urge to reach for her hand. "We'll get through this, Laurel."

She cleared her throat and gave a nod. "We have to. For Emma's sake."

Six

Laurel's eyes fluttered open to the play of early morning light on the gray walls. Upon the sight of the unfamiliar bedding and furniture, the previous day rushed over her like a rogue wave.

Mallory. Mike. *Emma.*

Her throat thickened with all the emotion she'd pushed back yesterday. And all the terrible things in store for today. She wished she could just close her eyes and go back to sleep. Wished she could sink into oblivion until everything went back to the way it was before. The feeling was as familiar as a pair of worn-in jeans.

A clanking sound came from downstairs. She wasn't alone with the child. It was barely seven o'clock, and she'd slept restlessly for all the obvious reasons. And also because she'd never thought she'd have to face Gavin again, much less under these conditions.

The quiet sounds of a child playing came from the nursery. Her heart gave a tight squeeze, and she closed her eyes. *Oh, God, You've got to help us here. Give us the words.*

Part of her wanted to stay here and let the girl enjoy a few extra minutes of normalcy. But Emma would soon tire of playing alone and begin crying.

Best Laurel caught her before that happened.

She crawled from bed and exited the room, only to nearly run into Gavin, obviously headed to the nursery too. Sunny was on his heels.

Gavin's hair was tousled in that familiar boyish way, and a pillow crease marked his stubbled cheek. "Morning."

She smoothed her hair. "Morning. Ready for this?"

"No."

"Me neither." But there was no sense putting it off. She swept past him, opened the nursery door, and flipped on the light.

Emma glanced up from where she sat in the crib with Bunny. Her blonde curls were a riot around her cherub face. Her green eyes lit up. "Waurel!"

Laurel's smile quivered. "Hi, sweet angel. Did you sleep well?"

"Gabin!" Upon sight of Gavin, Emma pulled to her feet and held out her chubby arms. "Gabin, take."

Laurel stepped aside and let Gavin lift Emma from the crib. He kissed her cheek, then Emma held Bunny out for a kiss. When Gavin accommodated with a loud *smack,* Emma giggled.

Gavin peered at Laurel, his eyes asking "What now?"

"Time to change your diaper," Laurel said, "and then we'll have breakfast, okay?"

"Gabin do."

Laurel's gaze met Gavin's. "You heard the girl."

Gavin laid Emma on the changing table while Laurel grabbed a Pull-Ups from the shelf. Emma played with Bunny while he changed her.

"We might as well get her out of her jammies." Laurel withdrew a pair of shorts and matching shirt from a drawer and set it on the table. She leaned against the wall and watched him change the child with the competence of a man who'd done it many times before.

Watching him now, Laurel could almost imagine the clock had rolled back five years and he was changing Jesse. Once he'd gotten past the fear he'd somehow break the newborn, he didn't seem to mind the less glamorous side of childcare. When he'd been around to do it.

She watched those nimble hands working now and noticed a slight tremble. Was Gavin thinking of their son too? Or was he just nervous about facing Emma's questions?

"All right, Emma Bear. All clean." Gavin picked her up.

As they left the room Laurel flipped off the light and followed them downstairs. Sunny led the way, her fluffy tail swishing back and forth.

The question came as they entered the empty living room.

Emma peered at Gavin with wide, innocent eyes. "Mama? Dada?"

He stopped in his tracks.

Laurel's gaze flickered to Gavin, just long enough to see the panic crouching in his eyes. "Let's sit down a minute, sweetie."

Gavin sat on the sofa beside Laurel and turned the child to face him on his lap.

Sunny nosed into the middle of them, seeking attention.

"Go sit down," Gavin said firmly and the dog obeyed.

Emma's expression held no hint of worry or concern. Simply a question.

Laurel hated that the answer was going to change everything. "Sweetie, we have something very sad to tell you."

When she paused, Gavin gave her a slight nod.

"Honey . . . your mom and dad had an accident." She forced the final words out of her mouth. "And they won't be coming home." Tears burned behind Laurel's eyes. She wanted to wail. She wanted to promise Emma she would be all right. She wanted to gather the child in her arms and never let her go. Did she understand at all? If nothing else, she knew what *sad* was and what it looked like.

Emma blinked up at Gavin, who watched the child as if his heart had just broken in two—as if he was afraid hers might too.

Laurel fought the strong urge to keep talking. But the articles said to go at the child's pace and keep things simple. So she forced herself to wait for Emma's response. For more questions. *God, give me the words.*

Emma's gaze, more somber now, returned to Laurel. "Waurel make pancakes?"

Laurel's breath froze in her lungs. Her gaze darted to Gavin, whose expression reflected the same shock and relief she felt. Her breath tumbled out. Her smile wobbled. "Yes, angel. Laurel will make you pancakes."

Gavin set Emma down in the living room by her basket of toys. "I'm going to help Laurel make the pancakes."

Emma walked over to the bookrack instead and pulled one down. "Princess book!"

"Are you going to read your princess book?"

"Yeah!" She plopped down on the floor and Sunny curled up beside her.

"All right, Emma Bear. I'll be in the kitchen."

He found Laurel pulling out a bowl and a whisk.

He got down a mug and poured the coffee he'd brewed earlier. "That is not what I expected," he whispered.

"Am I wrong for feeling profoundly grateful she didn't understand?"

"I feel like I just got pardoned for a heinous

57

crime." He added a bit of cream and a little sugar, then handed her the mug.

She set down the box of pancake mix and took the cup. "Thanks."

While Laurel made the batter, he refilled his own mug, then began setting the table.

Before he finished, his phone buzzed with a call. His mom.

"I have to take this." He slipped through the French door onto the back patio and answered the phone.

"Hi, honey," Mom said. "How's it going? I just can't believe this is happening."

"I know. It's . . . still sinking in."

Mom sniffled quietly. "Do they have any idea what caused the accident?"

"I haven't even asked. I've been too worried about Emma to think about that."

"Poor child. How is she this morning? Has she asked about . . . ?"

"Yeah, she asked. She doesn't understand the answer, of course. She's reading right now and seems okay. It's going to be a rough road."

God, where are You?

"Cooper said you were searching for a will."

"We actually found one last night. It's an old one, but it should buy us a little time."

"That's wonderful news. Wait, we? Who's with you?"

He winced at the slip. He'd hoped to keep Laurel's presence under wraps.

"Laurel drove up last night. She was concerned about Emma too."

The heavy silence said more than words ever could. Laurel had been one of them for five years. But the divorce had changed all that, of course. Sides were taken, and Mama Robinson was always going to side with her sons—even if the split had been Gavin's fault. He'd fallen into a black hole after the accident. Moved back to Riverbend, taken the first job he was offered—campground manager.

It was only because of God's grace, his loving family, and his friend Mike that he'd come out of that death spiral. Well, that and Katie—ancient history, given that the woman was now married to Cooper.

"Honey . . ." His mom's voice held that treading-cautiously tone. "Do you really think that's . . . healthy?"

"We're just trying to do what's best for Emma right now. She needs familiarity and Laurel stayed with her a while back so she knows Emma's routines."

"Of course, but . . . why don't you let me come over and I'll help you with her. Surely Laurel has to get back to her job, and I have all the time in the world. Emma and I get on like a house on fire."

Laurel had made it clear she wasn't going anywhere. "Thanks, Mom, but we'll know more here soon, and Mike's parents are on their way."

"Oh! That's great." The relief in her tone came through loud and clear. Gavin wouldn't be alone with his ex-wife. "I mean, not great—those poor people."

A warm breeze ruffled his shirt and whipped across the rolling acres. Rows of trees, their branches laden with ripe apples, dotted the landscape as far as his eyes could see.

The harvest. He set his hand on top of his head. Didn't even want to think about all that work and who was going to handle it. Mike and Mallory had sacrificed a lot to get their business up and going. It was finally paying off—and they weren't even here to enjoy it. He blinked against the sting in his eyes.

"Honey, are you there?"

"Yeah. Listen, Mom, I'll call you when I know what's going on."

"And if there's any way I can help. In the meantime I'll pull together the food for the funeral suppers. We can have them here if that works out best."

"Thanks, Mom. I'll let them know."

"Give that precious girl a squeeze for me."

After he disconnected he entered the house. In the living room Emma was lying against Sunny's side, pretending to read to her. The dog licked her hand, then set her head on her paws. Thank God for Sunny. The child would need something normal in this uncertain season.

Laurel stood at the counter, ladling batter onto a griddle. She seemed so young in her leggings and a long pink T-shirt that draped off one shoulder. She had a sensitive spot at the cradle of her neck. Had always hunched up her shoulder and gave that husky laugh of hers when he tried to kiss her there. Sexy as all get-out.

Did she have a man in her life now? Someone else who knew these intimate details about her? His gut twisted and he shook the thought away. He couldn't be thinking like this right now.

He resumed setting the table, his mother's words ringing in his ears. Definitely not healthy to be sharing this house with his ex. But it was just for a short period of time. Once they got an answer from Darius—no matter what it was— he'd talk Laurel into heading home. If it came to it, between him, his family, and the Claytons, Emma would be in good hands. The funeral would be a few days away, and Laurel could return for that.

"Any news?" Laurel asked quietly.

"Not really. I did track down Darius's number earlier this morning. And Mike's parents confirmed that they'll be here around ten. They had a slight delay in Chicago." He didn't mention that they were unaware of any guardianship plans, which meant Mike and Mallory hadn't asked them to fulfill the role.

"How long have you been up?"

He wasn't sure he'd ever really gotten to sleep. "A while. I thought I'd wait until eight to call Darius though. I let Cooper know about the will we found. That'll stave off CPS at least."

Laurel did a double take. *"CPS?"*

"Apparently, if a child is orphaned and the parents left no plan in place, their first course of action is to place the child in foster care at least temporarily until a family member petitions for guardianship."

"Emma can't go to foster care. That's the last thing Mike and Mallory would've wanted."

"We should be thankful for that will, even if it is out of date. It gives us the right to care for her until their updated plan can be located." He imagined CPS showing up and carrying Emma off and shuddered.

"And if there is no updated plan?"

He didn't even want to think about that. "We'll cross that bridge when we come to it."

Seven

Was time running backward? Laurel had made pancakes with blueberries and maple syrup, then they'd eaten and cleaned up the kitchen. She'd sat Emma on the potty while she read at least ten books to her, but those efforts had been fruitless.

And still it wasn't eight o'clock.

Gavin played with Emma between phone calls (Cooper and Avery, his sister). The Robinsons were a tight-knit family. For a while she'd felt like one of them. The split had not only torn her from her husband but from the family that had folded her into their loving arms.

Not that she didn't have her own family. Mom had always been there for her in her own way. And her stepdad, Brad, who'd come along when she was graduating from high school, was great. But she was a little cautious about fathers in general, and her mom wasn't exactly the nurturing type.

Emma handed her a LEGO block. "Build."

"You wanna help me build a house?"

"Build house."

Laural connected her block to Emma's. "Is it a pink house?"

"Yeah."

"So pretty." Laurel checked her watch.

Gavin entered the room. "I'm going to go ahead and call Darius."

"All right." *Please, God. We need a plan here. Something that'll give Emma the security she needs.*

She placed another block as Gavin returned Darius's greeting. "I'm sorry to bother you at home so early on a Sunday. I'm not sure if you heard what happened yesterday."

Gavin was quiet for a long minute. "Thank you. They were fine people." His gaze fixed on Emma. "She's hanging in there, I guess . . . Right. I'm sure you can guess what I'm calling about. I'm at their house now, and we found an old will dating back five years, but I'm sure they must've updated the guardianship . . . Of course. I'll wait."

His gaze met Laurel's, a thread of tension connecting them. They hadn't been on the same page in a long time, but right now, they couldn't be more unified. There had to be another plan in place.

"Do again, Waurel."

Oh, right. She placed another pink block, her fingers trembling. So much was riding on this. Emma's entire future hung in the balance.

"Okay," Gavin said. "No, that's fine."

He's checking, Gavin mouthed.

Laurel nodded. *Not to be a pest, God, but this*

is kind of important. And if You could just make sure those updated guardianship papers are in his files, that would be terrific.

"Yeah, I'm here . . . Right." Gavin turned toward the kitchen. "I know. Yes, I understand."

He frowned as he presumably listened to Darius. Whatever the attorney was saying took a couple of minutes.

"Do you have any idea when that'll be?" Gavin glanced at her. "Okay . . . No, I appreciate your help . . . That would be great, thank you. All right, I will." He said good-bye and lowered the phone. His shoulders rose and fell on a breath.

"What did he say?"

Gavin slowly turned around, his expression telegraphing the answer before his words did. "There's no updated will."

Despair settled over Laurel like a lead cape. "Is he sure?"

"He has all their records on his computer. He also handles the legal papers for Harvest Moon— the LLC and stuff."

She watched Emma placing another block, talking to herself.

Laurel's lungs felt as if they were full of cement. She had more questions, but not in front of the child. She got up and headed toward the island where Gavin had braced both hands on the granite top.

"It'll have to be Mike's parents then, right?"

she said. "They're the logical solution—the only living relatives, barring that aunt we haven't been able to reach."

The shadows in his eyes pushed back a bit. "They can't be that old, right?"

"Sixty-five is the new forty-five." Now that they'd talked about it, some of the weight eased off her shoulders. That made sense. Emma's grandparents would raise her. That happened all the time, after all. Of course it wouldn't be easy, but other grandparents managed.

"You're right. They love her."

"Did Darius say something else? He talked a long time."

"He was explaining my responsibilities as executor of the will. I have to offer the will for probate, pay their outstanding debts, and over-see the distribution of the assets—which I can't do yet since the assets will be held in trust by Emma's guardian until she reaches adulthood."

Gavin's gaze homed in on hers. "He also told me that whoever wants guardianship of Emma can petition for it. The court will then appoint a guardian ad litem to represent Emma. He or she will schedule a meeting with the potential guardians. Then there's a hearing that'll happen between ten and thirty days of Mike's and Mallory's deaths."

"We'll have this figured out way before then."

"We're going to have to. For now they'll

assume we're pursuing guardianship. And once Paul and Judy see there are no other options, they'll step up."

"Right. I'm sure they will. We should let Emma know they're coming."

"Finally, a little good news to share."

The sound of gravel popping under tires filtered through the house's walls.

"Mee-maw! Papaw!" Emma ran to the door, Sunny on her heels, tail swishing violently.

The couple had been delayed again, and it was going on lunchtime now. Laurel was in the kitchen, putting sandwiches together as Gavin edged past Emma and Sunny and opened the door.

Judy Clayton was retrieving something from the back of the car while Paul waited in the passenger seat. The couple appeared older than Gavin had expected, but maybe it was just the grief wreaking havoc on them. Judy's gray hair hung limply around her bare face, and Paul still wore yesterday's stubble on his pale cheeks. Their eyes were bloodshot. They were dressed in comfortable leisure attire, but nothing was comfortable about this situation.

Gavin let Emma past, and her little legs couldn't seem to navigate the two porch steps quickly enough.

"Mee-maw! Papaw!"

Judy's smile wobbled as she knelt to embrace her granddaughter. "Oh, precious, I'm so glad to see you. Mee-maw loves you, honey."

"Cookies, Mee-maw."

"Sure, honey, we'll make cookies later. Papaw can help too."

Emma gave the seated man a hug as they exchanged greetings while Sunny danced around them, seemingly oblivious to the mountain of grief.

Gavin approached the group. The strain on the couple's faces was heart-wrenching. They were trying so hard not to overwhelm the child with their pain. The closer he got, the older they appeared.

He introduced himself, and Laurel did the same as she approached. By silent agreement they didn't broach the obvious subject at hand.

"Emma will be going down for a nap after lunch," Laurel said. "We can talk then."

"Of course." Judy turned to the back seat of the rental.

"Let me get your luggage," Gavin said.

"That can wait a bit." She turned, unfolded a walker, and placed it in front of Paul, who used the metal frame to lift himself from the car.

Gavin met Laurel's gaze, exchanging the silent message. *Not good.*

Judy closed the door behind her husband. She was nearly as tall as Paul. "I don't know if Mike mentioned Paul had a stroke a couple months ago. He's doing great, though."

"Physical therapy has worked wonders," Paul said.

"I'm glad to see you're doing so well," Laurel said. "Are you hungry? I made sandwiches and soup."

"I hungry," Emma said and toddled toward the house.

"That sounds wonderful," Judy said.

Between their grief and Emma's unsettled future, none of them probably could've cared less about food right now.

They moved slowly toward the house, and Gavin positioned himself at the steps.

"Can I help you up, sir?"

"Thank you, honey," Judy said. "But we've got it."

Gavin watched Paul painstakingly navigate the two steps. Okay, so Emma's grandpa was a little disabled at the moment. He was recovering from a stroke. *Recovering* being the key word. He seemed otherwise in very good health. And Judy appeared strong as an ox, helping her husband up those steps—and also spry, the way she'd knelt to embrace Emma and popped back to her feet. They were holding up remarkably well under the situation.

Ten minutes later they sat around the table, making small talk. Since real conversation was ill advised, lunch revolved around Emma, and Gavin was fine with that. The adults ate little, mostly pushing food around their plates as they interacted with the child. Judy had to leave the table twice to get her emotions under control. Who could blame her?

Would Emma go down for her nap so soon after her grandparents' arrival? But shortly after the meal was over, she went willingly with Laurel while the others got up to clean the kitchen.

Once Emma was upstairs, Judy sagged onto an island stool. "That poor baby." Her voice quivered. "She's going to miss her mom and dad so much. Dear Jesus, why?"

Her husband cupped her shoulder, his eyes going glassy.

"I'm so sorry for your loss, both of you."

"Thank you for being here for Emma," Paul grated out. "It was one less thing to worry about."

"Of course. I'm here to help in any way."

Judy wiped the tears from her face. "Does she . . . does she know what happened?"

"Well . . . we told her they were in an accident and that they weren't coming back. But she's so young . . ."

"She can't possibly understand," Judy said. "*I* can hardly comprehend it."

Paul blinked back tears. "Maybe that's a blessing."

She would come to understand slowly, day by day, as her parents failed to come home. It seemed cruel. She'd be left wondering about the two most important people in her life.

The stairs creaked and a moment later Laurel appeared in the kitchen. Seeming to take in the somber mood, she gave the Claytons a tremulous smile.

"Did she go down okay?" Gavin asked.

"Like a champ. Can I get anyone a cup of coffee?"

The Claytons rejected the offer.

Gavin waved them toward the sofas. "Why don't we have a seat in the living room and talk through some things—if the two of you are feeling up to that."

"Yes, of course," Paul said. "There's a lot to be settled."

"First things first," Judy said after they were seated. "What's going to happen to Emma? Did they have a plan in place?"

Gavin glanced at Laurel, who gave him a nod. "Well, they did but . . . they made Laurel and me her guardians."

Judy blinked, then nodded slowly. "Well, okay then. I know how much they loved you both."

Paul put his arm around Judy. "And Emma feels comfortable with you—that much is obvious."

Gavin didn't like how easily they'd accepted that information. And it seemed odd that Mike

71

wouldn't have mentioned the divorce to them back when it happened. But then they hadn't known Laurel and Gavin personally. Or maybe Mike had told them, and Paul and Judy had just forgotten.

"It's not quite that simple." Laurel's gaze shifted to Gavin, seemingly waiting for him to deliver the blow.

"Laurel and I divorced three years ago."

"Oh dear," Judy said. "We didn't know."

"Obviously the will was drawn up when we were still together," Laurel said. "When Mallory was pregnant the first time."

Gavin weighed their reactions. Somebody had to broach the topic. Might as well be him. "We were actually wondering . . . would the two of you be able to care for her?"

The older couple regarded each other, and a moment later Judy spoke. "Of course we can. She's our granddaughter. We've been talking about moving here anyway, haven't we, Paul? There's nothing holding us in Colorado now that the store's closed."

Hope rose inside as if riding in a helium bubble. This would be the perfect solution. "I think Emma would like that. I know how much she cares for you both."

Laurel leaned forward. "Stability is so important for her right now. You could move in here with her for the time being. There would be a

72

lot of people to help out, including me. I'm free every weekend."

"And me, too, of course. You'll have all the support you need."

Judy stared off into the distance, seeming to space out for a moment.

Gavin followed her line of sight. The fireplace mantel. The family photo? She was probably lost in some memory.

She blinked and seemed present again. She clasped her hands in her lap, then gazed intently at Gavin. "But what about Emma? What's the plan for her?"

What? Gavin swung his gaze to Paul. Then to Laurel. Her furrowed brow and blank look mirrored his confusion.

Paul gave them both a grimace and placed his hand over his wife's. "We've become a little forgetful lately, haven't we, sweetheart? Emma will be fine, honey. We'll figure it out." He squeezed her hand and let go. "Gavin, you think you could help me with something in the kitchen?"

"Uh, yes, of course." He gave Laurel a slight shrug as he followed Paul and his walker into the kitchen, leaving Laurel to keep Judy company.

When Gavin reached the island, Paul stopped him with a hand on his arm. "I'm afraid Judy's been having memory issues for months. She refuses to go to the doctor—keeps chalking it up to normal aging."

Paul's lips trembled. "But since yesterday's phone call . . . it's gotten bad. Really bad. I've had to tell her twice now that Mike is gone . . . I don't know if I can do that again."

Gavin winced. "Oh, Paul. I'm so sorry." Poor Judy. How awful to realize over and over the death of a child as if you were just hearing it for the first time.

A tear trickled down Paul's face. "I wish so badly we could keep Emma. We love her so much. But with Judy's possible dementia, I just don't see how. I'm afraid to leave her alone, much less with a child. She could forget that Emma's in the car or leave her home alone while she's napping. We're just in no shape to raise a small child, Gavin. But I'm very worried about what's going to happen to her."

Gavin cupped the man's shoulder. "So are Laurel and I. But we'll figure it out. I—I'm not sure I could raise a child alone right now—I'm just getting my new business off the ground, building custom homes, and I still work part-time at the campground. I have long workdays. I don't think that's in Emma's best interest." He felt so selfish saying that. Would Mike want him to raise his child? But how could he do that and make a living too? Then there was the orchard . . .

"And Laurel?" Paul asked. "Would she be willing to raise Emma?"

Gavin lifted a shoulder. "She loves her as much

as I do. But she lives in Asheville and also has a demanding job. It's definitely best for Emma to stay here at least for a while. She needs familiarity now more than ever. Is there anyone else you can think of? A relative on your side of the family perhaps?"

"There's no one else on our side—except some distant cousins who barely know Mike and never even met Emma. But I think Mallory had an aunt she was close to."

"Laurel mentioned her. She lives in Florida, but we've been unable to reach her."

"And Emma knows her?"

"Apparently."

Paul's eyes lit up. "Is that who they stayed with when they went to Florida in the spring?"

"I think so."

"I recall Mike mentioning something about that. I got the impression she was younger than Judy and me and well-to-do. They went out on her sailboat."

Something came to mind. "I think I saw her in a beach photo I came across upstairs from their trip to Florida. The woman in the photo was maybe in her fifties. That had to be her."

"Maybe she's the answer. Maybe she's the right person to raise Emma."

A ray of hope. Gavin would cling to it for all it was worth. In the meantime, they just had to reach the woman.

Eight

The kiss on Gavin's back patio had changed everything. Laurel began to love those smoldering looks he gave her across the classroom. She'd always enjoyed school, but she'd never had more fun with a project than the one they worked on together. Being partners with Gavin was stimulating in multiple ways. He was so smart, and working as a team was even better than competing with him.

He was fun to be with too. She tried to be serious, but it was hard when Gavin was determined to make her laugh. They met at the library and at his house, where they were building the model. He insisted he needed her help, but he was doing all the work—and he was skilled at it. At least once during each meeting he'd palm her neck and pull her in for a breathtaking kiss. He was good at that too. So good. It didn't take her long to catch on—he didn't need her help on the model. He just wanted her company.

The thought made a private little smile curve her lips. Gavin Robinson wanted her. He'd even taken her for ice cream once after a session at the library, and he sometimes called her just to chat.

But as the end of the month neared, despair

seeped into her thoughts. The model was finished, and all they had left was final edits on the paper. She could easily handle that herself, but they'd agreed to work on it together at the library after school.

Ten minutes after they'd found a seat at an abandoned corner table, they sat poring over the essay. His arm pressed against hers, his warmth sinking into her flesh. She covertly inhaled the woodsy scent of him.

This was their last official meeting. What would happen after today? It was almost summer, and the thought of not seeing him every day made her chest feel hollow. Would the end of the project also be the end of . . . them? Was there even a *them?* Her friends thought he really liked her, but he hadn't asked her out on an official date yet. Yes, he kissed her sometimes. But what if he was kissing other girls too?

Laurel had never felt so vulnerable, and she didn't like the feeling.

"What's wrong?"

She blinked up at Gavin . . . so close. She got lost in his eyes for a beat. "What?"

"You seem distracted."

Words tumbled around her brain, nothing that made sense. Certainly nothing she was brave enough to admit. "I . . ." She gave up and shrugged. "I don't know."

His gaze sharpened on her eyes. Then they

dropped to her lips. He leaned forward and brushed her mouth with his, lingering even after the brief kiss ended.

"Know what I know?" his breath whispered across her lips.

"What?"

"I don't want this to end." He put a little space between them until their gazes connected. Locked in. His beautiful eyes were filled with wonderful things: affection, attraction, devotion.

Things that made her heart feel floppy.

"I want to go out with you, Laurel."

"Are you asking me on a date?"

"I'm asking you to be mine."

Oh. What those words did to her. She felt all floaty and melty inside. The wonder of it. She was just a normal girl—a book nerd, really. And while she was all right in the looks department, she'd never been outgoing enough to have a passel of friends. Gavin was athletic and social and so handsome. More importantly, he was kind and respectful. He could have any girl he wanted.

And he wanted *her.*

He gave her chin a little pinch, humor flickering in his eyes. "Hasn't anyone told you, you shouldn't leave a guy hanging?"

She breathed a laugh. "Sorry. I—I'd like that."

His lips turned up at the corners just before he kissed her again. This one was longer and deeper, making her forget she was in a public library until the squeaky wheel of a book cart pulled her back to the present.

Everything changed after that. That last week of school he sat with her and Bethany at lunch and walked her to class. Sometimes in the hallway he took her hand in his big, callused one. At the end of the week, they celebrated the 98 percent they'd received on the Shakespeare project with dinner at the Trailhead—their first real date.

Eating out was a luxury Laurel and her mom didn't enjoy very often, but Gavin seemed familiar with the menu and staff. She wished there were a band playing so she'd have an excuse to get her arms around him. They talked and talked until long after the food was gone.

Her mom had dropped her off, and as the evening wore on, Laurel worried about what would happen when he took her home. What would he think of where she lived?

"Tell me about your family," he said. "I know you don't have any siblings, but what are your folks like?"

"It's just me and my mom. My dad left when I was little."

His eyes softened. "I'm sorry. That must've been hard. Do you ever see him?"

She shrugged. "I have no idea where he is or if he's even alive."

"That's rough."

She thought of his picture-perfect family. He

wouldn't have a clue. But it wasn't his fault he had it all. "It was a long time ago."

"Still leaves its mark. You know anything about my dad?"

"Not really, but he seems nice."

"Jeff's my stepdad. He married my mom when I was twelve. My biological father's an alcoholic. He wasn't much of a dad or husband even when he was home. Couldn't hold down a job. My mom worked a lot of hours to make ends meet. Eventually he abandoned us, and Mom divorced him."

Laurel sat back in the booth. "I didn't know. I thought—"

"That we were the perfect family?"

Her face heated at his razor-sharp accuracy. "I guess I shouldn't jump to conclusions."

"Coop's my biological brother, and Avery's technically my stepsister, but she's as much my sibling as Cooper. And Jeff's pretty awesome too. But don't tell him I said so—I like to keep him on his toes."

"Do you ever see him—your dad?"

"He used to live here in town, and I saw him around. When he left it was actually a relief." A flush crawled up his neck. "It was kind of embarrassing, you know, the messes he'd get himself into, everyone talking about him."

Compassion squeezed her chest. She knew the shame of having a dad who'd rejected her. But he'd also borne the humiliation of his father's behavior. She set her hand on his.

He turned his hand over and laced his fingers with hers.

She had the feeling it was as difficult for him to talk about his dad as it was for her, so she changed the subject. "I always wanted siblings."

A saucy brow cocked. "You can borrow mine. They're a pain in the butt sometimes."

They shared a grin, and she felt so connected to him just then. Having that little piece of his history, finding they had this big thing in common, made her feel so much closer to him. He didn't have a perfect family. His dad had left them for alcohol while her father had abandoned his family for another woman.

When he took her home, her palms grew sweaty at the thought of him pulling in to her potholed driveway and seeing her small, shabby house. Too bad it wasn't light out so he could also see her beautiful azaleas, hydrangeas, and the lush blue carpet of creeping phlox she'd planted last summer.

When they reached the property, he said nothing as he walked her to the door. A moment later as they stood under the porch light, Laurel tried to block out the peeling paint on the windows and the dark spot on the door in the shape of an old door knocker.

"Is your mom home?"

"She's working."

"I'd like to meet her sometime."

"Sure."

He drew her close and brushed her lips once. He might've ended it there, but Laurel pressed closer and the kiss continued. The feelings he evoked were . . . she didn't even have the words. She just knew that kissing Gavin was addictive. The more he kissed her, the more she wanted, as if she could never get enough.

When he ended the kiss, they were both breathless. "I should go."

"You should definitely go."

"One more."

"Okay."

He kept this one brief. "I'll call you tomorrow."

As his headlights chased across the living room wall, Laurel's lips tipped in a smile. He'd never said anything about her dilapidated house. Hadn't even seemed to notice.

When their grades were published the next week, Laurel was thrilled her GPA had edged ahead of Gavin's. She worried it would change things between them. But when they spoke on the phone that night, he seemed genuinely happy for her. He teased her about being a genius, but surely he realized she had to work twice as hard as he did.

As the weeks of summer passed, Laurel fell deeper and deeper for Gavin. For all that he seemed like such a tough guy, he had a softer side. He was empathetic when she mentioned her dad or her mom's long work hours. As if sensing her need for family, he often included her in the Robinsons' outings.

He wasn't hotheaded like some of the other athletes. On the contrary, he was cool and collected, even when he had a bad game. She also liked that he was affectionate, always holding her hand or wrapping an arm around her shoulder. In his family, touches were doled out like candy on Halloween. It was a good kind of different from what she was used to.

She didn't have to wonder what he liked about her because he told her. He praised her work ethic and determination. He liked that she had goals, and he loved the way she blushed. He didn't seem to mind that she was sometimes socially awkward or that it took her a while to open up to people.

They had little in common outside of school, but it didn't seem to matter. She taught him about plants and gardening, and he taught her about baseball and football and home improvements.

When Gavin noticed her porch rail was wobbly, he brought his tools and fixed it. Before she knew it, he'd repaired a leaky faucet, replaced some rotted roof shingles, and cleaned out the gutters. At first she was appalled—he probably felt sorry for them. But he had a way of putting her at ease.

"Relax. You're helping me build my résumé." Then he flashed that gorgeous grin of his, and all the fight went right out of her.

One time he had confided that his mom had struggled to maintain their house because his dad was too busy getting drunk. Her heart broke at the thought of that little boy, too young to help his mother. He was helping Laurel now instead, and at the same time, reminding her she wasn't alone.

Her mom liked Gavin well enough, but she warned Laurel not to lose her head over him. *"They always leave, Laurel. You're gonna get hurt."*

And Laurel did try to temper her feelings. But despite her efforts she began to understand all the clichés about love. The sky did seem bluer, the grass greener. There were surely bluebirds fluttering around her head and happy tunes floating on the breeze.

One day late in the summer, they hiked up to Lover's Leap to watch the sunset. Gavin leaned against a tree trunk, and she sat between the V of his legs, lying back against his chest. Laurel could hardly think about the stunning colors sweeping the skyline. In the comfort of his embrace, his heart beating against hers, all she could think was how perfect things were.

As the sun touched the horizon he tipped her chin up. Their gazes tangled for a long moment.

Surely he could feel her heart thudding against his chest. But the way he was gazing at her, she couldn't bring herself to care.

"I love you," he whispered.

Her breath hitched. She took in his unusually solemn expression, the quick flicker of uncertainty.

She touched his face in wonder. "I love you too."

His eyes softened and his lips curled up just before he took her mouth in a delicious kiss. She'd tried to be careful with her heart. But somehow Gavin had wormed his way right past her defenses. She'd fallen in love with him. How apt that term was. It did feel as if she'd lost her footing, was at the mercy of gravity.

But everyone knew what happened when you fell. At some point there was a hard landing. And despite the joy and giddiness his love evoked, Laurel couldn't help but brace for impact.

Nine

Emma was definitely missing her parents. Gavin sat at the island, across from Laurel and Paul, watching Judy pace the back patio with Emma. The girl had been fussy since she'd woken from her nap.

"I've already reached out to the funeral home," Paul said. "We have an appointment in the morning. But I was wondering if it might be a good idea to have a single funeral service for both Mike and Mallory."

"That would be up to Mallory's aunt, I guess," Laurel said.

They'd left Patty an urgent voice mail. The woman didn't seem to have any social media accounts. Cooper had also called to inform him that they'd made contact with Mallory's estranged mother. The woman wouldn't even be coming for the funeral. Unbelievable. He couldn't imagine any situation in which his mother wouldn't attend his funeral.

"Did the will appoint her aunt as power of attorney?" Paul asked.

"Well . . ." Gavin glanced at Laurel. "Since her mom's not interested, the aunt's next of kin."

Paul took a sip of water. "Sometimes the will spells out who should do what."

"I didn't even think of that." Gavin jumped up from the stool and went to grab the document. He was glad to have the Claytons here, and not only for Emma. He'd gone through his son's death and funeral, of course, but the details were a blur. He'd been enveloped in a cloud of grief and guilt.

In the office he grabbed the document from the desk and returned to the kitchen.

Paul leaned in. "It would probably be under 'power of attorney' or something in regards to their health care. Being as young as they are—were—they may not have—" His voice gave way. He blinked several times and cleared his throat. "Sorry."

Laurel set a hand on his forearm. "You have nothing to be sorry for."

"I just . . . I still can't believe this has happened."

"I know." Gavin set down the will. "It doesn't seem real."

"I don't want it to be real. But there are things to be done, and we should get on with them." He nodded at the document. "First things first."

Gavin found a page titled *Durable Power of Attorney for Health Care*. "I think this is it." On the first line the Claytons were listed as Mike's agent. "Mike named you and Judy, of course."

He skimmed down a few lines, then he lifted his gaze to Laurel. "Mallory named you."

Laurel leaned back against her seat. "I don't remember her mentioning that. So I'll be planning her funeral? What about her aunt? What if we can't reach her?"

"Surely she'll be in contact soon," Paul said.

"You mentioned having a double funeral," Laurel said. "I think Mike and Mallory would've liked that."

"Me too." Gavin glanced out the patio door where Judy was still trying to comfort Emma.

"It'll be easier on Emma too," Laurel said.

Gavin's gaze shot her way. "Are you sure she should go?"

"Of course she should. It's her parents' funeral. She won't remember it, but one day she'll want to know she was there."

He thought of the overwhelming grief and pain of his son's funeral. And he was an adult. How would a child comprehend that kind of emotional display? "But won't it be . . . I don't know, too emotional for her? Won't it scare her?" Gavin looked to Paul for backup.

"You two have been around her more than Judy and me."

"If things get too emotional," Laurel said, "we can always take her from the room. But I think she should be there."

Gavin wasn't sure that was right decision. But

Laurel seemed so certain, and she knew more about little ones than he did. "We haven't talked about this, Paul, but what if we left the caskets closed? I wouldn't want Emma seeing her parents that way. It might confuse or scare her."

Paul gave a nod. "Judy and I already discussed this. Mike's body was . . . It's probably best to have closed caskets. Those who want to see them one last time could do so before the funeral."

Emma's wails carried through the patio doors. She was having a meltdown, and Judy was struggling to hold the child.

Laurel rose from the stool. "We can talk more about this later."

Gavin swept Emma into his arms. Hoping to settle the child with a quieter house, Laurel had taken the Claytons on a walk around the orchard.

Emma whined in his ear, but he couldn't distinguish any words.

"What's the matter, Emma Bear? What can Uncle Gavin do?"

She struggled in his arms so he let her down again. She threw herself on the living room rug and lay there, facedown.

Who could blame her? He felt like doing the same. Actually, he'd prefer to punch a wall. He watched the child, lying so still, her chest heaving. Should he console her? Give her some space? He needed a manual.

He eased down beside her and rubbed her back.

She edged away, turning her face the other direction.

He withdrew his hand and regarded her small, still body. He wished he had the words that would help her heal. He had to try. She didn't have the vocabulary to express what she was feeling.

"Are you sad, Emma Bear? I'm sad too. And I'm so sorry this is happening." His throat tightened. "I know you miss your mom and dad. I miss them too. But we're going to get through this. I'm not going anywhere. Do you hear me? Uncle Gavin will be here for you no matter what." He blinked against the sting behind his eyes. He had no idea what the future held, but he meant those words. As long as Emma needed him, he'd be here. Would do whatever it took to make sure she was okay.

He was the one who lived in Riverbend. If Aunt Patty didn't come through, it was up to him to take care of her. He didn't know how he'd do it with his business, but he'd figure it out. He wouldn't let this child down.

He reached out to rub her back again, and this time she let him. *Please, God, help her through this. Comfort her. Give me the wisdom to know what to do and what to say. I feel so helpless.*

A few minutes later Emma wiped her eyes and pushed to her feet. "Gabin read book."

He blinked at the abrupt change in her

demeanor. "You want me to read you a book?"

"Princess book."

At the ordinary request a weight slid from his shoulders. "All right, Emma Bear. Go get the book and I'll read to you."

Ten

Exhaustion swamped Laurel as she walked across the funeral home parking lot. She got into her car, started it, and lowered her window to expel the oppressive heat. Once the Claytons' car pulled from the lot she sagged back in her seat. She needed a moment before she returned to the house.

The morning had dragged by, but the planning was over. Who cared if the casket had a vault or what color or model it was? Mallory wouldn't care about such things. She hadn't been materialistic. She'd lived in the moment and brought joy to those around her, balancing out Laurel, who tended to be deliberate and pragmatic. Mallory had been the only one who could drag Laurel out of her shell. Make her forget to be careful. Years ago she'd been the one who'd encouraged Laurel to lean into those feelings of love she'd developed for Gavin. She'd been their biggest cheerleader—and eventually Laurel's maid of honor.

Not to mention Laurel's main source of support through the divorce. As opposed to her mother, who, when the marriage fell apart, only frowned at her, "I told you so" etched blatantly in her expression.

What was she going to do without Mallory? She'd always been the one Laurel could talk to about her mother, even though she seemed like a dream compared to Mallory's narcissistic mother. But it was a point of connection for the two of them.

Now her very best friend was gone, and no one waited in the wings to take her place.

"At least they went together," Judy had said inside the funeral home. *"They loved each other so much, and they didn't have to grieve one another. I guess we can be grateful for that."*

It was small comfort, but it was something. It was so easy to get lost in the tragedy and lose sight of anything positive. Grief was like that.

The Claytons had been muddled at the funeral home, uncertain of their decisions. Laurel had tried to help them, but she kept having flashbacks to her own son's funeral. Between that and the loss of Mike and Mallory . . . it was hard to separate the grief.

In one way she was jealous of the Claytons. They'd had thirty-five years with their son; she'd only had three with Jesse. Mike's body would inhabit an adult-size casket while Jesse's had been heartbreakingly small, propped all alone at the front of Riverbend Community Church. She shook the image from her mind.

She shouldn't compare. Grief was grief, and losing a child was impossibly painful. Laurel was glad to have the planning out of the way. The visitation would be Thursday morning with a double funeral following. She thought of all that lay ahead, including Emma's uncertain future. It was overwhelming. Best to take one thing at a time.

Her next hurdle would be Mallory's obituary, and she dreaded the task. How could she condense her friend's life into a few paragraphs? She thought of Mallory as a little girl, as a teenager, as a grown woman and wife and mother. There had been so many lovely facets to her personality. Laurel wanted to somehow capture them all.

But she felt so empty. So drained. She pressed her hands to her eyes. She needed a few more minutes before she returned to the house where Emma waited. Where her ex-husband waited.

God, help me. I can't do this without You.

Her mother had stopped by this morning to offer help, but Laurel didn't even invite her in—having her and Gavin in the same space would've only made things more stressful. There was enough tension in the house without adding her mother to the mix.

This morning Laurel had let her supervisor know what had happened and notified her that she'd need the week off. It was bad timing with the promotion within arm's reach, but it couldn't be helped. She could commute, but Laurel couldn't imagine leaving Emma with someone else all day. Diane seemed okay with the sudden request, and heaven knew Laurel had accumulated plenty of PTO. She would worry about work later.

Getting through this week was all that mattered right now. The grief was all-consuming, but she couldn't fall apart at the house. She had Emma to consider. And she wouldn't let Gavin see her that way. She no longer trusted him with her emotions—he'd let her down so badly.

In addition, it was odd to be parenting with him again. Going through all the motions of changing diapers, feeding Emma, playing with her. They'd found that rhythm again much too easily. It was disconcerting.

Furthermore, the house was crowded, and Emma didn't need them all hovering around her. Laurel would convince Gavin to go home. She and the Claytons were here for Emma, and Aunt Patty would surely reach out any moment. There was no need for Gavin to derail his life this week. Laurel would see it through.

That afternoon neighbors began arriving at the house with food: casseroles, stews, soups, pies. In the kitchen Laurel took a covered dish from Gavin. He was starting to look tired around the eyes. Of course, with the Claytons here, he was still sleeping on the couch.

"Lasagna," Gavin said.

Last night Laurel had given the Claytons the spare room and taken Mallory and Mike's bedroom herself. Their presence was so heavy in that room, in the happy colors and simple décor. A Dan Brown novel sat on Mike's nightstand, open to the middle and turned over as if waiting for his return. A half-empty water glass sat on Mallory's side. And even after changing the sheets, her friend's floral scent lingered, keeping Laurel awake late into the night.

She marked the Pyrex dish and made room for it in the freezer while Gavin returned to his laptop at the kitchen table where he'd been working on a bid most of the afternoon.

They'd already eaten supper (chicken casserole), and the sun was getting ready to set. The Claytons had taken Emma and Sunny outside, where they were both presumably running off their energy. Now was a good time to address the subject that had consumed her all day.

She poured herself a cup of decaf and took a seat across the table from Gavin.

He glanced up, brows raised at her appearance.

So yes, she'd been avoiding him today. The memory of their son's funeral plans didn't exactly inspire warm, fuzzy feelings for her husband. Best to ease into this conversation. "I don't know why it's a tradition to bring food to grieving families. No one wants to eat at a time like this."

"Gives folks something to do, I guess. Some way to show they care."

"I suppose. There's already enough food in there for a month." Who would be heating up all those meals? It was impossible not to fret over the future. The planner in her didn't like having anything up in the air, much less Emma's future. She glanced out the window where Paul lifted Emma into his arms. "She doesn't seem herself today."

Gavin glanced outside. "You think it's sinking in?"

"Or she's just missing them. She asked me about them after her nap."

"What did you say?"

"Same thing I said yesterday. She just stared at me." The look in her eyes had nearly broken Laurel's heart in two.

"A part of me wishes she could understand. Another part hopes she doesn't."

"I don't know which would be worse. She didn't go on the potty at all today. Mallory had her almost trained."

"I read some regression is normal."

"I read the same."

He'd changed a little since she'd seen him last. A few gray hairs threaded through the hair at his temples, and faint laugh lines fanned from his eyes, even though he wasn't smiling at the moment.

"I wonder why Patty hasn't called," he said.

"Maybe she lost her phone or broke it or something."

"Maybe."

"I'm sure she'll call soon." Check them out, being so adult. Putting all their hostility aside to deal with the tragedy at hand. But it was time to get down to business. She cleared her throat. "I've been thinking . . . there's really no sense in both of us hanging around here all week what with Paul and Judy being here."

Something flashed in his eyes. Relief? "I agree."

That was easier than she'd expected. She allowed the smallest of smiles. "The sofa must be hard on your back. You'll probably be glad to be back in your own bed."

His expression fell. "I'm not going anywhere. I thought you were going back to Asheville."

Her spine lengthened. "I'm not leaving Emma."

"*I'm* not leaving Emma."

She huffed. "She doesn't need all of us here."

"Feel free to go then."

She gritted her teeth. She'd rather yank out her teeth one by one than abandon that child right now. She knew all too well what that felt like. Not to mention the consequent trust issues that could follow. "I'm more familiar with her daily routines—and she's more familiar with me."

"What about your job? I live in town, and I've

got plenty of work I can do from my laptop. And don't you have a . . . a boyfriend or something to get back to?"

She crossed her arms. No way was she answering that loaded question. "I've already taken off work. I'm not leaving her, Gavin."

He pinned her with an unswerving look, his jaw set. "Then I guess we're both staying."

Eleven

The day of the funeral had finally arrived. Gavin shifted a sleeping Emma in his arms. She'd been up through the night and out of bed at five this morning. Laurel had put her in a beautiful maroon dress and gathered her blonde curls into a ponytail. The church was full of people who'd loved Mike and Mallory. All morning the receiving line had stretched out the door and into the parking lot.

Up front Laurel stood beside the Claytons as Mallory's only representative. It was fitting since they'd been lifelong friends. Still, Mallory's mother should've come. He hated that her aunt was missing the event. They'd finally reached the woman's neighbor. Aunt Patty, who was apparently a competent sailor, had just left on an expedition from Florida to San Juan. They'd done everything possible to reach the woman, and it wasn't fair to the Claytons to delay the funeral.

Judy broke down and excused herself from the line again, heading toward the bathroom. She wasn't holding up well. She'd been very forgetful this week. Paul, leaning stoically on his walker, must be getting tired too. But the visitation was almost over. The pews were almost full.

Four years ago, in this same church, Laurel and

he had stood beside a small casket, accepting condolences. How had they ever made it through that day? Through those weeks?

Not well, that's how.

A crowd gathered around the photo boards they'd assembled over the past few days. The Claytons had brought Mike's childhood photos from home, and Laurel printed out pictures of Mallory from her phone. Gavin dug through the photos stored at Mike and Mallory's house. Laurel had written a beautiful obituary for her friend, while Paul had penned Mike's. Both had appeared in the *Herald* yesterday.

Gavin had kept to the back of the room, trying to shelter Emma from the emotional scene up front. Neighbors kept stopping by, extending their sympathies, staring at Emma, who'd finally fallen asleep, with heartbreak in their eyes.

His gaze swung back to Laurel. She had that guarded look about her today. That shell that kept everyone from getting too close. The funeral was no doubt resurrecting their own tragedy. And it couldn't be easy, facing all these people who were close to the Robinson family.

His sister waited in line to pay her respects. When Avery reached the front, she gave Laurel a stiff nod and must've said something because Laurel's lips moved in response. His family was protective of him, but he could trust them to be polite.

He turned and came face-to-face with Laurel's mother and stepfather. The woman's lips pursed even as her slender frame lengthened to her full five-feet-two height. She still wore wire-framed glasses and styled her brown hair in a cropped cut that aged her ten years.

He nodded. "Donna, Brad." He tried to add "Nice to see you" but couldn't quite get there.

"Gavin." Brad extended his hand and Gavin shook it. Brad had always been the congenial one. Even through the bitter end, he'd never been anything but polite.

Donna's gaze softened as it fell on Emma's sleeping form. She reached out toward the child, her emotions obviously teetering between sympathy for the child and disdain for her ex-son-in-law. Which would win out?

She withdrew her hand and made that prunish face he'd become so familiar with. Then she dragged her husband toward the receiving line.

Up front, Laurel was starting to wilt. She'd insisted on staying up with Emma in the night. When Emma had cried out at dawn, Gavin had gotten to the nursery before she awakened anyone else. Despite his discomfort around Donna, he was glad she'd come for her daughter's sake.

Gavin's gaze swung toward the closed caskets. His friends' bodies were lying in there, lifeless. Mike's parents had chosen his navy-blue suit, and Laurel had picked out a cheerful sundress for Mallory. They'd opened the casket prior to visitation for family and close friends, but Gavin had opted out.

Seeing his son that way, all plastic and rigid and lifeless, had haunted Gavin for months. Even now, the image pushed forward, unwanted. He'd rather remember his son running around the playground, laughing, singing his silly songs, full of life.

His throat tightened. He wandered over to the board for distraction. The crowd was gone, so it was just him. But the pictures blurred in front of him. All he could think about was Jesse. If he were still alive he'd be seven, and Laurel and Gavin would still be together. Instead, Jesse was gone.

And it was all his fault.

The music shifted to a rendition of "Somewhere Over the Rainbow," and his heart kicked against his ribs. This had played at Jesse's funeral and had somehow come to symbolize that awful day. When the song came on the radio, he turned the station. If it played at a store or restaurant, he left.

He turned, searching for escape, but found his mom instead.

Mom's gaze sharpened on him, and her brow furrowed. "Honey, are you all right?"

His lungs felt too small for his breath. His skin too tight. He had to get out of here. He eased

Emma off his shoulder and toward his mom. "Can you . . . ?"

"I've got her, go on."

Gavin turned for the foyer and headed down a short hall, seeking an empty room. He found one on the left and pushed the door shut behind him.

She just needed a minute, was that too much to ask? But the last woman in line had done yoga with Mallory and seemed to think that made Laurel her new best friend. She'd spent at least five minutes consoling the woman.

She glanced at her friends' caskets. *Why did this have to happen, God?*

And why was she asking the same Person she'd asked last time she'd been standing up here? She'd gotten no answers then either.

It seemed her grief over Mallory's and Mike's deaths was compounded by memories of her son's funeral. It was all too familiar: the creamy, clove-like scent of lilies, the low, sad murmuring of people, the overwrought melodies humming through the speakers. How could the pain still feel so raw after four years? Sometimes it just hit her like a tidal wave. Sometimes she just *missed* him so much. She ached for the weight of his body, for the always-sticky fingers, and the softness of his baby-fine hair.

Laurel had been pushing her emotions down

for two and a half hours, and she wasn't sure how much longer she could manage. The Claytons were working their way toward the front row. The funeral would be starting soon.

Laurel patted the woman's shoulder. "I'm so sorry for your loss, uh, Francine, but I have to slip out for a moment. Thank you for coming."

"Of course. I'll catch you later."

Laurel kept her gaze on the floor as she sped from the room. Her mom had saved her a seat a couple of rows back and was no doubt trying to flag Laurel down. But she needed to collect herself.

She pushed through the door of what she remembered to be a prayer room. Light filtered through a sole window, spilling onto someone seated in one of the chairs. Her steps faltered.

Gavin. Still unaware of her presence, he hunched over, elbows on his knees. He sniffled.

Her heart squeezed tight. She was intruding on his pain. These past few days, their past a canyon between them, they'd grieved in private. At least she assumed that's what he did.

She would just slip out unseen and find someplace else to collect herself.

But as she stepped backward the floor creaked beneath her.

His head came up and his gaze connected with hers. His face was flushed, tears still streaming from his tragic eyes. His hair hung over his forehead, reminding her of that boy she'd fallen in love with so long ago.

The sight of him so broken propelled her forward. He held out his arms and she stepped into them, cradling his head to her stomach. His arms came around her.

After the initial period following their son's death, they had grieved separately. Gavin was neck-deep in guilt, and she was devastated. He withdrew from her, leaving her isolated in her pain. Losing their son was hard enough, and grieving alone only added to the misery.

But four years had passed, and now she wasn't so consumed with and blinded by her own grief. And as Gavin wept in her arms, her residual anger evaporated, making room for compassion.

This one time she could be here for him the way she now wished she could've been before. This was the way they should've grieved their son.

Her throat thickened with emotion as she threaded her fingers through his hair. Was he thinking of their son? Of Mike and Mallory? Emma? There was so much to grieve. Tears trickled down her own face, one loss melding into another.

She lowered her face to his head and breathed in the familiar scent of his shampoo. She'd missed him. She didn't want to admit it, but there it was. When she'd lost Jesse, she'd lost Gavin too. And it was all just too much. She thought she'd never pull herself back together. Why even try?

Just remembering how difficult it had been, coming out of that fetal position, made her stiffen, put that wall back in place.

He must've felt her withdrawal. He loosened his grip and eased away, giving her a speculative look. His tear-ravaged face threatened to pull her under again. Tension wove around them like a bad spell.

She tore her gaze away, took a step back, and cleared her throat. "The funeral will be starting soon. Where's Emma?"

"My mom has her. She's asleep."

"Good. I'll see you out there."

Twelve

Gavin's shoulders sagged as he closed the door behind the last of the guests. It had been a long day, and it wasn't even suppertime yet. Not that he could even think about food.

He went to the office and let Sunny out, gave her a little affection. "Sorry, girl. You missed all the excitement." But the dog's nose was already leading her through the living room. She stopped by the coffee table where her tongue lapped out, capturing a cube of cheese.

He glanced toward the kitchen where Paul and Judy were tidying up. Mrs. Clayton had seemed more comfortable working behind the scenes today than mingling with the guests. He couldn't blame her.

He joined them in the kitchen.

Judy was rearranging the freezer contents at warp speed, and Paul pushed his walker one handed, a foil-covered pan in the other. He seemed to have aged ten years in the past several days.

"Here, let me get that." Gavin took the dish from Paul and set it on the island with a dozen other dishes. He'd thought they had a lot of food before.

"I'm putting labels on each dish so we know what's inside," Judy said.

"Very helpful. Where's Laurel and Emma?"

Paul lowered himself onto a barstool. "Out back."

Gavin glanced out the French doors and spotted Laurel in the orchard, Emma riding high on her hip. The wind fluttered Laurel's dress, and the sunlight glowed through its filmy material.

What would happen now? They'd spent the whole week planning for the funeral, but it was behind them now. He assumed the Claytons would stay awhile. But surely Laurel had to return to her job by Monday. Maybe she'd even leave tonight so she could work tomorrow. He swallowed hard at the thought of her leaving, his feelings all mixed up inside. It was hard being around her again. All the memories, good and bad, toyed with his emotions. And yet . . .

His mind flashed back to that moment in the prayer room. To the way Laurel had comforted him. When she'd entered the room he'd been lost in his own pain, buried so deeply he hardly remembered where he was.

Then Laurel's face had softened with compassion, and he needed to be in her arms. His heart squeezed tight at the memory. She held him like she cared, her fingers threading through his hair the way they used to. Did she know he was grieving their child just then? Did she know how much he needed her? Her touch was more restorative than the best medicine had to offer. It began to heal a festering wound that had been long disregarded.

Then he sensed her withdrawal.

Now the door opened and Laurel appeared, brown hair mussed, reminding him of so many lazy Saturday mornings spent in bed.

He blinked away the thought as Sunny sidled up to Laurel and Emma, tail wagging.

Laurel set the child down. "It's getting ready to rain."

"Wain," Emma said. "Get wet."

"That's right," Laurel said. "We don't want to get wet."

Emma toddled off to the living room. "Sunny, come!"

The dog followed, like being the girl's minion was her favorite thing in the world. Gavin was suddenly so grateful for that dog that his throat thickened.

"What can I do?" Laurel asked Judy.

"All these dishes need to be labeled and covered. Then we'll put them in the freezer. I rearranged things a bit so it would all fit. Mercy, there's enough food for months."

"It's a great community," Gavin said. "Mike and Mallory were well loved."

Silence fell as Laurel got to work at the island.

Gavin headed to the sink and began loading the dishwasher.

From the next room Emma squealed at Sunny's antics. She'd slept through the funeral and tolerated the compassionate stares and comments at the luncheon. Gavin's family did a great job entertaining her. His mom, especially, was a huge help. She offered to stay and clean up, but having her—all the Robinsons, really—here with Laurel set things on edge. His family had questions about what would happen next, but Gavin had no answers. In the end it was a relief to see them go.

"What am I doing?" Judy froze, dish in hand, cold air wafting from the open freezer door.

"We're putting the food away," Paul said.

Judy scanned the room. "Why are we here? Where's Mike?"

Oh, dear God.

Paul's eyes locked on his wife, his facial muscles tight with dread. "Honey . . . let's step outside a minute."

"What's going on?" she asked. "What's wrong? What's happening?"

"Come on, honey." Paul pushed his walker toward the door and Judy followed, fussing after him.

Once they were on the patio, Paul took her hand.

Gavin looked away, unable to bear the grief that would spread across the woman's face yet again.

Judy's wail carried through the sliding door.

A cold shiver swept over him as he closed his eyes. Poor Judy. Poor Paul.

Laurel turned up the music that had flowed through the room during the reception.

In the living room Emma chased Sunny's tail, blithely unaware of the trauma happening outside.

Gavin glanced at Laurel, but she was back to work at the island. He turned the water back on and tried to forget what was happening outside, but his heart was still crashing into his ribs. "How awful."

Laurel shut the freezer door and slumped against the counter. "How many times is he going to have to tell her?"

But Gavin realized the words applied to Emma too. How many times would they have to tell the child before she understood her parents were never coming back?

Instead of having supper, they picked at the leftover perishables. Laurel was now upstairs tucking in Emma, and Judy and Paul had disappeared into the guest bedroom a while ago. Gavin settled on the sofa, the TV on, Sunny curled up at his feet. But he hadn't heard a word of the local news.

He grabbed his laptop and opened a custom-home bid he'd been working on.

The stairs creaked and Laurel descended, looking tired despite the early evening hour. She didn't have her suitcase in hand. Did this mean she was staying tonight? Through the weekend?

Sunny got up and followed her to the sofa across the room, and once Laurel settled she scratched the dog behind her ears.

"Emma go down okay?"

"Yeah. She was tired."

"Did she ask about . . . ?"

"No."

Laurel wasn't making eye contact. Hadn't really looked at him since that moment in the prayer room. That wall was firmly back in place, and it wasn't coming down again, not for him. Message received.

Paul shuffled into the room and settled at the other end of the sofa. He took off his glasses and rubbed his eyes.

"How's Judy doing?" Gavin asked.

"She's asleep." Paul shook his head as silence settled in the room, the newscaster's quiet voice the only sound.

Sensing Paul had more to say, Gavin shut off the TV and waited.

It didn't take long. "Listen, I don't know how to tell you this, but I've got to get her back home. She's not doing well here. Her condition has worsened tenfold, and I don't know how many more times I can . . ." His words crumbled as he squeezed the bridge of his nose.

"It's okay, Paul," Gavin said. "You're dealing with a lot."

Laurel patted his hand. "We understand."

"I feel terrible for Emma. I should be able to be here for her. I *want* to be here for her. But this is taking a terrible toll on Judy, and I think if she was back in her own surroundings, she wouldn't constantly be thinking of Mike. It wouldn't be so confusing for her."

"Take her home," Gavin said. "We've got this."

Laurel pulled her sweater together. "He's right. And I'm sure we'll be able to reach Patty soon."

"Maybe when she decides where she wants to raise Emma, we can move there—whether that's here or Florida. I want to be near Emma."

"I'm sure she'd love that." How would Judy's dementia factor into those plans? That was something Paul could figure out later.

The man blinked back tears, and his Adam's apple bobbed as he swallowed. "I can't get past the feeling that I'm dumping my grandchild on you guys."

"Hey," Gavin said. "We love Emma. We'll handle things on this end. You just worry about Judy. We'll stay in touch. Let you know how she's doing. You can FaceTime with her any time you want."

"Really, Paul," Laurel said. "We understand."

The man wiped his eyes and set his glasses back on his nose. "What a terrible day. A man shouldn't have to bury his son." His gaze flickered to Gavin. "I'm sorry . . ."

The statement punched Gavin in the heart. "Truer words were never spoken."

Laurel cleared her throat. "Would you like me to book your flight?"

"Would you mind? Judy usually does that but . . ."

"I don't mind at all. Happy to help."

"I'd like to get home tomorrow if it can be arranged." Paul wrote down all the details for the booking and handed the slip of paper and a credit card to Laurel. "Thank you. Thank you both. I don't know what we'd do if you weren't here."

"Well, you don't have to worry about that," Gavin said. "Why don't you get some rest. It's been a long day."

Laurel watched Paul head toward the spare room, all kinds of emotions swirling inside. Compassion for the couple, fear for Emma's future . . . Her gaze darted toward Gavin, then steered away once she found him staring right back. And what of the immediate future now that the Claytons—their buffer—would soon be gone?

Gavin was probably just waiting for her to drop a hint that she could handle things. Then he'd be out of here. Sure, he'd been adamant about staying through the funeral, but that was only a few days. Anyone could commit to that much.

But from here on things were pretty uncertain. Patty was an unknown. They had no way of ascertaining if the woman would take on Emma. Raising a child was a huge responsibility, and if she couldn't . . .

"What a terrible day." Gavin's low voice scraped across her heart, reminding her of the grief he'd unleashed on her earlier. She could still feel him quaking against her, his pain a tangible, awful thing connecting them. She could still feel the silky softness of his hair on her fingers.

She cleared her throat. "It's almost over now." Even though it was barely nine, she was so exhausted she could go to sleep right now. But they had things to talk about.

"You could probably head back to Asheville tonight if you wanted."

She bristled as her gaze collided with his. "I'm not going anywhere." She worked hard to keep her voice down.

"There's no reason for both of us to be here. I can take care of Emma until we reach Patty."

"We don't have any idea how long that might take."

"From what I've read," he said, "it's about a nine-day sail. She left last Saturday, so we'll reach her on Monday."

"That's if everything goes as planned. And

117

what if she can't take Emma at all? What'll happen then?"

"There's no need to go there just yet."

She shook her head. "We have to think things through and make a contingency plan, for Emma's sake."

"We should take things a day at a time and hope for the best. I live here and work here. It makes more sense for me to stay until things are settled. You've already taken four days off work."

"What's one more?"

"If we can't reach Patty till Monday, that would be two days. And that's *if* we reach her then. There's no reason for you to jeopardize your job."

She grinded her teeth. If only he'd been so supportive when they were married. It was always *his* work. *His* career. Just because his job had paid the bulk of their bills didn't make her work any less important. "Just go home, Gavin. You know you want to."

A muscle twitched in his jaw. "You have no idea what I want. You don't know me anymore, Laurel."

She knew he was a runner. He'd run when she needed him most. First emotionally, then physically. She'd never count on another man again. It hurt too much. And because she was so familiar with the feeling of being abandoned, she'd never leave Emma feeling that way.

She crossed her arms. "I'm staying until Emma's future is settled."

Gavin regarded her with a stubborn glint in his eyes. "So am I."

"Then I guess we'll just have to put up with each other."

"I guess we will." Their gazes clashed for a long moment.

Then Laurel got up and headed toward the stairs, feeling his eyes on her every step of the way.

Thirteen

Despite her mom's dire warnings about men, Laurel and Gavin breezed through their senior year of high school. Laurel was high on love. But, goals in sight, she poured herself into her academics, and in the fall she earned a full scholarship to Clemson. She couldn't stop staring at that acceptance letter. She'd done it. This was her way out, her way up.

Gavin took her to Asheville to celebrate and surprised her with a trip to the Biltmore after supper. As they walked through the gardens and grounds, she told him all about the plants and the history of the place. The grounds were a flora and fauna wonderland. And the rich history, going back over a hundred years, represented a kind of stability and continuity Laurel could only dream of. He listened and asked questions and didn't once seem bored by her passionate monologue.

At school she relished her role as Gavin's girlfriend. The football team had their best year in a decade, and shortly after the season ended, Gavin was offered a partial football scholarship to Appalachian State, where he would major in construction management.

They celebrated the offer, and the school year

seemed to fast-forward from that point. They attended prom, then graduation was upon them. She finished as class valedictorian while Gavin claimed salutatorian. And before she knew it, high school was behind them, and their uncertain futures opened up before them.

She confided in Mallory her worries about the upcoming school year. She and Gavin would go their separate ways, and the colleges were more than three hours apart. How would they remain close when they lived in separate worlds? He would be a campus football star. Surely some other girl would catch his eye, and Laurel would lose him for good.

But she couldn't give up a full-ride scholarship to a university so highly ranked for its horticulture program. And she surely couldn't ask Gavin to turn down the opportunity to attend his mother's alma mater. He'd had his heart set on AS since before he'd begun dating Laurel.

Her mom encouraged her to break up with Gavin, but Laurel couldn't even consider it. Still, her heart ached at the thought of a long-distance relationship. As July slid into August, Gavin seemed at ease about the impending separation. Once football season passed, they'd get together on weekends, and their relationship would continue as usual.

Laurel hid her fears from him, pretending to be confident that they'd breeze through these long four years apart. But really, how often did high school sweethearts make it long distance? The deck was stacked against them, and in mid-August as Gavin and Mom helped her settle into her dorm room, a dark cloud hovered over Laurel's head.

Her mom gave her a hug on the steps of her dorm building and patted her back awkwardly. "You're going to do great, honey. Stay focused on your academics—that's what matters."

But as her mom headed toward her car, Laurel couldn't even remember what classes she'd signed up for. Gavin stood in front of her, holding her hands, that boyish grin tilting his lips, and suddenly she just wanted to grab him and never let him go.

Once he left, he would be headed straight for his campus, where he'd meet other girls. Prettier girls with more to offer. Girls who'd feel more comfortable in social situations. Girls who were more fun and spontaneous.

Pain unfurled in her chest at the thought of days on end without him. Without hearing his laughter. Without kissing those lips. A sense of doom filled her. Her mother had been right. She never should've let herself fall in love with him. She'd just been asking for—

He cupped her face. "Hey, look at me. We'll see each other in two weeks, remember? And until then we'll talk on the phone every day. You'll get tired of all my texts." His eyes twinkled. "You're not going to forget about me, are you?"

Never. She forced a saucy expression. "Doesn't sound as if you're going to let me."

He chuckled and drew her into his arms and whispered into her ear, "I will be the biggest pest in the universe."

She clung to him, letting her body say what her mouth would never admit.

"You're going to be late for orientation," he said a long moment later. He kissed her softly, calming her in a way only he could. When the kiss ended, he pressed his lips to her forehead. "I'll call you when I get to campus. Cross your fingers my roommate isn't the jerk he seems on social media."

"I'm sure you'll make it work."

He held her again for a long moment. Time ticked away like a bomb.

"You're going to kill it here, Laurel." He whispered in her ear, "I love you."

"Love you too." She forced her lips into a smile as he pulled away and squeezed her hand. And then he was walking away. And her heart was beating so hard she pressed a palm to her chest just to make sure it didn't burst from her body.

The first days of college passed in a flurry of classes and meetings. Laurel poured herself into her schoolwork, organized her schedule right down to each meal break, and missed Gavin every second in between. She missed her mom and Mallory. She missed the Robinsons too. Since the time she and Gavin had started dating, they'd become her second family.

Her roommate, Sarah, was a nice girl from Asheville. Even though she was also a freshman, she seemed to have made a lot of friends already and invited Laurel to parties and girls' nights out. Laurel mostly turned her down, opting to study instead.

Gavin had been true to his word, calling every day and texting in between. He seemed to have settled in on campus, and between football and classes, he had a heavy load. Still, he made time for her. Maybe she'd been wrong about them. Maybe they had what it took to survive these four years apart.

As the second weekend approached she anticipated his visit. She couldn't wait to show him around campus and take him to the football game on Saturday night. She wanted to introduce her handful of friends to him—she was so proud of him.

But when he called the Wednesday night before his visit, she heard a foreboding tone in his voice. Maybe he'd gotten a poor grade on his English paper or had a setback on the team. "Is something wrong? You seem upset."

"Football hasn't been going very well. The coach isn't too happy with us."

She sagged against the pillows at her headboard. "Well, it's a bye week, right? You have all next week to prepare for your next game."

"That's just it. Coach doesn't think it's enough." The silence weighted the air. "He called for practice over the weekend, Laurel."

Her stomach sank like an anchor. "But . . . you can't come to see me?"

"I'm sorry. I'm disappointed too. I've been looking forward to this."

Her eyes stung with tears. The expectation of seeing him again was all that had gotten her through these two weeks. She'd been clinging to it like a life preserver. But maybe there was another way . . .

"What if I came there?" She really shouldn't spend her money on gas. Her part-time job on campus only paid minimum wage, and textbooks were expensive. "I could leave at four tomorrow, after my last class."

"Hon . . . I have a seven-o'clock study group that goes till ten, and I need it to get through my English exam. Then I have practice all day Saturday, and we're watching game tape on Sunday. We'd hardly get to spend any time together."

Study group? Did he really need that? Or was there something else behind his reluctance?

Maybe he didn't miss her as badly as she missed him. Maybe he didn't love her as much as she loved him. The thought made her chest feel hollow and achy.

Not only would she not get to see him this weekend, but his next bye week was months away. She swallowed against the knot in her throat.

"Laurel? You there?"

"I'm here." She worked hard to keep the devastation from her voice.

"I'm really sorry, baby. We'll just have to plan something else."

"Your next break isn't until Thanksgiving."

"I don't know what to say. We'll just have to make do with FaceTime and phone calls. Time will go by fast, you'll see. I'm sure you're as busy as I am."

It sounded as if he was perfectly content to wait until Thanksgiving. The thought tugged at the knot in her throat. "Of course. Time will fly by."

Time did not fly by.

August dragged into September, and the deeper they got into the school year, the less Laurel heard from Gavin. At first it was just a missed call here and there when their schedules conflicted. Soon the calls came every other day, and the texts were fewer and further between. She knew football and classwork kept him busy but couldn't knock

127

thc feeling that he wasn't pining away for her. Laurel poured herself into her schoolwork. She asked for extra hours at her campus job.

By the time October rolled around, the calls were coming only a couple of times a week and they were growing shorter. He sounded rushed and happy and always off to something else.

Though Gavin rarely got on social media, Laurel saw pictures in which he was tagged. He smiled from group shots when he was eating out or messing around on campus. He was obviously popular and well liked.

She couldn't deny her fears any longer. He'd already begun moving on without her. Sure, he still finished each phone call with "love you," but he said it so casually. Habitually. He was on his own for the first time. He was changing. And his feelings were probably changing too. They were growing apart, just as she'd feared.

These feelings swirled around for the better part of a month. She didn't talk about them with anyone. Her mom, who'd begun dating someone early in the summer, had somehow put aside her distrust of men and seemed optimistic about a relationship for the first time in Laurel's entire life. But even so, Laurel was sure if she confided in her, she'd hear the usual negative comments—and those were already filling her brain.

Mallory had her own struggles. Shortly after graduation her mom had moved to Chicago, leaving her to figure out her own housing. She moved into an apartment in Riverbend and worked her way up to assistant manager at the Iron Skillet. She was overwhelmed with real-life problems.

And Laurel knew better than to whine to Sarah about her relationship. Her roommate thought high school relationships were a waste of time. She was all about being free as a bird in college—and Laurel was starting to understand why. Her worry over Gavin was distracting her from schoolwork, and waiting for the other shoe to drop was making her miserable.

When Gavin FaceTimed her on a random Thursday in early November, Laurel had a bad feeling. He knew her schedule, of course, but they always arranged video calls in advance. As it happened she was in her dorm, studying alone. The sight of his name on the screen made her heart flutter with nerves.

She sat up on the bed, accepted the call, and tried for a smile as she propped the phone on a pillow. "Hey. I wasn't expecting to hear from you."

He was sitting at the desk in his dorm, his Braves poster visible right over his shoulder. "What are you up to?"

She held up her textbook. "Studying for my biology exam."

"Of course you are. You'll probably graduate summa cum laude."

Was he making fun of her? "Some of us are

129

here for the academics, not the social life." Her words had come out sharper than she'd intended.

His face fell. "Hey . . . I'm just teasing. I admire how hard you work."

Her skin flushed with heat. Did he compare her to the other girls he knew? Did she seem boring and predictable to him now? "Sorry, I'm just tired. How's football going?"

He told her about the last football practice, some of the terminology foreign to her. She tried to hang on, but negative thoughts persisted. He was a jock on campus and obviously a popular one. She thought of the latest photo she'd seen him tagged in with a group, including two attractive women, one of whom had been caught staring at him, midlaugh. Did she have a thing for Gavin?

Did he like her?

Her throat thickened at the thought. They hadn't talked in almost a week, and now he was rambling on about something he'd normally talk about with his buddies. And look at him. He was so handsome—and so sweet. How could girls *not* be attracted to him?

It had been quiet for a few beats.

"Well, anyway . . ." He gave an uncertain grin. "That's what's been going on with football. What's up with you?"

Laurel opened her mouth to respond.

But she was interrupted by a female calling Gavin's name.

He turned away from the phone and glanced somewhere off-screen. "I'm on a call."

"Come on, Gav, we're going to Boonie's."

Gav?

"Go on without me. I'll be a while."

"Booor-ing!" A door slammed shut.

Gavin faced Laurel again. "Sorry about that. Everyone avoids the dining hall as much as possible. The food's getting pretty old."

"Who was that?" Laurel tried to keep the raging jealousy from her voice, but the burning sensation in her stomach made her wince.

"Just a girl from upstairs. You were about to tell me what's going on there. How are your classes going?"

This woman had presumably barged into his dorm room. Were they that close? Were they more than friends? Was that why he wasn't calling and texting as much? Why their conversations had grown stilted sometimes?

Was he waiting until Thanksgiving to break up with her in person? Her mom's voice rang in her ears. *"They always leave, Laurel. You're gonna get hurt."*

Laurel pressed a hand to her chest. She couldn't handle three more weeks of this awful dread. Her mom was right. It was never going to work. Might as well just get it over with now.

"Laurel?"

She took a good long look at his face, knowing

in her heart this was the last time she'd see it on her phone. Fear sucked the moisture from her mouth. The spaghetti she'd eaten for supper churned in her stomach.

"What's wrong?"

"This isn't going to work," she blurted. And it wouldn't. The waiting for something bad to happen was eating her alive. Best to just get it over with now.

His expression fell. "What do you mean, it isn't going to work?"

"This. Us. It's not working. I can't do this anymore."

His posture stiffened and the corners of his eyes tightened. "I know being apart is hard but—"

"I can't, Gavin. It's too much. I need to focus on my schoolwork. If I want to achieve my goals I have to work hard. I can't just show up to my classes and earn straight As."

"That's not fair. I study plenty. And I know how important your grades, your future, are to you. But how exactly am I keeping you from your schoolwork? We only talk a couple times a week." Something flickered in his eyes. "Maybe something else is taking up all your time."

"Like what?"

"I don't know. Maybe you've met someone else."

If that wasn't a case of projection she didn't know what was. She gave a wry laugh as she brushed at the tears flowing down her face. "I'm not the one with girls barging into my dorm room."

"Fee's just a friend."

"Fee?"

"Felicity. Everyone calls her Fee. This isn't about me anyway. This is about you. Dumping me."

She snorted. "I'm just saving you the trouble, Gavin."

"What's that supposed to mean?"

"Never mind. It's like I said. This long-distance thing isn't working for me. We were stupid to think it would."

"Stupid, huh?"

"We're just a couple of high school sweethearts, destined for a clichéd breakup. Can't you see that?"

He stared down for a long moment, his jaw twitching. When he glanced back up, there was a different look in his eyes. A look she'd never seen before.

"Well . . . I guess your stupid high school boyfriend won't be calling you anymore."

Like a glacier calving, a chunk of her heart crumbled off. "I think that'd be for the best."

He gave her a long stare, those blue eyes burning a hole through her. "You got it."

Fourteen

Friday turned out to be the worst day since Mike and Mallory died. Laurel hadn't spoken to Gavin since the night before—she wouldn't even spare him a glance as they went about their daily routine with Emma.

That afternoon as the Claytons packed their things for their flight home, Judy was a mess, moody one minute, tearful the next. Paul was flustered when Gavin pulled him aside before they left.

"I just got off the phone with my sister, Avery. She's a doctor and runs the clinic in town. She's had some experience with dementia patients."

"I'll take all the help I can get."

"She said that when Judy asks about Mike, just go along with it. Change the subject or divert her attention by asking questions. Whatever you need to say to mollify her. She says there's no sense tormenting her with the truth when she's in a forgetful state."

Paul let out a deep breath. "That sounds so much kinder than what I've been doing."

"You didn't know. I didn't either." He put his hand on Paul's shoulder. "You'll get through this. We all will."

By the time the two of them got into their rental and drove off, Gavin was relieved to only have Emma's despondency to contend with. He shifted the girl's weight, then dried her tears. His heart broke for her. Too bad her grandparents couldn't have stayed longer. She needed all the support she could get.

Sunny trotted up to them, her blue rubber ball in her mouth.

"Look, Emma. Sunny wants you to throw the ball." Gavin started to set the child down, but Emma clutched at his shoulders.

"Let me take her," Laurel said. "You should get going anyway."

He handed Emma over. He was going to be late for his family supper, but he didn't want to further upset Emma by leaving on the heels of her grandparents.

Laurel addressed Emma. "Uncle Gavin has to leave for a while, but he'll be back later."

Emma laid her head on Laurel's shoulder, her body shuddering in the aftermath of her tears.

Gavin tugged Emma's ponytail. "Bye, Emma Bear. Be back soon."

Laurel toted Emma toward the house, distracting her by talking about what they would have for supper.

Gavin watched them go, guilt pricking him for leaving at all. She'd be fine. Laurel was good with her. And man, could he use a break.

• • •

By the time he arrived at his parents' house, the family was already gathered around the picnic table in the backyard. It was a perfect evening— barely into the eighties with big, fluffy clouds hanging on a backdrop of clear blue. He drew in a lungful of oxygen and blew it out as he approached the group.

Jeff was the first to spot him. His blue eyes lit up as he lowered his burger. His light hair had receded in recent years, but he was still attractive for a man nearing sixty. "Hey, come join us. We just started."

Cooper and Katie, who'd celebrated their first anniversary earlier this month, made room on their bench.

Avery handed him a water bottle. "Hey, Bro. Take a load off."

Wes, Avery's boyfriend and Gavin's business partner, gave him a fist bump. "How's it going, man?"

"All right."

"We hoped you'd make it." Mom had gathered her blonde hair into a ponytail, and her left dimple was present and accounted for. "Where's Emma? I thought you'd bring her. I dug up some old toys to keep her entertained."

"She's back at the house."

Mom forked a burger onto his plate. "With the Claytons?"

137

"No, they left this morning. Emma's with Laurel."

His family exchanged silent glances while he added condiments to his burger, pretending not to notice.

"She's still in town?" Mom's casual tone sounded forced.

"The Claytons had to leave on account of Judy's health. It was for the best. They could really use our prayers."

"But when's Laurel going back home?" Mom asked.

Jeff set a hand on hers. "How's Emma doing since the funeral?"

"About the same. She doesn't understand what's going on, but she's been pretty moody the past couple days." He addressed Avery. "I told Paul what you said about Judy. Thanks for that."

"No problem. As far as Emma goes, you can probably expect some regression. I have a colleague in Asheville who specializes in children and grief. I'd be happy to give you her number if you'd like."

Always the doctor, his sister. "I might take you up on that."

"Some play therapy might be helpful."

Cooper's brown eyes fastened on him. "Any luck getting hold of the aunt yet?"

"We don't expect to reach her until at least Monday. She's on a sailing expedition to San Juan at the moment," he added for the benefit of those he hadn't told yet. "I'm sure she'll come once she finds out about Mike and Mallory. They seemed fairly close."

"Is that the plan then?" Jeff asked. "That she'll become Emma's guardian?"

"That's the hope." Gavin bit into the sandwich, wishing for a change of topic. His brain needed a respite from worry.

"But won't she want to move Emma to Florida?" Cooper asked. "She's still working, right?"

"I think so. Obviously it would be better if she stayed here for a while at least. Plus there's the orchard to consider. But that would be up to Patty, of course."

"Isn't it about harvesttime?" Jeff asked.

Mouth full of food, Gavin nodded. Harvest Moon had meant so much to Mike and Mallory. Mike had maintained his job at an auto parts distributer, but the plan had been to grow Harvest Moon to the point where he could quit. They would never reach that goal now. The thought punched Gavin in the gut.

"You know, honey," Mom said. "I'd be happy to help out with Emma this weekend and next week. There's no reason for Laurel to miss more work. And I'm sure you have a lot on your plate with that house you're building."

"Thanks, Mom. But Wes is covering for me when necessary, right bud?"

"I'm all over it."

"And I've been working on a new bid from my laptop." Though his heart hadn't really been in it. That was only to be expected after such a terrible shock. Before he'd gotten news of the accident he'd been raring to find office space for Robinson Construction. Now, that couldn't seem less important. He cut Wes a look. "Speaking of bids, we should probably get together this week and go over some stuff."

"Sure thing. Let me know what day works best for you."

"But what about Laurel's job?" Sometimes Mom was like a dog with a bone. "I'm sure she's needed at the Biltmore."

He gave careful consideration to his response. While he was frustrated with Laurel, his loved ones needed no extra ammunition to use against her. "She doesn't want to leave Emma any more than I do, Ma."

His family exchanged glances over the table again.

Gavin rolled his eyes. After the rough week, maybe he was a bit on edge, but all this speculation and second-guessing was getting under his skin. He set down his burger and regarded his family with a scowl. "What? Does someone have something to say?"

A long beat of silence followed.

Avery glanced his way. "We're just worried

about you, Gav." She turned her gaze to Cooper, who picked up right where she left off.

"Being trapped in a house with your ex has disaster written all over it, don't you think?"

"Maybe if Laurel won't leave, you should," Mom said. "It'll only be for a few days, until the aunt turns up, and I'm sure Laurel can handle Emma just fine on her own."

Something dark welled up inside him at the thought of leaving the child. "I'm not deserting her."

Mom hiked a delicate brow. "Laurel or Emma?"

Gavin frowned at her. "*Emma*. Everything I'm doing is for Emma. I'm over Laurel." His heart bucked at the declaration.

"Of course, honey, but maybe you don't have to stay there, that's all."

"You could always visit Emma in the evenings," Avery said.

"Laurel might even welcome a break," Katie added.

Mom tilted a smile at him. "Caring for a child twenty-four seven is a big responsibility, to say nothing of the trauma she's experienced. It's a lot to deal with."

Gavin pressed his lips together. His family was just concerned. They were worried being with Laurel would put him in that same pit of despair he'd fallen into after the death of his son and subsequent divorce. But didn't they understand

141

he wasn't the same person now? A man didn't go through all that and come out unchanged.

But one thing that *had* changed was his priorities. He'd never again prioritize work over someone he loved. He would no more desert Emma than he would cut off his right arm. Just the thought of it made him sick.

Meanwhile, his family was still discussing what he should do—each of them having an opinion.

He crumpled the paper napkin, tossed it on his plate, then stood and stepped over the bench. "When you all decide what I should do, let me know. Thank you for having me over, but I'm going to leave now."

"Oh, honey, don't go. You just got here."

He tossed his paper plate into the trash. "If you need me, you know where to find me."

Fifteen

Bedtime was not going according to plan. Laurel set down the book and pressed a kiss to Emma's forehead. "Time to go to sleep."

Emma grabbed her arm. "Read book!"

"We already read three books. It's night-night time now."

"Princess book! Pease!" The tears wobbling in Emma's eyes made Laurel ease back against the rocking chair. It was so hard to know what to do. Sticking to the child's routine was good for her, but Laurel had to allow for grief. Didn't she?

"One more book." Laurel winced because she'd said that last time.

She opened the book and began reading. Despite the long day and short nap, Emma seemed determined to stay awake. After Gavin had left for his family gathering, Laurel kept her busy to distract her from the fact that everyone else was gone.

Even so, Emma kept asking about her grandparents and Gavin. She asked about her parents, too, and Laurel repeated the words she'd said before. By suppertime Emma was irritable, refusing to eat even the foods she normally loved. Laurel had finally let her fill up on blueberries. Mallory had been diligent about feeding the child a healthy, balanced diet, but one night without protein wouldn't kill her.

"Gabin home soon?"

Laurel stopped reading midsentence. "Yes, honey, he'll be home soon." She continued the story, making it through three more pages before Emma interrupted again.

"Want Gabin," she whined.

"I know you do, angel. He'll be home soon." Was the child worried he wouldn't come home at all? After all, her parents had probably told her they'd be home soon too.

Sorrow compressed Laurel's chest. How was Emma to trust anything at this point? Her parents had disappeared without warning.

God, are You there? Help her. Comfort her. I don't know what to say. I don't know what I'm doing.

When Laurel was almost to the end of the book, she heard the faint sound of an approaching car engine. A minute later the door downstairs clicked shut. Laurel pulled out her phone and shot Gavin a text. *Can you come to Emma's room?*

A moment later the stairs squeaked, then Emma's door opened quietly.

Gavin's face softened at the sight of the child in Laurel's arms. "Hi, Emma Bear. Is Laurel reading you a bedtime story?"

Emma bolted upright and held her arms out to Gavin. "Gabin read!"

His gaze darted to Laurel and when she nodded he said, "Of course I'll read to you." He stepped forward and lifted the child into his arms, then switched places with Laurel. "What have we got here? The princess book—my favorite. Rapunzel is so smart."

Emma settled into his arms with her floppy bunny, and Gavin began reading in that soft, steady voice he reserved for the girl. Laurel had a feeling Emma would fall asleep to the sound of his voice, and the feeling brought a pang of relief.

While Gavin finished putting Emma to bed, Laurel went downstairs, loaded the dishwasher, and cleaned the kitchen. She wished she could wipe away the image of Gavin reading to Emma as easily as she wiped up the mess under the high chair. She couldn't help but recall the gentle way he'd had with Jesse. The way he gazed at his child, lips curling into a tender smile as the boy slept. Yes, he'd worked too much—but he was a good dad. The man had the patience of Job. Never lost his temper. Laurel wished she could say the same.

Now that their marriage was in her rearview mirror she saw a lot of things more clearly. She understood why he'd worked so much. He'd been trying to provide her the sense of security she craved. Trying to prove he was a better man than his dad—a notion that had never been in question for Laurel. But for a man with an alcoholic, deadbeat dad? Yeah, it made sense.

She gave the thoughts a resolute shove from her mind. Emma wasn't Jesse, and Laurel and Gavin were no longer married. They might be sharing a house at the moment, sharing parental duties, but emotionally they were on opposite sides of the world.

She had to admit he was doing his part, though. Surprisingly, he hadn't run from the responsibility even when she'd tried to let him off the hook. He'd even picked up the slack with household chores. Maybe she wasn't the only one who'd changed over the past few years.

Laurel set the rag in the sink and headed to the office to tackle some tasks she'd been putting off. She would save a copy of Mike and Mallory's will onto a flash drive. Aunt Patty would need a copy eventually. After that, Laurel would see what she could find related to the upcoming apple harvest. Some of the fruit was ready to come off the trees.

She grabbed the will, stuck a flash drive into the port, and opened the copier lid. A document was already on the printer, facedown. She picked it up, her heart stuttering as she read the first line.

Gavin laid the toddler in the crib, then gently eased away, hoping she wouldn't stir. Emma's body relaxed, arms winging out to the side, tiny hands closed. Her chest rose and fell beneath her Minnie Mouse sleeper. Her delicate lashes fanned out against her upper cheeks, a mere shadow in the dim light.

Sweet dreams, Emma Bear.

He treaded quietly from the room and pulled her door closed behind him. He'd read four books before Emma finally dozed off. Laurel preferred they put her down awake as Mallory had done, but everything in him wanted to make Emma's life as easy as possible. She already had so much to contend with.

Gavin considered going straight to the spare room. But Laurel had finally broken her silent treatment with that text, and he should probably build on that. It would just be the two of them for a few more days, and they had to communicate— for Emma's sake at the very least.

As he descended the stairs his thoughts went back to his family's warnings about his living situation. He agreed it wasn't ideal. He just didn't have a better solution.

Laurel wasn't in the living room or kitchen. The patio seemed empty in the waning light. He made his way to the office. The light was on, and she stood by the desk, reading a document.

"She's down for the night. It only took four books." And two songs, but she'd practically been asleep for those.

"Have you seen this?" She extended the papers.

He took them and skimmed the contents. "They got a contract from a grocery chain."

"That's exactly what it is. Clean Eating is a chain in the Charlotte area. Mike and Mallory had been pursuing this contract for more than a year."

He flipped to the last page where both parties had signed. "And they got it. That's great news."

"That must be why they were flying to Charlotte—to meet with the CEO."

His stomach felt leaden at the realization. Why did this tragedy have to happen just when they were finally achieving their dreams?

"Have you looked at the desk calendar?" Laurel asked.

He glanced at the gridded schedule sprawling on the old desk. He hadn't been able to bring himself to read Mallory's scripted notes. And now that the will was in probate he needed to dig out all the ongoing bills and get them paid. "No."

"Harvest should begin soon. I don't know all the details, but I know there's a good deal of work to be done. And that contract means a lot of money for the orchard."

"I agree. But with everything up in the air . . ."

"We have to get those apples in. They worked too hard to make this happen to let them die on the trees. And this is Emma's inheritance we're talking about."

Mike and Mallory would want Emma to have

provisions for her future. "Of course. I just have no idea what an apple harvest entails. Do you?"

"I know a little, and we'll have to figure out the rest—the mortgage bill came in the mail today along with their bank statement. And trust me on this—we're going to need that harvest."

Sixteen

Gavin reached the edge of the property line and turned the riding mower around. The September sun beat down on his shoulders, and sweat trickled down his chest. The scent of mown grass permeated the air as a hot breeze cut across the property. It had taken all afternoon to mow the orchard in preparation for the harvest, and he was now tackling the front yard.

His thoughts went back to the bank statement. Mike and Mallory had barely been making ends meet. His friend's regular salary kept their household in the black, but not by much. The mortgage on this place wasn't cheap, and last year's crop had yielded fewer apples, thanks to a late-spring freeze.

Gavin didn't know much about selling apples, but he remembered Mike saying that the grocery contract they'd recently secured would be a big boon for the orchard. He owed it to his friends to see this year's harvest through, regardless of what happened with Emma. It would increase Harvest Moon's value should Patty decide to move the child to Florida.

His stomach burned. He didn't even want to think about that.

The sight of an approaching Jeep caught his eye. His sister pulled in to the driveway, and when Gavin reached the end of the row, he shut off the mower and removed his hearing protection.

As Avery jumped from the Jeep and headed his way, the sunlight picked up hints of red in her long brown hair. Her teal scrubs suggested she'd just come from work, and the sprinkle of freckles on her nose attested to hours spent in the summer sun. She seemed healthy and happy. He was glad she'd hired that doctor at the clinic last summer. Her boyfriend also seemed to have a relaxing effect on her—though it had taken Gavin a long time to admit it.

"You picked the hottest day of the week to mow," she said as she neared.

"Tell me something I don't know." He took a long swig from his water bottle.

And when she didn't say anything else he said, "Did you stop by just to bring me the weather report?"

"I came to apologize for yesterday, grouchy." Her features softened. "I'm sorry we piled on. I know this is an impossible situation, and you're just doing the best you can."

"Okay . . . I appreciate that."

She glanced toward the house, then back to him. "No offense, but I'm glad you happened to be outside. I was dreading having to face her again."

"She's not the Wicked Witch of the West, you know." Why did he always feel so compelled to defend her?

"I know that. How's it really going in there? Must be all kinds of awkward between the two of you."

Sometimes the tension was so thick he had to leave the room. Sometimes he wondered what was at the root of the tension: regret, anger, chemistry? Because, yeah, that was still there.

And he kept it buried with all the rest. "We're mostly focusing on what needs to be done. There's Emma, then there's the orchard—harvest begins soon. There's plenty here to keep us busy."

"Is Laurel—does she still . . . ?"

"Hold our son's death against me? No doubt, but we don't talk about that. No reason to get into it at this point. We have more immediate concerns."

"Of course. I just don't want her making you feel bad."

No one could possibly make him feel worse than he'd made himself feel. "Or getting her hooks into me again?"

"I didn't say that."

"Didn't have to."

His family had never fully understood Laurel. They were all so open with their affection, but Laurel was more reserved. All those walls that had been so hard to climb over protected a soft, vulnerable heart. When they were together his family had accepted her as their own. But they'd never really seen the vulnerable side of her.

"And you don't have to worry about me." He almost added again that he was over his ex-wife, but the last time he'd said it, his heart rejected the statement. Besides, there was a point at which you were protesting too much, and Avery was too perceptive to miss it.

"I also wanted to offer my help. I'm available to babysit in the evenings if either of you needs a break. Emma knows me from the clinic and church, so I'm familiar to her." She cocked a brow. "And I do know all the Disney princesses."

"She's really into all that. Thanks for the offer. I'll keep it in mind, but I'm sure we'll be able to reach her aunt soon."

Avery's gaze sharpened on him. "You think she'll take on Emma's guardianship?"

"I have every reason to think so. She's apparently financially secure, and she's obviously in good health if she went on a sailing expedition."

"It takes a lot more than health and wealth to raise a child."

Having Emma's future hanging in the balance . . . sometimes it was overwhelming. And the hearing deadline didn't help. He pulled off his ball cap and wiped his forearm across his face. "I'm just trying to take one day at a time here, Ave."

"Right. Sorry. Is there any other way I can help? I know you were looking for an office to lease for the business. Wes and I could take that on for you—meet with Realtors, inspect potential properties."

"Thanks, but I think it's best to put that on hold till all this is settled. Between Emma, the business, and the executorship, I don't have the time or energy to make that decision right now."

"I understand. Let me know if I can help in any way. I'd even be willing to cook a meal."

He gave a wry grin. "The stockpile of casseroles in that freezer will last us through the holidays." Except there was no "us," and Laurel would be gone long before the holidays. He bit the inside of his mouth.

Dismay flickered in Avery's eyes. But the next moment her lips lifted in a wan smile. "Well, I'm just a phone call away if you need me."

"Thanks. I appreciate the offer."

As his sister walked away, Gavin put his hearing protection in place and turned on the mower, all the while wondering if that slip of the tongue had been more telling than he wanted to admit.

By the time Gavin returned the mower to the barn, the sun had slipped behind the mountains. The air was thick with the scent of rain, and the temperature had dropped several degrees. He made his way through the burgeoning apple trees and onto the back patio, anticipating a shower.

As he entered the house cool air washed over his skin. Even though it was almost suppertime, the past week had taught him to enter quietly in case Emma was sleeping or Laurel was trying to put her down. Since the child was sometimes up in the night, her nap schedule had been erratic.

He entered the living room and stopped short at the sight. Laurel had fallen asleep on the sofa, orchard papers in hand, hair tumbling over the throw pillow. More documents were fanned across the end table beside the nursery monitor, which displayed Emma, sleeping in her crib.

Laurel had always been able to fall asleep anywhere. In the passenger seat of a car, watching TV on the sofa, sitting on their back deck. On their honeymoon she'd fallen asleep during their couples' massage. Afterward he teased that it was the most expensive nap she'd ever take.

Her expression was unguarded in sleep, her muscles relaxed, her lips slightly parted. Her arms were toned and sun-kissed from all the hours she worked outside. Chill bumps lifted the skin on her arm.

He pulled a lap blanket from the back of the recliner and gently placed it over her. When she didn't stir he let out a breath—she wouldn't thank him for the caring gesture.

He was about to leave the room when her

phone, sitting on the coffee table, vibrated. A banner came across the screen with a text notification from a Connor Martin.

How's it going? Let me know the minute you're back. We'll grab a bite to eat or something and celebrate your—

The notification ended there, and while he was curious to read more, he couldn't exactly open her phone.

He frowned at the cliffhanger. At the text in general. Who was Connor Martin? Did he hold a significant place in Laurel's life? More importantly, why did Gavin even care?

Seventeen

Gavin had been true to his word. After the terrible FaceTime breakup, he didn't call Laurel back. She removed his contact information from her phone and unfriended him on social media so she wouldn't have to see the photos he'd been tagged in.

But she couldn't eradicate him from her thoughts even after he was gone from her life—even after that other shoe had finally dropped. Okay, so she'd caused it to drop. But it was better this way. She'd simply left him before he could leave her. Anyway, he sure hadn't put up much of a fight, had he?

Only . . . she hadn't known she would feel so hollow inside. Didn't know that the days looming ahead without Gavin would feel so empty.

She called Mallory often, and her friend did her best to console her from afar. Encouraged her to work toward her goals.

But as one meaningless day rolled into another, she missed some of her morning classes, opting to sleep instead. The classes she did attend left her numb and tired. She moved through her days like a robot.

Class.

Study.

Sleep.

She slept a lot. In fact, afternoon naps became the norm. They sometimes slid into the evening. And weekends she barely dragged herself out of bed at all.

Much to her mother's disappointment, she didn't go home for Thanksgiving weekend. Told her she needed to stay and work on a paper that was due next week. In reality the paper was finished, but Laurel couldn't bring herself to go home where she'd have to face Gavin.

Sarah and pretty much everyone else had gone home for the holiday weekend and Laurel was glad. With the dorm hall empty, she could pull the blinds and sleep the weekend away undisturbed.

Later that weekend when a clatter woke Laurel, she was uncertain of the time of day. The hall light flooded into the dorm, then the overhead light flickered on. Her sleep-hazed eyes focused on Sarah, overloaded duffel bag drooping from her shoulder.

"Turn off the light." Laurel fell back into her pillow, closing her eyes. Part of her was relieved the weekend was over. She wouldn't have to picture Gavin back in Riverbend without her. He was back at college now, miles away in an unfamiliar world. The thought was supposed to make her feel better but somehow didn't.

The covers were ripped away from her body, and cold air washed over her.

"That's it." Sarah's duffel hit the floor. "You need to get up and get in the shower."

"Give me back my covers!"

"I knew I shouldn't have left you. This has gone on long enough, Laurel. In the shower."

"I don't want to."

"I know you don't, but I'm worried about you. It's been weeks since the breakup and you're not coping well."

Laurel jerked the cover from Sarah's hands and fell back into her pillow. "Leave me alone."

It was quiet for a minute. Maybe Sarah would go away and let her fall back into oblivion again. Tomorrow would arrive soon enough, and Laurel had to attend her morning bio class. She'd missed two already.

"If you don't get up and get in the shower, I'll call student affairs tomorrow."

Something red and hot swelled in her chest. "This is none of your business! I'm just tired."

"You're not tired, Laurel. You're depressed. And sleeping all day isn't going to fix it."

"Of course I'm depressed! We broke up and I still love him." Her words crumbled off and tears tumbled down her cheeks. A sob stole her breath. She loved him so much! What had she done? She wrapped her arms around her pillow and buried her face in it.

God, will this pain never end?

Maybe she'd made a terrible mistake. But if he'd really loved her as he said, wouldn't he have fought for her? And if she'd broken up with him, why did she feel so . . . abandoned?

The mattress sank under Sarah's weight, and she rubbed Laurel's back for a long moment, letting her cry it out. How many tears would she have to shed to be rid of this awful ache in her chest? When would she get over him? Why had she ever let herself fall in love? It was awful! Her mother had been right. She'd never let this happen again. She'd been so stupid.

Sometime later her sobs ebbed, leaving her pillow drenched and her muscles weak.

"When was the last time you ate, sweetie?"

"I don't know."

"You've lost weight. If I didn't see how much you were suffering I'd be jealous. Now, come on. Let's get you in the shower, then we'll get you in clean clothes and find you something to eat."

"It's too much. I don't have the energy."

"Look at me." Sarah gently turned Laurel's face toward her. Compassion filled her hazel eyes. "We're going to get you through this. One thing at a time. Let's get you in the shower, and we'll worry about the rest later. Come on. I'll help you."

Laurel allowed Sarah to help her up and walk her to the bathroom.

But even after the shower, clean clothes, and a bit of food, she still felt hollow inside.

Laurel dragged herself through the following weeks. By sheer force of will she went to class, studied, and even went out with Sarah and her friends a couple of times. Mallory called often, sharing silly stories from the diner that took Laurel's mind off her troubles. Mallory also needed her support. Though her mom was now living in a different state, that hadn't stopped Darcy's spiteful comments or manipulative behavior.

The ache in Laurel was starting to abate at least enough to allow her to breathe again. Every time she thought of Gavin she turned her thoughts to her goals instead. Despite her somewhat rocky semester, she *would* graduate summa cum laude. Then she'd get a good job, buy a nice home, and be financially independent.

Before she knew it the semester was winding to a close and winter break loomed ahead. Her mom was going on a Christmas cruise with her boyfriend, and Mallory was busy with her work, so there was no reason to return to Riverbend Gap and torture herself with the sight of Gavin. Surely he'd moved on. He probably had a girl-friend already. Might even bring her home to meet his family. She didn't want to subject herself to that.

But staying here in the empty dorm seemed ill

advised. She was afraid she'd fall back into bed and tumble into that deep well she'd fallen into last month. So when Sarah's family invited her to spend Christmas with them she jumped at the chance.

Christmas in Asheville was a nice distraction. The holiday passed in a flurry of events, home-cooked meals, and presents. Sarah's family was warm and welcoming and Laurel's mom FaceTimed with her on Christmas Day from some Caribbean island. She was having a fabulous time, and though Laurel had told her about the breakup, she'd never divulged the depth of her heartache.

Just after Christmas Mallory came down to spend a day with her. They ate lunch out, shopped the afternoon away, then went to the Biltmore to see the Christmas decorations. Laurel wandered through the gardens, amazed at the transformation. The conservatory was abloom with red and white poinsettias. On the grounds, white twinkle lights and Christmas greenery decked every available surface.

The day's light was fading, the mountains in the distance just a silhouette against the evening sky. "I'm going to work here someday," she reminded Mallory on the front lawn from beneath a massive decorated Christmas tree, lit with a zillion lights.

Mallory took her arm, pressing close. "You'll be running the place by the time you're thirty."

As nice as the holiday was, Laurel was glad to return to her college routine. She was determined to make straight As from this point on. Focusing on schoolwork beat thinking about Gavin. *This* she could control. *This* wouldn't break her heart and leave her in the fetal position. *This* would get her one step closer to her dreams.

With the summer stretching ahead, Laurel applied for a summer internship at the Biltmore in the Human Resources department—there were no openings in horticulture at present.

Having no desire to return to Riverbend for spring break, she worked right through it, adding to her savings account. And the next week she received news that the Biltmore had offered the internship to another student.

The rejection left her in a quandary about where she would spend her summer. She didn't have the money to stay in Clemson, and Sarah was going home. Laurel tried to convince Sarah and a couple of friends to share an apartment in Asheville, but they preferred to go home and save for tuition.

Much as it pained her, Laurel needed to do the same. So as June neared she contacted her old boss, Nancy Owens, and secured summer employment at the nursery. When the last day of the semester arrived, she went home for the first time since the breakup. Mallory was thrilled to see her and excited for a whole summer together.

Laurel's mom, blooming with love, was a

lighter, brighter person these days. Laurel was happy for her, but what had happened to all her reservations about men? And Laurel fervently hoped Brad wouldn't break her heart.

But Laurel had her own life to worry about. The nursery was even busier this summer than last, so they gave Laurel all the hours she wanted—and Laurel wanted all the hours. It would go a long way toward expenses that weren't covered by her scholarship, and it kept her from dwelling on Gavin—whom she'd heard was also home for the summer.

She was in the greenhouse, deadheading the tea roses when she heard someone approaching from behind. She snipped a dead bloom from the cane at an angle, then opened her mouth to offer assistance.

"Hello, Laurel."

At the sound of his voice, her breath caught in her chest. She somehow managed to keep hold of her shears. Steeling herself, she turned to face him.

He seemed taller than she remembered, but that couldn't be right. His shoulders had broadened, though, under his rigorous training schedule. And that lovely jaw of his sported a five-o'clock shadow. He offered a tentative smile, those blue eyes laser focused on her.

The shears trembled in her hands. "What are you doing here?"

His smile slipped. "I heard you were home for the summer and working here again. I thought I'd stop by. You know. See what you were up to."

It had taken months to get her act together. And a single sighting of him made her feel like the floor had dropped from under her feet. "I can't talk right now. I'm working."

She turned back to her roses. The shear's blade slipped on the cane, an incomplete cut. Drat. She caught sight of her boss helping a customer with the hydrangeas.

"I just wanted to talk. Maybe we can—"

"I'm sorry but I'm working. Unless you want to buy a plant you should probably go."

He didn't respond.

Nothing but quiet. Just conversations going on around the greenhouse. The snipping of shears somewhere behind her. A car engine coming to life outside. Gavin must've left, though she hadn't heard retreating footsteps. Maybe that was his truck firing up. Maybe even now he was pulling from the—

A shuffle sounded behind her. "Fine. I'd like to buy a plant then."

She cut him a look. "Really. What kind?"

"Something for my mom. You pick it."

Laurel gave a huff. "Indoor or outdoor? Plant or flower?"

"Indoor flowering plant."

She wandered down the row and selected a

167

potted African violet, blooming in Lisa's favorite color. She held it out to Gavin. "I think she'll like this."

"Purple's her favorite color."

Still holding the pot, Laurel's chin notched up. "Are you going to take it or not?"

His lips twitched as he relieved her of the plant. "I believe I will. Thank you."

"You can pay for it inside." She tried to step around him.

He edged over and blocked her path. "Should she keep it in the sun or shade?"

Laurel frowned at him. "Indirect light." She started to pass him again.

"How much water?"

"Your mom has been tending plants longer than I've been alive. She'll know how to care for a violet. Is there anything else?"

"Would you like to catch up over coffee?"

"Thank you for the offer, but I don't think that's a good idea."

"Why not?"

What was she supposed to say to that? Why was he here, messing with her sanity? She threw her hands up. "I have to get back to work, Gavin." She nailed him with a long look.

He moved aside to let her pass.

She didn't relax until his old truck pulled from the gravel lot.

For the next few weeks she was on edge at

work, worried (hoping?) he'd show up again. But he didn't. She spotted him once at the Trailhead, eating with Cooper and Avery. But she'd only come for takeout, so she ducked out unseen.

But the first week in July she turned from helping a customer, and there he was again. Her thundering heart betrayed her excitement at seeing him again. He approached, those faded jeans making the most of his long legs, that T-shirt stretching around his sculpted biceps, those eyes homing in on her. It just wasn't fair what he did to her.

Why was he here? Why did he keep coming around? She went back to her hydrangeas.

"Not even going to greet your customer?"

"Are you here to buy another plant?"

"I believe I will. My mom loved the violet. Thank you."

"No need to thank me. You're the one who bought it." She blew out a breath. "Are we really going to do this again?"

"Do you have any potted peonies?"

Her favorite—but he wouldn't remember that. She'd only mentioned it once in passing. She gestured across the greenhouse. "They're over there."

"Can you show me?"

Willing herself to be patient and professional this time, she pulled off her gloves and walked to the end of the row. She wouldn't let him get to her. Wouldn't let him know that his nearness disrupted her heart's rhythm.

"Maybe you can select one for me," he said when they reached the right section.

She chose a flourishing plant with beautiful coral blooms. She'd been admiring their vibrant color all summer. "How about this one?"

He accepted the plant without even looking at it. "Perfect."

He didn't move.

Laurel crossed her arms. "Aren't you going to ask me how to care for it?"

"Nope." He offered a smile. "Thanks, Laurel." He carried the plant toward the register.

Laurel gave her head a shake. Was he just going to come in here every few weeks and knock her marbles loose? Give her lungs a workout? What was his deal anyway? Was he one of those guys who thought a couple could actually be friends after a breakup?

She huffed. Fat chance.

By the time her shift ended, she was ready for a nice, warm shower and a good book. But when she reached her car, her foot connected with something on the ground. There, right beside her car, sat that beautiful coral peony plant, and she didn't need a note to tell her who had left it.

Gavin didn't return to the nursery until late July. Laurel tried not to react when she saw him striding down the row of petunias toward her.

She continued watering the hanging plants. "Can I help you?" she asked when he stopped beside her.

He leaned casually on the table beside her. "Did you like the peonies?"

She'd never thanked him for the flowers. But she cared for the plant like it was a newborn baby. "You know I did since I picked it out myself. But you didn't have to do that. Can I help you find something?"

"Meet me for coffee, Laurel. Come on. I just want to talk."

"We really don't have anything to talk about."

"Speak for yourself." He continued staring at her. "I have plenty to say."

She kept working, but her hands wouldn't cooperate. The water dribbled down her gloves and into her sleeves.

"Are you dating anyone?" he asked.

Laurel pursed her lips. He was not going there. She told herself she didn't care about his interest in her romantic life, but her racing pulse refuted the claim. Maybe it wasn't only friendship he sought.

"Mallory said you're not."

She couldn't believe her friend had divulged that information. Then again, Mallory had always thought Laurel and Gavin were perfect together. "Mallory doesn't know everything."

He tilted his head. "So you *are* seeing someone?"

"What's this all about, Gavin? Why do you keep coming here?"

"Have coffee with me and I'll tell you."

"If I do will you stop bothering me at work?" Drat. She hadn't meant to say that.

His eyes lit with the win, and the corners of his mouth curled upward. "Yes. How about if I pick you up at four?"

Now she'd seem like a chicken if she tried to back out. Like she had something to fear, something to lose. There was no way out of this. But he wasn't picking her up like this was a date or something. "I'll meet you there at four."

He straightened from the table. "Thank you. I'll see you then."

After her shift, Laurel changed outfits three times. At a few minutes after four she approached the coffee shop in the most casual clothes she owned—a Clemson tee and cutoffs she usually reserved for gardening. But she had tidied up her ponytail and couldn't resist adding a coat of mascara and a natural-colored lipstick.

Now she shook her head at her foolishness. As she entered the shop the robust aroma of coffee filled her nose, and cool air skittered over her arms.

From a corner table Gavin waved.

Her nerves jangled even as she worked to keep her expression neutral.

He rose as she approached and gestured toward a drink on the table. "I hope you still drink chai."

She hung her purse on the chair and sank into it. "Thank you. I'll pay you back."

"No worries. I invited you."

She took in his freshly shaven jaw and the button-down—same shade of blue as his eyes. His hair, cropped a bit shorter than he used to wear it, made him seem a little older. More mature. More handsome.

"You look great," he said. "I mean . . . it's good to see you."

He was nervous too. Somehow that didn't make her feel better. She sipped her drink, made just the way she liked with coconut milk and a dash of vanilla. So what if he'd remembered her drink. They'd been together two and a half years after all.

"So . . . catch me up with what's going on," he said. "How'd your school year finish up?"

"It was fine. My grades are good."

"I had no doubt."

This was so weird. Maybe he was just trying to get them back on friendly terms so they could run into each other without this terrible awkwardness. Summer was almost over, but there would be many more breaks coming up. It would be best if they could at least exchange casual greetings.

Maybe someday seeing him wouldn't make her chest ache.

"And you?" she asked belatedly. "How did your classes finish up?"

He gave a sheepish smile. "Not as well as I would've liked. But I'm not in danger of probation or anything."

That probably meant he'd gotten a couple of Bs. "I'm sure football and baseball kept you busy."

He ducked his head, then glanced back up at her. "I, uh, didn't play baseball this spring."

She blinked. "Why not?"

"I just . . ." He shrugged. "I don't know. Decided not to. Better for the grades, I guess."

He loved baseball even more than football. But it was the latter that had earned him the scholarship so maybe he'd decided to focus his athletic efforts there.

"How's your mom doing?" he asked. "I've seen her around town this summer with Brad."

"Yeah, they're still dating. She seems happy."

"That's good. And Mallory? How's she doing?"

Remembering that Mallory divulged Laurel's single status, she quirked a brow. "Maybe you should tell me—you seem to be keeping up with her."

A flush creeped up his neck. "I run into her sometimes at the Iron Skillet . . . Does she enjoy working there? I guess she's assistant manager now."

"She likes it but I don't think it's her forever job or anything. She wants to own a farm or something like that. She's dating Mike Clayton now. He graduated a couple years ahead of us."

"I remember him. He set a couple track records."

"He's very nice. He just got his pilot's license."

"I think I heard that. He's attending Mars Hill, isn't he?"

"Yeah, he's studying business."

"Well, I hope it works out for them." Their gazes met, tangling for a long moment. Both of them seeming to realize that the platitude he'd tossed out wouldn't be true for the two of them.

His gaze grew intense, the corners of his eyes tightening. "I miss you, Laurel."

He wanted her back. Something inside went soft with longing even as warning flags waved. She was weak. So weak. She could not go that route again. It led to nothing but heartache. *Remember where you were. Remember those days in bed. Remember the slow climb out. Don't do this to yourself again.*

She pressed back into her seat, drawing as far away from him as she could. "Don't say that, Gavin."

He leaned forward, elbows on the table. His expression offered something she longed so badly to reach out and grasp. "Why not? It's true."

Fear flowed like a ribbon of poison through her veins. She reached for her purse.

He took her hand. "Don't leave. Please. Hear me out."

"I didn't come here for this. It won't work."

His eyes sharpened on her face, probably seeing far more than she wanted him to. "It's okay. Slow down. Talk to me."

She settled back in her seat, willing her heart to stop thudding in her chest. She would be okay. He couldn't make her do anything she didn't want. But that was the problem, wasn't it? Her stupid heart wanted him right back. And she was afraid she was too weak to turn him away.

"Tell me why it won't work," he said gently, his hand still on hers. His thumb stroking the back of it.

She jerked her hand away. "It just *won't*. We live hours apart, Gavin. You didn't make me a priority. I didn't feel like you were committed to me, to us."

"That's not true—"

"You were too busy with everything else to call and text, and I'm not doing that again. I can't. I won't."

"I'll admit I took you for granted. You have no idea how sorry I am for that. If you give me another chance, I'll prove to you that—"

"No. Long-distance relationships don't work. I'm not going through that again." Mallory's words flickered in her mind. Her friend was always encouraging her to open up again—sometimes even in reference to Gavin. She pushed the thought away.

Gavin's brows knitted and his eyes narrowed thoughtfully. A moment later his expression relaxed and he tilted his head back. Gratification flickered in his eyes.

She jutted her chin out. "What? What's that look for?"

Their gazes tangled for a long moment, that annoying triumphant look still twinkling in his eyes. "You never said you don't love me anymore."

Heat flushed through her, collecting in her cheeks. She had to get out of here. She stood and nailed him with the most confident expression she could muster. "This was never meant to be, Gavin. Go back to college and get on with your life. That's exactly what I'm going to do."

Eighteen

Gavin pulled his truck into the church parking lot and turned into an empty space.

From her car seat, Emma peeked out the window. "Church!"

"That's right, we're going to church."

He and Laurel had had a long discussion about it the night before. It was important for Emma to resume her routines, and church was a big part of that.

Gavin glanced at the traditional clapboard building with the towering white steeple. He and his family had attended here as long as he could remember. Laurel had gone with him when they'd dated and during summers while they were in college.

He glanced at her as she unbuckled her seat belt. "You don't have to go. I'm sure she'll be fine. I can handle anything that comes up." They'd been through this last night, but he wanted to offer her one last chance.

"I'm going." She unbuckled Emma from her seat and lifted her out. "Let's go see your friends, angel."

"Bubbles!"

Laurel glanced at Gavin.

"They have a bubble machine in her class."

"What fun." As she exited the cab Gavin thought he heard her murmur, "Can I come with you?"

They made their way across the parking lot. To a stranger they would look like the perfect family heading to church. But they were nothing of the kind. Not anymore.

At the door, cool air and the happy sounds of chatter greeted them. Worship music filtered through the building, and fresh flowers and pine cleaner scented the air. Gavin cut through the foyer, greeting folks briefly as he went.

By the time they reached the children's hall, tension had stiffened Laurel's spine. This was basically enemy territory for her. It was a terrible thing to say about a church, but the members didn't really know Laurel, and they were protective of their own. He wished he could set a hand on her shoulder for support, but she wouldn't welcome his touch.

This was partially his fault. The Robinsons were a bedrock family in the community, in this church. In the sixties when the town's silver mine was failing, Jeff's grandfather had petitioned to have the Appalachian Trail brought through Riverbend Gap, right down Main Street. When the idea was approved, it brought new life to the town. That reason alone endeared the Robinsons to the community.

The family was still heavily involved in the town: Jeff was on the Better Business Bureau board, Avery ran the medical clinic, and Cooper was county sheriff. Their mom participated in the Rotary and Garden Clubs, and she'd pioneered and now spearheaded Trail Days—their annual fall festival that had proven to be a big boon for the local businesses.

Gavin stopped at the sign-in table, now staffed by a very familiar woman—Mom was also director of the children's department. The couple in front of them finished signing in and slipped away.

Mom turned her smile to the next in line, and when her gaze fell on Laurel, it faltered.

"Morning, Mom," Gavin said.

"Good morning."

He bent over the table to sign in. "Emma's looking forward to class today."

Mom beamed at the child. "Good morning, honey. We're so happy you're here. The bubble machine is on, and your friends are already playing in your classroom."

"Pop bubbles," Emma said.

Mom beamed. "Yes, you can pop the bubbles, sweetheart. You're going to have so much fun."

Emma was pretty darned adorable this morning in a denim dress with white sandals. A daisy adorned each of her curly pigtails.

His mom pressed a name tag onto Emma's back.

"She goes to classroom two. Have fun, sweetheart."

Gavin ushered Laurel in front of him as they headed toward the classroom. They'd worried Emma might balk at leaving them. But when Laurel set her down, the girl toddled right into bubble mania with the other children.

He and Laurel slipped away, trading a look of relief. One hurdle down.

On the way to the sanctuary Gavin greeted more friends and neighbors. He tried to keep the conversations brief, but everyone wanted to know how Emma was doing and what was going on.

While he chatted, Laurel lagged behind him, checking her phone. As much as he wanted to draw her in, she was more comfortable in the background. Especially when the folks here probably still blamed her for his post-divorce misery. He'd never exactly set them straight on that. In his defense he'd been deeply depressed, and with Laurel all the way in Asheville, people's opinions hadn't seemed to matter.

But now, with Laurel at his side and surrounded by his church family, it seemed very relevant. True, this would be her one and only Sunday here, but maybe if he showed he had no hard feelings, she'd be more comfortable returning home to visit her mother.

The sanctuary was filling up. His family had taken their usual pew up front, on the left.

Everyone was already there except his mom.

"Go sit with your family," Laurel said. "I'll be back here."

He touched her arm. "Come sit with us. There's plenty of room."

She snorted. "No thanks. I'll see you after church." She turned left and edged down the second-to-last pew and took a seat at the far end.

Gavin paused only a moment. Then he followed her down the row and sank onto the bench beside her. Let everybody get a big eyeful. They might think he and Laurel were back together. Oh well. What was the worst that could happen? Anyway, it was a small town. By now word had circulated about Emma's guardianship situation. He'd already fielded several questions about Emma's aunt. Apparently, it had been a matter for the prayer chain. So they must know Laurel was sticking around for the child's sake.

"What are you doing?" Laurel whispered.

He cut her sideways glance. "Sitting beside you."

"You should go sit with your family."

"I'm fine right here."

She gaped at him. "What will everyone think?"

"I really don't care."

"Your family keeps looking back here."

Just then Avery turned and gave a little wave, then whispered something to Wes, who also turned.

Gavin waved at him too. "Don't care about that either."

She huffed.

He bit the inside of his mouth to keep from smiling. What was it about riling Laurel that amused him so much? Even now, after all they'd been through? She'd always been so unflappable. It was just fun getting a rise out of her, seeing some emotion leak past that heart she guarded so closely.

"People are staring," she hissed.

Good. Maybe they'd realize Laurel wasn't the enemy. He opened the bulletin and skimmed its contents. Budget was looking good. There was a church-wide bonfire coming up. The youth were taking an overnight hike to Max Patch. The church was already collecting canned goods for the Thanksgiving boxes they would deliver to families in need.

"I don't mind sitting by myself," Laurel whispered.

Gavin closed the bulletin as the worship leader took the stage. "Shhh . . . The service is starting."

She gave another loud huff.

And Gavin had to bite his lip again.

Nineteen

On Sunday night when Laurel saw the name flash across her phone screen, she didn't want to answer the call. But she didn't dare let it go to voice mail. Emma was helping Gavin load the dishwasher, so she slipped into the living room and took her boss's call.

After exchanging pleasantries, Richard got right to the point. "Listen, Laurel. I realize you're in a tough spot with your friends' daughter. I admire what you're doing, I really do. But I just wanted to give you a heads-up that your absence around here has not gone unnoticed. Greg's got his eyes on my job, and he's been getting pretty cozy with Diane."

Laurel's stomach bottomed out. Diane would make the final decision about who would replace Rich. "Are you still recommending me for the job?"

"Of course. But that only holds so much weight. Greg's been here a few years longer than you, and he has a way with people. He's taking advantage of your absence, Laurel, and I'm afraid what'll happen if you're gone much longer."

He didn't need to state the obvious: Laurel was much better with plants than she was with people.

"You mentioned you have some help with Emma. Have you considered commuting? Or even bringing her to Asheville until a more permanent arrangement can be made?"

Gavin would never agree to that. "We're expecting to hear from Emma's aunt any day now. I'm sure it won't be much longer. Anyway, I can't uproot her after she just lost her parents."

A weighted silence filled the gap. "I understand. Poor kid. I'm not trying to coerce you into anything you're uncomfortable with. I just . . . I wanted to make you aware of what's happening. If you take much more time away, I'm afraid Greg will end up getting the promotion, and I didn't want you blindsided by the news when you return."

She was *this* close to getting her dream job. The thought of losing the opportunity made her hands tremble. If Greg secured it, he'd almost certainly be there till he retired, and he was only a few years older than Laurel. It was now or never.

But she couldn't abandon her best friend's daughter. "I appreciate the call, Rich. I'll do everything I can to wrap things up here as soon as possible." She winced. She'd made Emma sound like a chore to tick off her list. "How's Anna doing?" His wife's diagnosis with ovarian cancer had pushed up his retirement by a year or so.

"She's doing her treatments. We won't know

for a few months how much effect it's having."

"That must be very difficult. I'm praying for you both."

"Thanks, Laurel. We'll take all the prayers we can get."

When she got off the phone Laurel looked for Ruby's contact and tapped the number. The dining supervisor answered on the second ring. "Hey, sweetheart. I've been thinking about you. How's it going with the kiddo?"

"She's doing about as well as can be expected." Laurel began picking up toys and returning them to the box in the corner. Amazing the mess a two-year-old could make in one day.

"Any word from her aunt?"

"No, but we expect to reach her soon. How are things in The Dining Room?"

"Oh, much the same. Connor keeps asking about you." The last was said with a teasing note.

Connor was head chef. He and Laurel had gone on a date a few days before she'd gotten the call about Mallory. "He's been checking in with me occasionally."

"I'll bet he has. Boy has it bad for you, honey."

"He barely knows me. We've only had one date."

"Must've been some date. He's counting the days until your return. Kayla said he asked about you—wanted to know if you might like to go to the theater. Of course Kayla told him you weren't too fond of musicals."

"Well, he gets an A for effort, I guess." She really didn't want to talk about Connor. Sure, he was nice and attractive, but he seemed a million miles away right now. "Listen, I was wondering if you'd heard any gossip regarding the promotion. I just got a call from Rich, and he seems concerned my absence might be causing some problems."

"Oh no. I haven't heard a word, but I'll keep my ears open. Diane would be a fool to give that job to anyone else."

"Even Greg?" She turned to pick up the magnetic blocks and found Gavin leaning on the wall between the kitchen and living room. How long had he been standing there? How much had he heard?

"Especially Greg! He spends more time watering the grapevine than those garden plants he's supposed to be tending."

"Thanks, Ruby. Well, listen, I have to run. You have a great week. I'll let you know when I'm coming back." Laurel disconnected and began picking up the blocks. "Where's Emma?"

"Playing outside."

She glanced past the screen door to the patio, where Emma was jabbering away. She turned her sand bucket upside down and set it on Sunny's head while the dog sat patiently, panting.

"I didn't mean to eavesdrop," he said, "but are you up for some kind of promotion at work?"

Laurel stacked the blocks into the Rubbermaid container. She couldn't see any reason not to tell Gavin about the job. "Rich is getting ready to retire. He's recommending me for his job."

Gavin straightened, beaming. "Hey, that's amazing, Laurel. Why didn't you tell me?" He seemed so . . . proud of her.

A rush of pleasure flushed through her body. Nobody knew better than Gavin how much she'd had her heart set on that job. "It's not a sure thing yet. He's not the one who gets to make the call."

"Diane's always liked you, though. She's still calling the shots, right?"

"Yeah, she is . . ." But Rich was right to worry about Greg. Everyone liked him—probably even Ruby, though she appreciated the woman coming to her defense. It was impossible not to like Greg, and he was an excellent gardener. She could easily see him stepping into the position.

Gavin knelt on the floor and helped with the blocks. "Your being here is causing a problem."

"I'm sure everything will work out the way it's supposed to."

He took her hand. "You can't risk that promotion, Laurel. It's your dream job. Why don't you just commute? I can figure out Emma's care."

The familiar weight of his hand, the concern on his face tugged at her heartstrings. Made her wish things had worked out differently. "Patty's supposed to return tomorrow. This'll all be over soon, and I'll go back home and resume my job, right?"

Their gazes tangled for a long moment. Something shifted in his eyes. His brows smoothed out as his gaze drifted over her features. "Right."

"Gabin, see Sunny!" Emma called from the patio, laughing.

Their gazes held another instant. Then with one last wistful look, Gavin got up and went outside.

Twenty

Time to check the apples. Laurel finished loading the dishwasher, then gathered her supplies on the island. Though it was too early for bedtime, Gavin was upstairs playing with Emma. From the sounds of her laughter filtering through the ceiling, all was well.

She lined up three apples—Red Delicious, Golden Delicious, and Jonagold, along with the refractometer and a butter knife. She'd learned a lot just from helping Mallory out with the orchard a few times. Harvesttime for each apple type varied, and many factors determined the right time to pick the fruit, including their ultimate purpose. These apples would be sent to Clean Eating. She'd already been in contact with them and ironed out the details.

She sliced the Red Delicious in half, finding the seeds nice and dark. She took a bite of the flesh, and the juices burst from the fruit with a mild, sweet flavor.

Now to measure the sugar content. She put a drop of juice on the refractometer's slide, closed the lid, and peered through the eyepiece. After turning the focus ring, she read the scale. Ten degrees Brix. Between the sugar content and taste test, the Red Delicious apples were ready for harvest.

She moved onto the Golden Delicious and found the fruit not quite ready. The Jonagold tested the same.

When she was done she finished off the Red Delicious apple and cleaned up the mess. It was time to get Emma into the tub. It had been quiet up there for a while—or maybe Laurel had been too focused on her task to notice the sounds.

She went upstairs, her mind already on the harvest. She'd call Emilio in the morning—she'd touched base with the crew supervisor last week and told him they were getting close. But what would happen after Patty came and Laurel had to leave? There was a lot to running an orchard, and it was a critical time in the growing season to be on the wrong side of the learning curve. She couldn't risk Mallory and Mike's hard work. But what other choice did she have?

As she hit the top of the staircase, quiet sounds of play carried from the nursery. When she reached the open door, she peeked inside.

Emma rooted through her toy box and came up with a pair of flamingo sunglasses. She walked them over to Gavin, who sat on the floor by the rocking chair—wearing a bejeweled tiara and a hot-pink feather boa. His hand grasped a plastic scepter capped with a huge pink jewel.

Biting back a bubble of laughter, Laurel

stepped fully into the doorway, posture perfect and pasting on an expression worthy of the queen's royal court. She lowered her weight in a deep curtsy, bowing her head. "Your Majesty."

Gavin scowled at her. "Very funny." He dropped the scepter and pulled the boa from his neck. "Emma's playing dress-up."

"Looks like you're the one playing dress-up." Laurel didn't remind him about the tiara, still perched atop his head.

"Gabin princess!"

"I see that." Laurel turned loose her smile. "He makes such a beautiful princess."

"Bootiful." Emma placed the flamingo sunglasses on his face, temples spread wide to accommodate his head.

"Now, these are cool," Gavin said. "How do I look?"

"Too wittle." Emma took them off.

Laurel checked the time. "Guess what, angel? It's bubble time. You want Gavin to give you a bath or me?"

"Gabin *and* Waurel."

Laurel's gaze connected with Gavin's.

"All right by me." He stood. "I'll run the bath."

He stood, still looking pretty regal in that sparkly tiara. Laurel arched a brow at him, biting back a grin.

"What?" he asked.

"Nothing."

He rolled his eyes and headed toward the bath room.

She lifted Emma into her arms and whispered, "He forgot to take off the tiara."

Emma giggled. "Gabin princess."

"Silly Gavin," Laurel whispered as the bathwater came on in the next room. She rummaged through Emma's drawer, found her *Frozen* pajamas, and pulled them out.

"Oh, ha-ha," Gavin called out over the sound of gushing water. "Very funny, Laurel."

She burst out laughing, and Emma covered her mouth, giggling.

Laurel lifted a dripping wet Emma from the tub, and Gavin wrapped a thick, fluffy towel around her. He grabbed the thick-toothed comb and ran it through Emma's baby-fine curls while Laurel dried her off.

He listened as his ex-wife carried on a conversation about the things they'd done and seen today. The bunny in the orchard. The spider web on the deer fence. Emma listened intently, repeating key words and phrases, as Laurel helped her into her pajamas. She was so good with Emma. Always seemed to know just what to say, what to do.

Gavin grabbed the girl's toothbrush from the medicine cabinet and was just about to squirt on a dab of toothpaste when his phone buzzed in his pocket.

He pulled it out and froze at the number on the screen. "It's a Florida area code."

Laurel sobered. "Take it. I'll get Emma to bed."

He slipped from the room and as he went downstairs, he answered the call.

"Gavin?" a woman replied. "This is Patty Dupuis—Mallory's aunt."

He sighed. Finally. "Of course. You got my message."

"I'm so sorry I missed your calls. I was on a sailing expedition. I just arrived in Puerto Rico this afternoon and charged my phone."

"Your neighbor filled us in. That sounds like quite an undertaking."

"It's quite exhilarating. Is everything okay? Is Mallory all right?"

He'd been so eager to reach the woman, he hadn't given much thought to how he'd break the news. "I'm afraid I have some terrible news, Patty. It's about Mallory and Mike. They were flying back from Charlotte and . . . their plane went down. There's no easy way to say this— they both died in the crash."

Shocked silence filled his ear. A moment later she burst into tears. "Oh no. No, it can't be true."

He ached for her. "I'm so sorry for your loss. I know this is a terrible shock."

"When did this happen?"

"A week ago yesterday."

"My sweet little Mallory." She gasped. "Emma! What about Emma?"

"Emma's fine. She wasn't with them. She's here at her house with Laurel and me."

"Oh, that poor child. She must be so confused. Did Mallory—was it quick? Do you know?"

"My brother was present on the scene—he's the sheriff. Mike was already gone by the time help arrived. Mallory was unconscious. They took her to the hospital, but she passed during surgery. I don't think she was aware of anything. I don't think she suffered."

Patty wept quietly, and Gavin forced himself to wait. To let the news sink in before he had to hit her with the question about Emma's future.

"I can't believe this has happened," Patty said a while later. "I was out *sailing* when my niece was dying in an awful plane crash."

"You couldn't have known. There's no reason to feel guilty."

"I—I should come in for the funeral. When will it be?"

He winced. "I'm sorry to tell you, but the decision was made to have a double funeral, and out of respect for Mike's parents, we went ahead and had it earlier this week. I feel awful you weren't able to attend."

"She's already buried?"

"Yes, ma'am."

Gavin was silent, letting Patty come to grips with what he'd said.

"I understand. Mike's poor parents. I never had any children, but it must be the worst thing in the world to lose one."

Indeed it was. Even as a hole opened in his gut, he pressed forward. "They're taking it pretty hard, understandably. They were here several days, but they had to go back to Colorado."

Patty was quiet a moment, sniffling a time or two. "Mike and Mallory were just here in the spring. Still so in love."

He swallowed against the lump in his throat. "There's not much of a bright side here, but I keep telling myself at least they didn't have to grieve each other. They went home together. That's something to be thankful for."

"But that poor child. What'll happen to Emma? You said Mike's parents left. But are they coming back? Are they going to take her in?"

"I'm afraid they're getting up in years. Judy's dealing with dementia, and Paul has some health problems of his own. They're unable to raise Emma."

"Oh no. Then what's going to happen to her? Who did you say was there with you?"

"Laurel, my ex-wife. Mike and Mallory drew their will up a long time ago—when Laurel and I were still married. They named us as guardians

197

of any children they might have. But obviously now . . ."

"Right. You're divorced. Is one of you taking her in then—or are you asking me to?"

Gavin weighed his response. "Laurel and I don't feel either of us would be ideal. We feel it would best to keep her life as stable as possible by keeping her here in Riverbend, in her home, at least for a while. But I've just started a business that promises to be time-consuming. And Laurel's life is in Asheville now.

"There's also the orchard to consider. As I'm sure you know, Mike and Mallory invested everything into building Harvest Moon. The business is going pretty well, and it's harvesttime. All of this has to be properly managed, and Laurel and I wondered if you might be willing to take it on. I know this is a lot to dump on you."

"Oh, Gavin. I just . . . I don't know what to say. I don't even know if Emma will remember me. It was months ago that I saw her last."

Fair point. "I'm sure Mallory talked about you with her."

"Yes, I just . . . I never even had kids of my own—I already said that. Sorry, I just feel so overwhelmed right now. And I'm afraid I got a bit dehydrated on my expedition. My thinking is a little fuzzy."

"Of course. I really am sorry to have to tell you all this. Maybe you should give it some thought and call me back when you're ready to talk."

"Yes, I'll do that. I don't know how long that'll be." She sniffled. "That poor child. How's she doing with all this?"

"About as well as can be expected. She's had a little regression, but otherwise she's coping pretty well. She's in her own home and she has her dog. She's young. She'll recover from this."

"She won't even remember her mom and dad. That's so awful!" Patty broke down.

Gavin offered words of comfort, but they seemed so lame. So futile in light of what was happening.

When Patty collected herself, she agreed to call back soon.

Gavin tapped the End Call button. How long was "soon"? He ran a hand across his face. Breaking the news had been awful, but it was over with now. He'd really hoped Patty would jump at the thought of raising Emma. But maybe that wasn't fair. She was probably exhausted from her trip, and he'd just hit her with terrible news. Maybe she just needed time to process it all.

Twenty-One

"When did Patty say she'd call back?" Laurel had put Emma down and joined Gavin and Sunny in the living room.

He regarded his ex-wife from the recliner, where he'd been fretting for the past thirty minutes. The lone lamp cast a golden glow on her beautiful skin. Disheveled waves cascaded over her tee-clad shoulders. As gorgeous as she'd been when she dolled up for a night out, he'd always preferred her this way—casual, a little rumpled. When she'd come home from her gardening job, strands of hair loose from her ponytail and a streak of dirt on her cheek, he wanted to drag her into the shower—and sometimes he'd done just that.

"Gavin?"

He gave his head a shake. *Stay in the present, idiot.* "What?"

"When's Patty calling back? Did she sound like she might want to take Emma?"

"She said she'd call soon—I don't know if that means hours or days. She was overwhelmed and worn out from the sailing trip."

"I'm sure she was shocked and devastated by the news. We all were."

"And wc've had a week to process this. It's only fair we give her a little time."

"But the deadline . . . that hearing Darius mentioned. I guess I was hoping she'd be eager to take Emma, and we could get all this settled. Was she upset about the funeral?"

"She didn't seem too upset about that, but I was dumping a lot of information on her."

"I hope going ahead without her wasn't a mistake."

"Nothing we can do about it now."

"You're right." Laurel picked up a teddy bear and straightened his polka-dot bow tie. "I tested the apples while you were upstairs with Emma earlier. The Red Delicious are ripe, so a crew's coming to harvest those tomorrow."

"I'm glad you know what you're doing with those trees. I wouldn't have a clue."

Her lip curled upward at the corner. "Plants are kind of my thing."

"And you're very good at it. I saw you planted the funeral flowers out front. They look nice."

"They'll grow well there in the sun." She set the bear down and leaned forward as if she was about to stand.

"Tell me more about your promotion," he blurted.

She shrugged and settled back against the sofa. "Not much to say, really. It's a matter of waiting to see what Diane decides."

"When does Rich retire?"

"Beginning of the year. His wife is battling ovarian cancer, and he wants to be there for her."

"I'm sorry to hear that. She can't be that old."

"Just fifty-six. She's lucky, though. They discovered the cancer early because of an unrelated injury."

"I think Avery's mentioned that's a tough one to catch early."

"How is Avery doing? I saw her at the funeral"—Laurel gave a humorless smile—"but she didn't exactly stop to chat."

"She started a clinic here in town and is busy running it. She's doing well. I'm proud of her. She's dating a guy named Wes Garrett now. One day last summer he came off the trail sick as a dog, and the two of them hit it off. He's my business partner, though he's still working his full-time job till the business gets off the ground."

"And you're still working at the campground?"

"Just part-time now. Enough to justify my living there." They hadn't found a replacement for him, so the office manager kept begging him to come back. There were times he was tempted.

"And Cooper? I heard he's sheriff now and married to boot."

He couldn't tell if she had the scoop on Katie— namely that Gavin had dated her first, then lost her to his brother. Good times. "Katie moved here to work at the clinic as a nurse—old friend of Avery's from undergrad."

"She must be very special. Never thought I'd see the day Cooper settled down."

"They're a good match." He could finally say that and mean it. Once he'd realized his feelings for Katie were more about wanting to live again, moving on got a lot easier. Besides, when he remembered the way he'd felt about Laurel, it was obvious he'd never been in love with Katie at all.

Laurel pulled her phone from her pocket, checked the screen, and thumbed something in.

Recalling the text she'd received from that guy yesterday, his stomach soured. "That your boy-friend?"

She arched a brow at him, her thumbs still moving.

A memory flashed in his mind of that summer after their freshman year of college when he'd been so desperate to win her back. Despite his efforts, she refused to engage with him, but Mallory had been on his side. He fished all the information he could from her.

But Mallory was gone now. And there was no hope of reconciling with Laurel this time. He'd burned down that bridge long ago.

Twenty-Two

When August rolled around Laurel was both relieved and depressed to return to Clemson. On one hand, she wouldn't come face-to-face with Gavin anymore. On the other hand, she wouldn't come face-to-face with Gavin anymore.

Which must be why, when she was exiting her dorm building, late for her second day of classes, she thought she spied Gavin. The man faced the other direction, ball cap tilted just so, black T-shirt stretched across broad shoulders. He looked down at something in his hands, his posture and movements screaming *Gavin*.

She gaped, unblinking. She must be losing it. She'd heard of this happening when someone close to you died—seeing your loved one in a crowd. The mind could play terrible tricks.

But then he turned and their gazes connected.

It really *was* Gavin.

Her heart dropped like an anchor even as liquid fear shot through her veins. Her feet froze to the pavement, and their gazes held for a long moment. What was he doing here? Sure, his classes started a week later than hers (yes, she'd checked), but Clemson was more than two hours from Riverbend and certainly not on the way to Appalachian State.

He walked toward her, lowering the paper he'd been studying. He had the nerve to smile at her as if their last meeting hadn't been full of friction. As if it hadn't tied her stomach in knots and stolen her appetite for days.

"Hey," he said.

She blinked at him. *"Hey?"*

"Your dorm's hard to find. Even GPS couldn't help me. And this campus—jeez. A man could walk for days. Don't even get me started on the parking situation."

"What are you doing here, Gavin?" She gave her head a shake—why give him the chance to sweet-talk her? "Never mind. I'm late for class. You need to go." She headed toward the science building.

"Hey, wait up." Gavin caught up to her and strolled beside her as if they were still in high school, and he was walking her to calculus.

She told her stupid, traitorous heart to chill out. It didn't listen. Thank God the science building was close by. She could see it from here—just twenty yards ahead. She quickened her pace. He could only do so much damage in that short amount of time.

"Don't you want to know why I'm here?"

"You shouldn't have come, Gavin. We already talked. I met you at the coffee shop like you asked, and you said you'd leave me alone after that."

"Actually . . . I said I wouldn't bother you at work again and I didn't."

He was still smiling—she could tell by the tone of his voice. Her blood pressure ratcheted up about twenty points. "And I told you this wouldn't work."

"You said you couldn't do the long-distance thing again."

She reached the building's door and turned. "Exactly. Now I have to go. My class started five minutes ago. Good-bye."

He opened his mouth to say something, but she darted into the building—heart quivering, legs quaking—before he could speak.

Two hours later as she left class, she couldn't remember a word of her professor's lecture. And when she exited the building, if her stomach squeezed a little at the sight of the empty grounds, she wasn't about to admit it. Not even to herself.

The next day Laurel found her English II class and headed inside the lecture hall. She was only a few minutes early, but there was an empty seat in the front row right next to—

Gavin. She gasped.

He glanced up just then and their gazes collided.

Someone ran into her from behind. She'd forgotten to keep walking.

"Sorry," Laurel muttered as the guy slid around her and headed up the stairs along the wall.

Her adrenaline had spiked, giving her that fight-or-flight sensation. The flight option was very tempting. She was so close to the doorway, and it would be so easy to just—

Gavin's mouth curved into a knowing smile.

He could read her like a chapter book, and just now that ticked her off. Really, this was ridiculous. The man must've gotten hold of her schedule somehow—sweet-talked one of the girls in registration or something. She stiffened her shoulders and made a beeline for the empty seat beside him. Then she slid into it.

The classroom was quiet, so she lowered her voice and hissed, "What are you doing? You are not allowed to be here."

"Good morning to you too."

"Leave now or I will turn you in."

The professor entered, and Gavin pulled his laptop from a book bag she hadn't noticed before.

She gaped at him. "I mean it, Gavin."

But just then the professor stepped up to the lectern and introduced herself.

Laurel couldn't bring herself to raise her hand and complain about Gavin. Who wanted that kind of attention on day one? She shot Gavin a withering look and then, hands shaking, she withdrew her own laptop.

At least it would be a short class—they'd likely only go over the syllabus. Good. Because she didn't know how long she could sit here with Gavin beside her acting like everything was fine.

While the professor droned on about upcoming assignments and exams, Gavin took notes as if he were just another student.

Fired up, Laurel spent the class mentally composing her case, fed by the memory of her misery from last fall. By the time the professor dismissed class, she had an arsenal of reasons Gavin should go away and leave her alone.

Gavin stashed his laptop in the book bag. "Hungry? Want to have lunch together?"

"This is ridiculous!"

One of the exiting students glanced at her on his way past.

She lowered her voice. "First you show up at my work all summer and—"

"Three times."

"—then you come to my campus, and now you're practically stalking me. What kind of game are you playing?" She shouldered her book bag and headed out the door.

He followed. "I assure you, this isn't a game."

"Then what are you doing?"

"If you hadn't run off yesterday you'd know that—"

"I had a class."

"—I transferred here."

"You can't just—" His words sank in. Her feet came to an abrupt halt, heedless of the students bustling in and out of the building.

Gavin took her arm and pulled her out of the fray.

She must've misheard. Or misunderstood. "You did what?"

"I'm a student at Clemson now, Laurel. Just like you." His mouth tilted in a grin. "And it seems we share an English class."

She shook her head. It couldn't be true. He'd transferred here? "What—what about football? What about your *scholarship?* You've always wanted to go to App State. It was all you could talk about in high school. You have to go back! It's not too late." He couldn't pass up that scholarship. He didn't have the money for tuition, and she didn't want him racking up school loans—Clemson wasn't exactly cheap. And the football team was so good, Gavin wouldn't even have a chance at first string, much less a scholarship.

A smile lifted both corners of his lips, but those blue eyes of his remained sober. Wistful. "You know, in all those reasons you just gave me for getting out of here . . . none of them were about you wanting me gone."

She gave him a little shove—completely ineffectual. "Stop being foolish, Gavin. App State hasn't even started yet. You can transfer back and talk to them about reinstating your scholarship. If you call them today maybe they'll—"

"Slow down there, Jenkins. I'm not going anywhere. I'm playing baseball for Clemson—you know that's my first love anyway. And I got a nice scholarship. You don't have to worry about me." He touched her arm. "But I kind of like that you do."

She took a breath. Had someone vacuumed the oxygen from the air? "Is it a full ride?"

"Not exactly, but I'll work it out just fine. You'll see."

She huffed. He'd grown up with so much. He didn't know what it was like to scrape and borrow. "You're throwing away so much."

He stepped closer and touched the side of her face, his eyes softening. "I don't want to lose you, Laurel."

Her throat thickened and her eyes stung. He'd come here, given up what he wanted for *her.* Her heart gave a hard squeeze. The thought was heady. But it was also awful because surely he'd come to resent her. "But you'll regret it. When football season starts and you're in the stands or down the road when you're making student loan payments and—"

He set a finger against her lips and waited till he had her full attention. "I love you, Laurel Jenkins. And if coming here is what will get you

211

back . . . I promise you, I will never regret it."

His features went blurry as her eyes filled with tears.

"But I'd never want you to feel obligated to me. If you really don't want this, don't want us . . ."

"No," she squeezed out through a swollen throat. "I do."

He leaned forward and brushed her lips with his. Every reservation, every fear faded in the wake of his touch. She kissed him like a woman starved for his affection—and that's exactly what she was. He made her forget everything but her need of him.

Some part inside warned her that was dangerous. But right now her need was greater than her fear. She wound her arms around his neck and pressed closer, feasting on him.

A long moment later he drew away, just far enough to meet her gaze. He swept away a tear with his thumb. "Do you still love me?"

Her heart was beating so fast. She tried to make herself remember how hard losing him had been. But her life without him had been so empty. She'd missed him so much. Missed the way he teased her from a bad mood. Missed the gentle way he touched her. But mostly she missed the way he knew her and understood her and loved her anyway.

His brows furrowed as worry flickered in the depths of his eyes. "Laurel?"

She should say the words he wanted to hear—because it was true. Her love for him ran so deep, she thought it might kill her if she tried to root it out. But fear sprang up like pernicious weeds, constricting her lungs and strangling her throat. "I'm—I'm afraid."

His expression softened as he framed her face with his hands. "Look at me, honey. There's nothing to be afraid of. I'm here now and everything's going to be okay. We're going to do this college thing together, you and me. We're going to go the distance because there is no one else for me. *No one*." His eyes lit with affection. "All right?"

Though her heart quaked and her soul trembled, Laurel did the thing that scared her most of all: she decided to trust him.

"All right."

Twenty-Three

Gavin had dreamed of this day when he lived in Asheville, and now his dream had finally come to fruition. He maneuvered the trailer into the driveway of the job site. He got out and unhitched it, then went inside to check on the drywallers. Once inside he greeted the crew, then glanced around Robinson Construction's first custom build, scanning the solid framing he and Wes had done themselves.

He took in a whiff of raw wood and sawdust. He'd missed this smell. This work. Taking a building from the ground up and turning it into someone's home. It was one thing to do the job for a builder. Another to own the company doing the work.

He took in the rafters overhead, currently being covered with drywall. A dozen men worked, some on the ground, some on scaffolding that reached the cathedral ceiling, and some walking on stilts. A sunbeam sliced through the haze of drywall dust blooming through the house. The whir of screw guns and lively music filled the space, along with the clunking steps of the men on stilts.

His spine lengthened as he surveyed the work.

This house would come in on time and on budget if it was the last thing he did. He'd contracted the electric and plumbing, but much of the finish work he planned to do himself.

Seeing a need, he hoisted a sheet of drywall to a guy on the scaffolding. He didn't think he'd have time for this today. The harvest crew had shown up at the orchard at first light. Gavin headed out to help but quickly saw his efforts were wasted. The crew could pick five apples to every one of his.

"Let them do their thing, Gavin," Laurel had said. Even she couldn't keep pace with the crew and soon left them to their work.

Since Laurel was with Emma and Wes was working his day job, Gavin slid out to the construction site. Unlike his crews in Asheville, Gavin didn't know this team. Needed to make sure they didn't cut corners. He scanned the hung drywall. Small gaps between the sheets. Adequate number of screws. So far, so good.

"Hey, Bro." Cooper, in full uniform, entered through the construction door and winced at the cacophony.

"Hey, Coop. What are you doing here?" Gavin asked when the noise died down a bit.

"Had a call down the road and saw your truck." He scanned the space. "This is coming along. Last time I was here there was nothing but a foundation."

"Owners want to be in by Christmas."

Cooper's brows hiked up. "You've got a lot on your plate right now: this house, Emma, the orchard, and an ex-wife to boot."

Gavin rolled his eyes. "I'll manage. Emma's aunt checked in yesterday for what it's worth."

Cooper folded his arms over his chest. "How'd she take the news? Is she coming for Emma?"

The loud *zip* of screw guns started again, so Gavin gestured to Cooper to follow him outside. Once on the front porch he continued. "She was pretty shaken up, man. I had to tell her that her niece died and the funeral was already over . . . it was a lot to dump on the woman. She's calling back when she's had time to process everything."

Cooper frowned. "I get it but . . . that doesn't sound too promising."

"Give her some time."

"What will you do if she doesn't want her?"

Gavin should probably give some thought to that. "We'll cross that bridge if and when we come to it."

His brother was too perceptive to miss the *we.* Next he'd probably warn Gavin off Laurel like their mom had. Or at least tell him that sitting with her at church had been a bad move.

But Cooper did neither of those. "Hey, I know you guys are busy with the orchard and your business and everything. Katie and I were

217

talking . . . we could pick up Emma some evening this week, take her for a little hike. I know Mallory and Mike used to do that with her— posted pictures on Facebook. They have one of those carriers."

"Thanks, Coop. I'll keep that in mind. It's really one day at a time right now. Patty could show up tomorrow and take her off to Florida." His gut clenched at the thought. He really didn't want to see the child ripped from her home, from a community who cared about her. And the thought of not seeing her anymore . . . it made a spot inside ache—a spot that had long since been numb.

"Right . . ." Cooper said. "Well, I did come by to deliver some news I got this morning."

Gavin's gaze sharpened on his brother. "What's up?"

"It's about the plane accident. I got a call from the NTSB this morning. They determined that the plane went down on account of a mechanical issue—not a pilot error."

Gavin let that sink in. "It wasn't Mike's fault then."

"I'll spare you the explanation I didn't even understand. The gist of it is, it wasn't even something he could've missed in preflight."

Gavin exhaled, long and slow. As someone who'd been guilty of negligence, he was glad his friend—even dead—wouldn't have that on his record. It didn't change anything, of course. Mike and Mallory were still gone, and Emma was still an orphan.

"It'll be in tomorrow's paper, so I wanted to give you a heads-up."

Gavin would clip the article as he had all the others regarding the accident. Someday Emma might want to read them. And now she'd know her father wasn't to blame. Gavin wished he could say the same about his son's death.

"Thanks for letting me know."

Cooper squeezed his shoulder. "Of course, buddy. Listen, I have to run out to the Hollister farm."

"Edith's cat up a tree again?" The widow had 911 on speed dial, but since she had no family, the department accommodated her.

Cooper gave a wry grin. "You know it."

Laurel picked an apple off the ground and bagged it. The scent of freshly mown grass mingled with the earthy smell of apple trees. She loved fall. Today's high was a mild seventy-four degrees, and the sun peeked out from the clouds only occasionally. She loved working outdoors in weather like this, and she hadn't realized how much she'd missed living in the heart of the mountains.

"Over here, Emma," she called. "Get that one."

Emma scampered toward the apple and Sunny

219

followed, tail fluttering behind her like a furry flag.

The harvest crew had arrived at dawn and dispersed into the orchard. The migrant workers moved efficiently, bagging apples, then rolling their filled bags into the big bins sitting in the grassy rows.

Laurel tried to keep pace, but with Emma needing her attention, she gave it up and decided they'd be the cleanup crew instead.

Emma reached for the fallen apple, and Laurel held out the bag. "Careful . . . we don't want to bruise it."

"Careful." Emma set the apple into the bag. With the early arrival of the crew, Laurel hadn't taken the time to put up the girl's hair so her wild blonde curls framed her face.

"Good job. Do you see any more?"

Emma dashed through the grass to the next fallen fruit. "Got it!"

"You're so good at finding apples."

Emma studied the fruit in her hands, then took a big bite.

"Is that your way of saying you're ready for supper?"

"Supper!" she said around a mouthful of apple. "Emma hungry."

Sunny stared at Emma's apple, licking her chops. When that didn't work, she barked.

Laurel laughed. "I guess you both are." It was

after six. Laurel walked toward the nearest bin. The crew would work until twilight or till the last Red Delicious was picked, then the fruit would be off to the packaging facility.

Laurel paused to take in the orchard, smell the hint of fruit in the air. This work wasn't unlike her job at the Biltmore. In some ways, it was more satisfying because it was so personal. She could understand the appeal it had for Mallory— the tending of her own land, the ability to be self-sustaining, enjoying the fruit of her labors— literally. Laurel felt at peace working this property, much as Mallory had.

Laurel carefully rolled the apples into the bin. "Let's go back to the house so we can make supper. I'll bet Sunny needs a drink of water."

"Sunny thirsty."

"That's right."

Emma took off toward the house. "Gabin."

"He'll be home soon." Or so she supposed—he didn't exactly report in. But that was okay. He had a business to run and a campground he half managed. He'd always been a hard worker. And she was content to take care of Emma and oversee the harvest.

Once inside Laurel filled Sunny's water dish, then helped Emma wash her hands. When they were dry, Emma went off to put Bunny down for a nap while Laurel pulled a dish from the freezer and put it in the microwave to thaw. She'd add some veggies and the fresh loaf of bread Lisa had sent home with Gavin yesterday.

The doorbell rang and Sunny flashed by, claws sliding on the kitchen floor in her rush. Emma got up and ran toward the door. "Mama! Dada!"

Laurel's heart faltered. She went after Emma and caught her before she opened the door. She swept the girl into her arms. "Baby . . . Oh, honey, I'm sorry, but it's not your mommy and daddy."

Laurel peeked out the sidelight and saw her mother on the stoop. "See, it's Miss Donna."

Emma's lip quivered and her big blue eyes filled with tears before she let out a heart-wrenching wail. Laurel pulled the girl close. She pressed her hand to the child's back and swallowed the lump in her throat. "I'm so sorry, honey. It's going to be okay. I love you, sweet angel."

Laurel opened the door, letting her mom inside.

"Oh dear. Poor darling. What happened?"

Laurel shook her head and kissed Emma's temple. "I know you miss your mommy and daddy, sweetheart. I know you're sad. I'm sad too. But it's going to be all right. Laurel's here. I've got you."

Her mother followed her quietly into the living room where they sat down. But they were unable to talk over the wailing. Laurel continued to murmur whatever hopeful things she could think of, but the child was inconsolable.

Her mom tried to distract her with toys, but Emma was too distraught. Even Sunny couldn't cheer her up. Laurel gave up trying and just prayed. Maybe the child was starting to understand her parents were never coming home.

The front door opened and Gavin entered, his brows drawing together when he heard Emma's cries and found her wailing in Laurel's arms.

"What happened?" He barely acknowledged Laurel's mom as he dropped his keys on the table and headed straight for the child.

Upon hearing his voice, Emma turned and reached for him, tears streaming down her pale face. He lifted her into his arms and she clung to him. "It's okay, Emma Bear. I've got you."

He looked at Laurel for an explanation.

"When the doorbell rang a few minutes ago she thought it was . . ." Laurel nodded toward the picture of Mike and Mallory.

His face fell and pain flickered in his eyes. He cradled the back of the child's head. But Emma had already calmed down a bit. She shuddered in his arms and sniffled back tears.

Gavin walked toward the kitchen, nodding at her mom as he passed. "Donna."

"Gavin," she replied in her *back off* tone. Then she quietly addressed Laurel. "I'm sorry my arrival upset her."

"It's not your fault."

In the kitchen Gavin blotted Emma's face with a tissue and spoke quietly to her.

"I brought tomatoes and cucumbers from the garden. I know you have plenty of casseroles and such, but a growing child needs vegetables."

"Thanks, Mom."

Gavin carried Emma to the French doors and pointed at something outside as he kept a monologue going.

"It's hard to hear her cry," Mom whispered. "But she needs to grieve."

"I know. It just about tears me up though."

"You always did have such a soft heart."

She regarded her mother for a moment. Most people thought Laurel was as tough as nails. One guy in high school had deemed her the ice princess, and it caught on for a while. "You think so?"

"Please. When you were little you tried to rescue every stray animal you found. You cried buckets every time I said no. I finally let you keep one."

"Scrappy." She'd been in the fourth grade when she found a burr-covered mutt that had been injured by another animal. The dog wasn't much to look at, but Laurel loved him anyway. He died a few months after she took him in.

"I knew that dog wasn't going to make it. Should've spared you the pain and just said we couldn't keep him."

"Loss is a part of life," Laurel said automatically. She'd almost forgotten about that hopeful child she'd once been. But all that hope was dangerous. It left a person vulnerable to heartbreak.

Gavin slipped out the French doors with Emma and Sunny followed.

Mom watched them go. "Well, the child certainly seems taken with him. But frankly, I'm surprised he's stuck around this long."

"He loves her. And he's good with her." He'd been good with Jesse, too, when he'd been around. The boy had loved his daddy. Had imitated the way he stood, walked, and talked. She'd jokingly called him Gavin Junior.

"Just don't go getting any ideas," Mom said. "There's a reason it didn't work out the first time."

Laurel was not in the mood for a lecture. "I know that, Mom. I expect Emma's aunt to call soon and accept guardianship. Then I'll be heading back to Asheville, and everything can go back to normal."

Her mom's expression softened. "I'd like to spend some time with you while you're here. Maybe Brad and I can have you and Emma over for supper one night this week. He's very good with children, and I'll bet she'd adore Tootsie."

Their little terrier was pretty cute. "We'd like that."

"You can bring Sunny if you'd like. Tootsie would love it." Mom grabbed her bag of produce and carried it into the kitchen.

Laurel followed.

"How are they handling your absence at work? This won't affect your promotion in any way will it?"

"I had the PTO coming, so it's not a big deal." She didn't divulge the rest. If her mom knew what Greg was doing, she'd pressure Laurel to return to work. But Laurel wasn't leaving Emma. "The tomatoes look good." Laurel lined them up on the counter, stem side down.

"I used that organic fertilizer you recommended." Mom glanced out the window.

Gavin walked hand in hand with Emma, and Sunny flanked the child protectively. Beyond them, the harvest crew was still hard at work. They should be finishing soon.

"I see the apples are coming in."

"Just the Red Delicious. The bulk of the orchard are Cameo and Fuji." Those would ripen late September to early October. Laurel wouldn't even be here then. Who knew where Emma would be or what would happen to the fruit ripening on the trees?

Her stomach bottomed out at the thought.

The microwaved dinged. She'd forgotten about the lasagna she was defrosting. She removed the casserole, slipped it into the oven, and set the timer for thirty minutes. "I think I'll make a salad and use your fresh tomatoes and cucumbers." Then—and only because she felt she should—she asked, "Can you stay for supper?"

Mom folded the produce sack and glanced outside. Gavin and Emma were headed back in. She checked her watch. "Thanks for the offer, but I should get home to Brad. Call me when you hear from the aunt." Mom gave her a half-hearted hug and waved to Emma through the glass door before heading out.

Laurel began setting the table. After supper she or Gavin would give Emma her bath and the other would put her to bed. They'd slipped into a routine in the past week—and Laurel wasn't sure if that was good or bad.

Twenty-Four

Gavin knew he was dreaming, but try as he could to extricate himself from the nightmare, he couldn't seem to wake himself up.

Jesse was screaming from his car seat as Gavin hitched the trailer to his truck. "Hang in there, buddy."

The trailer coupler was now poised over the ball. He unlatched the coupler and lowered the trailer until the hitch was fully seated.

What was next? He'd done this a thousand times before, but his thoughts were muddled. He had to get this right. It was important—he couldn't quite put his finger on why.

But Jesse's cries distracted him. He couldn't think. He gave his head a shake.

Close the coupler. Right. He did that, his hands trembling, his heart thudding against the confines of his rib cage. What was wrong with him?

Think, Robinson!

The pin. Right, he had to slide the pin into place. As he did so Jesse's wails escalated. "It's okay, son. Daddy'll be right there."

But Jesse cried on. Was something wrong with him? Should he go get him? But no, he had to get this trailer hitched right.

If only he could figure it out. He blinked at the hitch and saw the dangling chains. He grabbed them and secured them in place. A memory flashed in his head, prompting him to connect the breakaway system and hook up the seven-way plug. He set the jack in place and secured it with the pin. There. He'd done it. Hadn't he?

He stepped back. Had he done everything right? Why were his thoughts so scrambled? What was he forgetting?

The sway bar. Thank God he'd remembered.

When he turned to fetch it, his truck was gone. His house was gone. In its place stood a construction site. A framed house squatted on a mound of dirt. From somewhere inside the building Jesse screamed.

His heart kicked into gear. "I'm coming!" As he ran toward the structure, the house morphed. Now the building was nearly complete with siding and stone and a front door. From its confines Jesse wailed on.

Then a plume of smoke rose from the roof and fire licked at the windows.

A cold chill swept up Gavin's spine. "Jesse!" he screamed above the sudden roar of fire.

He vaulted onto the porch and tried the front door, but it was locked. "I'm coming!"

He darted to the nearest windows, made a fist, and struck the glass. No good. He scanned the area. There. A cut piece of two-by-four. He grabbed it and jammed it into the window with all his might. But the window didn't break.

Laurel stirred from a deep sleep. Had a noise awakened her? Emma? Listening intently, she heard nothing but the tick of the wall clock. She rolled over and pulled up the covers. It seemed like the middle of the night, but if she checked the time it would only make her more alert.

Best she got some sleep while she could. Emma was prone to waking in the middle of the night. When she did, Laurel would rock her in the nursery until she was sound asleep again, then put her back into the crib. Sometimes Laurel fell asleep in the chair, too, and woke in the morning with a crick in her neck.

A cry jolted her from her thoughts. Not Emma. Maybe Sunny was having a dream. She slept just outside the nursery door.

Another cry rang out. This time she recognized the guttural sound, coming from the direction of the spare bedroom. Was Gavin hurt? When they'd been married he sometimes woke in the middle of the night with terrible thigh cramps. A heating pad was the only thing that relaxed the muscle.

She whipped the covers back and scrambled out of bed. Where would a heating pad be? The floor was cold against the soles of her feet as she used the night-light to navigate to his room.

Moonlight spilled across his form, the white

sheet a dim glow in the darkness. He thrashed in the bed, crying out, something about coming.

He didn't have a cramp. He was having a nightmare.

Laurel paused on the threshold. Should she wake him or go back to bed? Over the past few days they'd done a solid job of keeping things cordial. They took care of Emma and handled the chores, keeping to their own corners whenever possible.

But entering his bedroom and waking him from a dream drifted into spouse territory—and she was no longer his wife.

She turned to go, giving his shadowed form one last look. His legs fought the confines of the sheet, and his head whipped back and forth on the pillow. "No, please . . ." Then his anguished moan pierced the air. "Jesse!"

A shiver shot through her, kicking her heart into gear. She dashed forward and grabbed his shoulder. "Gavin. Wake up."

He thrashed, jerked away, mumbling.

"Gavin, it's okay. Wake up." She shook his shoulder. *"Wake up, Gavin!"*

He suddenly stilled. Stiffened. His breaths were loud and ragged in the quiet.

She lowered her weight to the bed, leaving her hand on his sweat-dampened shoulder. "It's okay. You were dreaming."

His shuddery breath shook the bed. His throat

released a pitiful squeak. He latched on to her, wrapping his arms around her middle, clutching her with the desperation of a dying man.

Or a man who'd lost his son.

He quaked against her. "Couldn't save him. I'm sorry. So sorry."

A vise tightened around her heart. "It's okay. It—it was just a dream." But was it really? He *had* lost his son. She had, too, of course. But he obviously still carried the weight of guilt—and she hadn't exactly helped with that.

"Couldn't get to him," he grated out, still in the throes of his nightmare. "Couldn't save him."

"Shhh . . ." She put her hand on his head and blinked against the tears gathered in her eyes. "You're okay. Everything will be okay."

Did he have these nightmares often? It had been four years. Their son had been gone longer than he'd been alive. She'd grieved her way through that first year, wondering how someone could hold so much pain inside and not die from it.

And yes, of course . . . she still thought of her son every single day. But now, all these years later, the bittersweet memories brought a smile. She could accept that God had called him home for whatever reason and that Jesse was in a better place now.

She glanced down at Gavin. Those strong arms wrapped around her as though he were holding on for dear life. Gasping for breath.

When their son had died, Gavin retreated into himself. Over the next weeks he became a stranger. She needed someone to grieve with her, and instead he withdrew, only engaging with her when he lashed out in anger.

Laurel had lost her son and then she lost her husband. She felt utterly alone. And nothing she did could draw him back to her.

After they'd separated, he returned to River-bend. The divorce went through—he gave her everything but his truck. She heard snippets about his new life. He'd forfeited his career to work at a campground and live there in a tin can. His family was worried about his state of mind. She took in the updates with a certain smugness, delight licking at her own wounds. He'd gotten what he deserved.

But now, years down the road, her wrath assuaged, she felt differently. She didn't want him to suffer anymore—he'd been through enough. They both had. Now she only wanted to comfort him. And that was a dangerous place in which to find herself. In five minutes flat he'd managed to tie her stomach in knots.

His breathing had settled. His grip loosened. His head grew heavy in her lap.

She cleared her throat. "You—you should probably try and get some sleep." She began easing away.

His arms tightened. "Don't go."

She hesitated. The raw anguish in his tone gutted her. His pain was her pain. How was that still so? After a separation and divorce, and all the time and miles between them, why did she still feel so connected to him?

"Please . . ."

She squeezed her eyes shut. She was helpless against his plea and hated herself for it. But she couldn't deny him. She eased back against the spare pillow.

"Thank you." He settled himself back on his side of the bed. Quiet bloomed around them like a spring fog over a valley.

"Do you want to talk about it?" she whispered across the space between them.

"No." He stirred, then settled again. "Tell me about your life. About your friends. Where are you living now?"

She sighed, relieved to return to solid ground. "I have a one-bedroom apartment on the north side near Aston Park."

"Fairview?"

"Yeah."

"I remember when it was going up. Nice place, safe neighborhood."

"There's a pool and a gym, and the price was reasonable."

"Does Ruby still work at the Biltmore?"

"Yeah. We're still friends. She took a new woman named Kayla under her wings. She's my age and divorced. We all go out sometimes. And I've got a couple neighbors I can count on to water my houseplants and such. What about you? What have you been up to?"

"Oh, you know. The usual: running the campground, keeping up with the family."

"And your new business?"

"Sure . . . there's that."

She got the feeling he didn't want to talk about that either, which was strange since it had been his dream. "Have you done much dating?" The darkness must've emboldened her.

"Little bit. Things are a lot different these days with dating apps and all. You? Are things serious with Connor?"

She whipped her head around. "How do you know about Connor?"

"I saw a text notification the other day."

Which message had he seen? And what was he doing, reading her texts?

"Is it serious?"

"Not really." Turnabout was fair play. "What about you?"

"I'm not dating anyone right now." He was quiet so long she thought he might not answer. "But I've dated a few women from that dating app—Flutter."

A ribbon of jealousy tightened around her stomach. She *had* asked. This information shouldn't bother her. Shouldn't she be over him by now?

"And Avery set me up with her nurse about a year and a half ago. We dated awhile."

He'd mentioned a nurse before, and Laurel tried to recall what he'd said. Surely not . . . She blinked at him. "Not the nurse Cooper married."

"She wasn't married to him then." Humor laced his words.

"You went out with her first? For how long?"

He chuckled. "Do you really want to hear about this?"

She propped her head on her hand. "Darn right I do. What happened?"

"I can't believe Mallory or Mike never told you. It was all over the town grapevine."

After the first year of their divorce Laurel forbade her mom and Mallory from giving her updates on Gavin or the Robinsons. It hurt too much. "Well, they didn't, so fill me in."

After a brief pause the story unfolded. He'd been dating Katie awhile when she'd met Cooper. As Gavin talked his tone didn't hint of heartbreak, though he must've felt betrayed by both Katie and his brother.

"Goodness," she said when he finished. "I'll bet that caused an uproar in the family."

"You have no idea."

"But there are no hard feelings now?"

"We're fine. We worked it out. I was never in love with Katie."

His words hung there suspended in the gap

between them. Did that mean Laurel was still the only woman he'd ever loved? And why did that matter so much anyway?

"You never changed your surname," he said. "I didn't realize until I saw it in the obituary."

"I thought about it but . . ."

"But what?"

She tried to assimilate her thoughts. "Going back to my maiden name would be too much like saying it never happened—our marriage. Jesse. It felt like I'd be saying his life hadn't mattered. Like he'd never been here at all."

When he didn't respond, she said, "Sorry. I didn't mean to make you sad."

"It's okay. I understand what you're saying. I just . . . I miss him."

The raw confession had taken courage. "I do, too, every day. He was so sweet and stubborn."

"And silly. I miss that silly boy most of all."

"Those big brown eyes. Gosh, he could work me over with just a look."

"He knew it too."

She smiled in the dark. "He did." She didn't regret it. Any of it.

Weariness closed over her suddenly, making her aware it was the middle of the night. She gave in to the feeling, closing her eyes. Cool air drifted through the open window, skittering over her skin.

Gavin spoke softly through her haze of fatigue. "Are you happy, Laurel?"

She slitted her eyes open, taking in his dark shadow on the pillow next to hers. "Happy enough." Then she closed her eyes again, her breaths deepening.

And then there was nothing but quiet.

Gavin awakened to a soft sound, but he didn't bother opening his eyes. He was too sleepy, too comfortable. He hugged his pillow tighter, inhaling a subtle fruity scent that reminded him of Laurel.

At the thought of her, he opened his eyes to dawn's early light spilling into the room. His gaze fell to the woman he was wrapped around. Her hair stirred with his breaths.

She still slept, facing the other direction, the slight weight of her hand resting on his.

His heart beat so hard the bed quaked beneath him. Last night rushed back. The horrible dream. Laurel waking him. The heavy load of grief and guilt. It had been a long time since he'd had a nightmare like that. The ragged remnants of the dream had haunted him, and he couldn't bear the thought of being alone. He'd asked her to stay— begged, really.

And she had. They'd even talked about Jesse— and it felt good.

Now in the bold light of day he took in their intimate embrace. She hadn't asked to be groped in the night. But thankfully, she was unaware he was currently wrapped around her like a porch around an old farmhouse.

Slowly—regretfully—he removed his arm from the familiar curve of her waist. Eased away from her while pulling his other arm from beneath her pillow.

When he managed to disentangle himself unnoticed, he heaved a sigh. He just settled back to his own side of the bed when the bed moved.

Emma appeared at the foot of the bed. She climbed onto the mattress. Her curls were in disarray, and her beaming smile cut through the faded morning light. "Hi."

Laurel stirred. Her eyes opened, falling on him first. Realization registered and her brows drew together a moment before she spotted Emma. Her eyes widened. "Emma. You climbed out of your crib."

"Emma climb!"

Gavin chuckled at the proud look on the girl's face. "Oh boy. We are in for it now."

"Oh boy." Emma repeated as she bounced across the bed and plopped between the two of them.

Twenty-Five

Thirty minutes later, showered and dressed in T-shirt and jeans, Gavin headed downstairs, Sunny on his heels. He was a little sheepish about falling apart in Laurel's arms last night— that was twice now. What was wrong with him? He needed to get it together.

In the kitchen he found Laurel dressed in black jeans and a burnt-orange tank top, mashing a banana.

"Emma eat." Emma announced from her high chair when she spotted him. She scooped a bite of oatmeal into her mouth.

"Can I have some?" He crouched down beside her and opened his mouth wide.

Laughing, Emma put a glob of oatmeal in his mouth.

"Mmm. That's good."

"I like how you shared." Laurel put the mashed banana in the oatmeal and gave it a stir.

"Share with Waurel."

She met Gavin's gaze for a beat before she opened her mouth for the bite. Then she playfully nibbled her way up Emma's arm, making the child giggle. "Do you want milk or water this morning?"

241

"Want milk."

"I'll get it." Gavin headed to the fridge while Laurel sat at the table with a whole banana. He was relieved she didn't seem awkward about last night.

He poured himself a cup of coffee, the aroma teasing his senses. "The harvest go okay yesterday?"

"They finished picking the Red Delicious. I think the Golden and Jonagold will be ripe in a week or so."

"Find apples," Emma said.

"That's right. We picked up apples yesterday, didn't we?" She addressed Gavin. "We were the cleanup crew."

Gavin poured Emma's milk into a cup, set it on her high chair, then took a seat at the table. "Sorry I wasn't around to help out."

"We had it covered, didn't we, Emma?"

"Had it covered." Emma sipped from her cup.

Sunny strolled over and licked up a bit of oatmeal that had hit the floor.

"What's on your agenda today?" he asked.

"I was going to do some trellis repairs, but that could wait. After this morning's event"—she pointedly cleared her throat—"someone needs a toddler bed. She could get hurt climbing from her crib."

Gavin hadn't thought about that. "I can run out and get one today."

"You're not going to find one around here. Asheville would have the best options—and anyway I was thinking about running home to check on my apartment—the mail, my plants, and stuff."

"Right." After last night's display she probably wanted to escape him. And that was a shame because they'd just started finding their footing. He didn't want her running off to Asheville alone—he wanted to spend the day with her.

Huh.

Even after the realization, it took a minute to get up the nerve to make the suggestion. "I could keep Emma if you'd like. Or I could, ah, come along if you wouldn't mind some company."

She regarded him from over the rim of her mug. "Don't you need to work? Check on your new build or something?"

He had planned to swing by the house. The crew would be applying another coat of mud. But they'd seemed perfectly capable. And he'd much rather spend the day with Laurel and Emma. "I can check in later."

A pretty blush bloomed in her cheeks. "Well . . . you are going to be the one putting the bed together after all."

He bit back a smile, playing it cool. "That settles it then. We'll head for Asheville after breakfast. Didn't you say your apartment has a pool?"

"You want to take Emma swimming?"

"Emma swim!"

Gavin and Laurel traded a look, then Laurel said, "We're going swimming at Laurel's apartment."

"Princess suit!"

"We will definitely bring your princess suit."

The forty-five-minute trip to Asheville passed in a rush. Gavin and Laurel kept up a steady flow of conversation. He told her about the house he and Wes were building, and she opened up about work.

Now standing in a fluorescent-lit aisle of an enormous big-box store, Gavin surveyed the many toddler bed options. His son had slept in a toddler bed, but Laurel must've picked it out. He didn't even remember Jesse's first night in it. What he wouldn't give now to have been there for those moments. His stomach gave a hard twist. But he pushed the feelings aside.

"This one converts to a table." He frowned at a complicated design. "I'm not sure why."

"Maybe we should just get a twin bed with rails. That way she could use it for a while."

"She seems so small for a twin."

"Dat one!" From the shopping cart Emma pointed to a pink crib.

"We're going to get you a big-girl bed," Laurel told her, then addressed Gavin. "Maybe you're right, though. She has a long way to go before she outgrows the crib mattress."

He read the box for a white, wooden-framed bed. "This one seems sturdy, has guardrails, and it's low to the ground so we wouldn't have to worry about her falling out." As if *we* would have to worry about anything for much longer.

"Hmmm. That's true I guess." There was a somber note in her voice.

"What's wrong? Is there another one you like better?"

"No, it's just . . . this is such a big milestone for a child."

He caught on. "And certain people aren't here for it."

"I hate this. She would've been so proud but also bummed that her baby was growing up."

"He would've called me to help put the bed together, stood back while I did all the work, then acted like he'd done it himself."

She gave a wistful smile. She was on to him. "They're going to miss it all: Emma dressing herself, losing her first tooth, learning to ride a bike. It's so unfair." She lowered her voice. "Why did this have to happen?"

"I don't know." It wasn't the first time they'd asked that question about the death of a loved one. "Maybe we'll never understand. Maybe we don't need to. Maybe we just have to figure out how to go on."

"That's a big cnough task all on its own."

"It is."

When their eyes locked, he didn't think either was thinking about Mike and Mallory anymore. He was still learning how to go on. Maybe she was too.

Her gaze swung back to the boxed bed he'd been examining. "Let's get that one."

"You sure?"

"Positive."

A rush of cold air brushed Laurel's arms as she entered the apartment building and headed toward the mailboxes. Gavin was on her heels, toting Emma in his arms.

As she checked for mail she tried to see the place through his eyes. The building was tastefully decorated in neutral colors. She'd chosen the apartment for its convenient location, amenities, and open floor plan. The complex was nice, attractive, and well kept, but it wasn't the most luxurious place in town. She could've afforded more—the sale of their house had netted her a nice nest egg. But she had yet to touch it. She enjoyed the security of having money in reserves.

She gathered the few pieces of mail and started up the steps, her legs a little unstable. When she'd agreed to let Gavin come to Asheville with her, she hadn't thought it through. Hadn't considered how it might feel to have him in her space. When she'd gotten the call about Mallory, she'd left in such a hurry . . . she couldn't even remember if she'd left it clean. Too late for that.

"Why didn't you ever buy a house?"

"I don't know. I guess I just never had the time to look for one." That was only partly true. The whole thought of settling down in an empty house made her feel lonely. At least in an apartment there were people around her. Noise. In an apartment, she wasn't really alone.

She stuck the key in the knob and gave it a twist. Warm, stale air greeted her. She went straight to the thermostat and adjusted it.

"Hot," Emma said.

"We'll fix that in a hurry," Laurel said.

Emma squirmed in Gavin's arms. When he set her down she scooted toward the entertainment center and tugged open the bottom drawer.

"You keep toys for her here?"

"Mallory brought her at least once a month," she said quietly. "We'd make lemonade and take her swimming, then put her down for a nap in my bed." Her heart gave a strong tug at the memory. There would be no more lazy Saturdays with Mallory. No more dishing about the Riverbend rumor mill or the cute Italian guy who lived in building three.

Laurel went through the mail Brandon had set on her kitchen island. Mostly ads with a few bills in the mix. Although she expected to return home permanently any day, she tucked the bills and the new edition of *Horticulture Magazine* into her purse.

When she finished, Emma was working a simple puzzle and Gavin wandered through the apartment, taking it in.

She tried to see the place through his eyes. It was a blend of old and new—her old married life and her new single life. New colorful pillows adorned their old gray leather sectional. Candles Mallory had given her as a house-warming gift embellished their old coffee table.

Gavin had picked up the one photo of Jesse she kept on a floating shelf. It had been taken at his third birthday party, which they'd hosted in their backyard. The snapshot captured joy on his face in that instant after he'd blown out his candles.

"He was a cutie," she said. "Those big brown eyes, that dimple . . ."

Gavin's Adam's apple bobbed. "Yeah. I keep his picture on my nightstand. I don't want to forget the way those eyes could sparkle when he was up to no good."

"He used to think he was so sneaky."

"His face gave him away every time." He set the photo down and moved on to the sun-loving plants lining the living room window: hibiscus, papyrus, and croton as well as sweet basil, thyme, and aloe vera.

Laurel knelt and inspected the croton's leaves,

then moved on to the others. They were faring nicely in her absence.

"Who's been taking care of your plants?"

"Brandon—he lives in the next building." She pinched a few dead blooms from the hibiscus.

"Friend of yours?"

"Good friend. I met him the day I moved in. He's been very helpful."

A shadow flickered in Gavin's jaw as his muscles clenched. "I'll bet."

"And he really knows his way around a plant." Surely he wasn't jealous. Did she want him to be? Maybe. The notion surprised her. Probably just a relic of their former relationship—as was his jealousy, most likely.

Gavin moved on to the French doors, leading to her balcony. "Wow, you've outdone yourself out there."

Her balcony was an outdoor oasis, sporting an old white glider she'd procured at a garage sale. The space was currently blooming with every color of the rainbow. Every morning she—

"I'll bet you have your coffee out there every morning in your ratty blue robe."

"It isn't ratty." She continued inspecting her hibiscus blooms.

"You probably read the newspaper out there too."

"I get my news online these days."

"But I'll bet you still read it with your coffee."

He'd win that bet. "You still forget your coffee in the microwave. Don't think I haven't noticed."

"You still think reheated coffee is the devil."

"It is."

They shared a smile.

"Emma swim now." The girl was rooting through her diaper bag, half the contents already spilled onto the floor. She pulled out the pink swimsuit. "Princess suit!"

"Let me clean out the fridge first, okay? Then we'll go swimming." She addressed Gavin. "I have no idea what I might've left in there, but it shouldn't take long."

"Take your time. I'll get her changed."

Twenty-Six

First there'd been Connor, now Brandon. Who was this guy she trusted with a key to her place? With her *plants?* And was he currently hanging out at the swimming pool?

With Emma in his arms Gavin eased through the chlorinated water, his gaze flittering over the sunbathers. Chances were slim the guy would be hanging around the apartment pool on a random Tuesday afternoon.

He dipped down into the water.

Emma squealed. "Water cold!"

"Wanna do it again?"

She giggled. "Yeah."

Gavin dipped her down again. She flapped her arms, water wings and all, splashing water on her face. She blinked and gasped. When she opened her eyes, she gave Gavin a toothy smile. Her pale lashes clumped together, and her bangs hung in wet strings. She had to be the cutest thing on God's green earth.

"Want me to let you go?"

"Over there." Emma pointed to the steps leading into the pool.

He waded that way, catching sight of Laurel approaching. A grass-green bathing suit hugged her slim figure, and a short white skirt fell to mid-thigh. Those legs hadn't lost their appeal. Nor had the rest of her. He'd always been attracted to her, from the first moment he'd seen her. Getting to know her had only magnified that attraction.

Emma squirmed in his arms. He'd already reached the steps, which he would've realized if he hadn't been gawking at Laurel.

He set Emma down and she plopped on the first step, barely in the water.

Laurel spread a beach towel on the lounge next to his. "Is the water cold, Emma?"

"Yeah."

"Get the fridge all cleaned out?" he asked.

"I did, but there was some pretty moldy produce in there. And dinner leftovers that had definitely seen better days."

It had been strange, being in her apartment, seeing the furniture that had adorned their home. The same sofa on which they'd eaten, cuddled, watched countless hours of TV, and made love more than once. But while their home had felt warm and inviting, her apartment was sparse. Minus the houseplants, it had all the warmth of a hotel room. Maybe she just preferred a simpler style these days.

"Your phone's vibrating," Laurel said.

He immediately thought of Patty. "Who is it?"

She checked the screen. "Your mom. Trade you places?"

"Thanks." He walked up the steps, passing Laurel, and grabbed his phone from the lounge chair. "Hi, Mom."

"Hi, honey. Sorry to bother you in the middle of the day. Do you have a minute?"

"Sure." He straddled the lounge and sat. "What's up?"

"I was just going over some things for Trail Days with Katie and realized we didn't have anyone covering the dunking booth on that Saturday at—what is all that noise?"

He was suddenly aware of the sounds of shrieking, laughter, and splashing water. "Oh, I, ah . . . I'm at the pool." He winced. "So what time is the slot you wanted me to fill?"

"Did one of your friends get a pool?"

"No, it's, ah . . ." There was no getting around it. "I'm at Laurel's apartment pool in Asheville. We needed to buy Emma a toddler bed. She climbed from her crib last night, and the nearest store that carried them was here. Plus Laurel needed to check on her apartment so we combined the trip. Emma wanted to go swimming." He squeezed his eyes shut. For crying out loud, why did he feel the need to explain? He wasn't in high school anymore.

"I see. Well, it sounds like you're busy. I won't keep you."

Why oh why had he answered the phone? "It's just an errand, Mom."

"Did I say anything?"

He rolled his eyes. "You didn't have to. Now what time do you need me for the dunking booth?"

"From two till four if you're free."

"Go ahead and put me down."

"I'll do that. Thank you, honey. Have you heard from Emma's aunt yet?"

"Not since Sunday. I'm sure she'll call soon."

"Well, if you still have Emma this Saturday, why don't you bring her to lunch? I'd love to see her."

"I'll do that."

After they ended the call, Gavin tried to put his mom's concern from his mind. His gaze drifted to Laurel. She sat on the steps with Emma and showed her how to blow bubbles in the water. Laurel was so good with her. That guardedness she'd always wielded had never extended to children. She was her truest, most open self when she was around kids.

He wished his family could remember how she'd been with Jesse and cut her some slack. Anyone with open eyes could see he was the one to blame for the demise of their marriage. That Laurel didn't seem to hate him anymore was a miracle.

"Laurel! Laurel, you're here." A boy in his late teens rushed alongside the pool, a towel wrapped around his shoulders. His pale stomach ended at a pair of dripping wet Hulk trunks. His face bore the distinctive physical characteristics of Down's syndrome.

"Hi, Brandon." Laurel stood and gave the boy a warm hug.

So this was the guy with her apartment key. Gavin felt a little foolish for that prick of jealousy he'd experienced earlier. But part of him also felt relieved.

"I came to check on my apartment," Laurel told the boy. "You're doing a great job with my plants."

"I watered them yesterday. Only the ones I was supposed to. Did you find your mail? Is she your friend, Laurel?"

"This is Emma. Emma, this is my friend Brandon. Can you say hi?"

"Hi." Emma went back to her bubbles.

Laurel turned toward Gavin. "And this is my other friend. Gavin, this is the young man who's been taking such good care of my plants while I've been gone."

"Hi, Gavin." Brandon gave him a cheerful smile.

"Hi there, buddy. I like your trunks."

"Hulk is the best Avenger. Avengers are the Earth's mightiest heroes. I like Iron Man, too, and also Black Widow, but Captain America is not an original Avenger. Most people don't know that."

Gavin grinned at his enthusiasm. "I didn't know that."

A middle-aged woman approached. "Hi, Laurel. It's good to have you back."

"Mom," Brandon said. "This is Gavin and Emma. She's not back. She's just checking on her apartment, and I did a good job with her plants."

"I'm Sheila," the woman told Gavin. "Brandon's mom, obviously."

"Nice to meet you."

"It's good to see you, Laurel. How's everything going back home?"

Laurel glanced at Emma. "About as well as can be expected. I should be able to come home soon."

"Well, no hurry on our account. Brandon loves taking care of your plants."

"And getting her mail. I get her mail too."

"I'm so glad I have you to depend on," Laurel said.

"Well, it was good to see you," Sheila said. "We have to be getting inside now. Brandon's drawing class starts soon."

They said their good-byes and the two of them headed through the gate.

Gavin gave Laurel a wry look. "You didn't mention your good friend Brandon was a teenage boy."

"Why would I?" She scooped Emma off the step and carried her deeper into the water.

Back in the truck again, Laurel leaned back and tried to rest. They'd let Emma play in the pool for two hours, then Laurel gathered a few items from her apartment, reset the thermostat, and locked up.

By the time they put her back in the car seat, Emma was overtired and fussy. And after the long drive to Asheville, she wasn't crazy about getting back into the vehicle. But by the time they hit the bypass, she was sound asleep.

Laurel glanced back at the girl. Her curls were still damp and wild, and despite the sunscreen Gavin had applied, her cheeks pinkened a bit in the sun.

"I think we exhausted her," Gavin said.

"She's out cold."

From beneath her lashes Laurel studied Gavin, remembering the way he'd looked in his trunks. She hadn't been the only one who'd noticed his great physique—though he'd seemed unaware of the gaping women at the pool. He'd always been so oblivious that way. It was one of his charms.

Yes, he'd stayed in great shape during their years apart. Still had that six-pack and those strong biceps she'd always loved. When he'd wrapped his arms around her she felt so safe. So adored. She missed that.

This morning when she'd awakened in his bed, he was snuggled against her back, his arms encompassing her. She lay there, eyes closed, heart thudding in her chest. For just a moment she let herself pretend they were still married. That she could turn around and press her lips to his. That his eyes would open with that sleep-dazed look before they focused on her. Then his lips would curl into a lazy smile, and his eyes would twinkle with an idea that was sure to please them both.

"I'm sorry about last night," he said.

She blinked. "What?"

"Last night . . . I know I shouldn't have . . ."

Apparently she wasn't the only one thinking about last night—and this morning. "You don't have to apologize. It was a nightmare—completely out of your control."

"Not that." He glanced at her. "I shouldn't have asked you to stay. That was crossing a line. Obviously I have some issues I'm still dealing with, but that's not your problem."

Anymore. "You're not alone in that. We both went through a lot—and yet here we are . . ."

"Stuck together?" He tossed her a humorless smile. A moment of silence passed before he spoke again. "What happened to Mike and Mallory was a terrible tragedy, and I'd do anything if I could undo it. But since I can't . . . I wonder if anything good could come from it."

Laurel weighed his comment. "I guess we both could use some closure." Right, closure. That's why she'd just been reminiscing about how it felt to be in his arms.

Gavin's phone buzzed on the console, intruding on the moment.

"Can you check that for me?"

Laurel did so, and when she recognized the name on the screen, her heart gave a leap. "It's Patty. Want me to answer and put it on Speaker?"

"Please." He signaled and drifted to the exit lane while Laurel put the call on Speaker. When she was finished she gave him a nod.

"Hello?" Gavin said.

"Gavin? Hi, this is Patty Dupuis."

"Hi, Patty. You have good timing. Laurel is here and I have you on Speaker."

Laurel exchanged greetings, adjusting the volume. Emma was still sound asleep, and she wanted to keep it that way.

"I'm glad to talk to you both," Patty said. "I'm sorry I haven't called sooner. All of this has been a lot to digest. I've thought of nothing else since we talked."

"We understand," Gavin said. "The news was a shock to us all."

"I'm sorry for your loss, Patty," Laurel said. "Mallory and Mike thought so much of you."

"Thank you. Mallory loved you as well. She talked about you often."

"I loved her like a sister."

"It was clear she felt the same way. Can you

tell me how Emma's doing? I've prayed for her so many times the past two days, I think God must be sick of me."

"She's doing pretty good." Gavin pulled off the street and into a parking lot. "All things considered."

"I'm glad to hear that," Patty said. "She's lucky to have you both. I understand this is a temporary arrangement though. And I'm afraid I wasn't thinking very clearly when we talked on the phone Sunday, Gavin. There were some critical factors I neglected to mention, and I thought a phone call was in order.

"First of all, I haven't fully made up my mind yet—I want you to know that right off. But there are some complications you might not be aware of. I don't know how much Mallory has shared with either of you but . . . I'm engaged."

Gavin put the truck into Park and exchanged an uneasy glance with Laurel. "Then you're not the only one making this decision."

"That's exactly right. Robert and I are getting married in January. Like me, he was married before. He and his late wife had three children—they're barely out of the house. Two of them are still in college. He wasn't counting on raising another child."

Laurel's stomach sank like an anchor.

"On top of that Robert owns a business here in Tampa. He details boats and yachts. That's actually how we met—I hired him to clean my boat."

Gavin winced. "There aren't many boats in Riverbend."

Patty's mirthless laugh carried across the distance. "He's worked hard to build his business, and it's quite successful. He enjoys what he does, and he's at least ten years from retirement."

"So," Laurel said. "If you did decide to take on this challenge, you'd need to stay there in Florida."

"That's what I'm getting at. I realize it would be better for Emma to stay in familiar surroundings. But children are resilient—that's what I hear anyway. I'm just talking out loud, you understand. This is a lot for a woman who's never had kids of her own."

"We understand," Gavin said.

"I guess I need to ask this, too, just so I know exactly where things stand: If Robert and I couldn't take Emma, what would happen to her? Is there some other family member on Mike's side who'd be able to step in?"

Gavin looked at Laurel, his face betraying the same despondency she felt. "There is no one else, Patty."

They had to make her understand. "If you're not able to take her, she'll become a ward of the state. They'll find her a foster family with the hopes she'll get adopted eventually." Laurel's stomach went sour at the thought.

"That could take years," Gavin added. "Or it might never happen at all. There's no guarantee she'd stay in the area either."

Laurel could not let that happen. She would take her first. She'd have to move her to Asheville, and Mallory and Mike's beloved orchard would go to ruin. The thought was a punch to the gut. But at least the child would stay with someone who loved her. Someone who could keep alive the memory of her parents.

"Oh, this is just awful," Patty said. "How can it have come to this? Mallory was such a good mother. How can she be gone? And Emma . . ." Her words choked off. "That darling baby girl. It's all so unfair."

"Believe me," Gavin said, "we're right there with you."

They hadn't gone over the financials yet. It sounded as if Patty and Robert might be financially set, but maybe knowing they could also petition for guardianship of the estate would alleviate some concern. "We can send you Mike and Mallory's will and financial documents. We should've done that already."

"It's really not about the money," Patty said. "I feel so awful. I do love that little girl. Oh, how I wish I could just jump on board with this, but my wishes are not the only ones that matter anymore."

"We understand," Gavin said. "But I'll send the

documents just the same. You should have all the information before you make a decision."

"Thank you." She gave her email address, and Laurel jotted it down. "I know this has disrupted both of your lives. I promise to give you an answer by Friday. Will that work? Can you manage that long?"

Laurel and Gavin traded a helpless look. They would have to.

"We'll wait to hear from you then, Patty," Gavin said.

They said their good-byes, and Gavin turned off the phone. A long silence settled in the cab between them. Patty was clearly torn between obligation and her commitment to her fiancé. While Laurel felt a little frustrated with her, she couldn't really fault the woman. She was in a hard place.

Gavin stared out the windshield, his hands still grasping the steering wheel.

"It's not sounding good," Laurel said finally.

"The business-owning fiancé is an unfortunate plot twist." He glanced over at her. "If you can't wait around until Friday, I'll figure something out."

"I'm staying. But my PTO will pretty much run out by then."

"I don't want you jeopardizing your promotion. Maybe you should commute."

He was probably right but . . . She glanced

back at Emma to find the child's lips parted in sleep. So young and innocent. She'd already lost so much. And Laurel wanted to be there for her in a way she hadn't expected. "I don't want to leave her with someone else."

Laurel turned her attention back to Gavin. "And I won't let her go into foster care." Her voice rang with all the resolution she felt. She didn't know exactly how she'd make it work, but she would find a way.

"It might not come to that."

"Maybe it won't. But I'm just telling you . . . I can't let that happen to her."

Twenty-Seven

The rest of college didn't pass uneventfully. Laurel studied hard to redeem her first semester. In the summers Gavin worked for a small local builder, learning the business from the ground up. Laurel worked at the nursery.

They were busy.

But during the school year they made time for each other by studying and eating together. And just as he had in high school, Gavin's winsome ways helped Laurel form new bonds. Having him at her side made everything better.

Oh, there were fights. Sometimes Gavin's friendliness attracted other women and Laurel's jealous side kicked in. Or sometimes in the spring he was so busy with classes and baseball that he forgot to call. Those moments threatened her peace of mind. Made fear flow like poison in her veins. But he would remind her how much he loved her, and somehow everything was all right again. As time went on, her academic achievements went a long way toward alleviating her insecurities, as had Gavin's obvious adoration of her.

Before she knew it, they'd graduated—it had taken them five years to earn their bachelors' degrees, and Laurel was determined to continue on for her master's.

Gavin accepted a full-time position with Burgundy Construction in Asheville. But she still had two more years of school and couldn't afford a place in Asheville. Gavin wanted to get married so they could be together, but Laurel wouldn't settle down into married life until her education was finished. That was a good way to get stuck with a husband and children and unfulfilled dreams. She wouldn't be supported by a man the way her mom had been only to have the wheels come off when he disappeared. If she'd learned anything from her mother's life, it was this.

Another argument ensued. But somehow she convinced him they should wait until she'd finished her master's.

The two years dragged by, but finally she graduated and moved back home with her mom. She'd gotten an assistant manager's position at an Asheville nursery, but it didn't start for a few weeks.

Gavin came to town her first weekend back home, flushed with excitement about his opportunities at Burgundy Construction. He filled her in over supper at the Trailhead. Tomorrow they'd hike up to Lover's Leap for a picnic.

That Saturday Laurel worked till three, then went home to freshen up for her date. In previous summers she and Gavin had hiked all the trails outside town and even done an overnighter up to Max Patch. She loved that he enjoyed being outdoors as much as she did.

At six o'clock he stopped by the house to pick her up and they set off. The first part of the trail ran along the rushing river, then it turned into the woods for the switchbacks up the mountain. The temperature was mild for June, so the uphill climb didn't seem so arduous. They chatted as lung space allowed. Laurel drew in the pine and earthy scent of the woods, allowing it to soothe her. While she'd been at college she missed living right in the mountains. If it weren't for her dream job she'd be content living here the rest of her life. But the Biltmore was in Asheville, and so was Gavin's job.

They were quiet during the final steep ascent. The river and town were far below them now, and the sun was sinking low in the sky.

When they reached Lover's Leap, Gavin slid off his backpack and handed her a water. "It's been a while since we hiked this one."

Laurel put her hands on her hips, catching her breath as she surveyed the vista. The Blue Ridge Mountains rolled across the skyline, hazy in the evening sunlight, and the French Broad River snaked through the valley, meandering along the town's edge. "I could never get tired of this view."

"I know what you mean." He pulled out a

blanket and spread it open on the ground. "Have you ever heard the legend behind 'Lover's Leap'?"

"It's of Native American origin. Something about a maiden?"

"A beautiful Cherokee maiden who was deeply in love with a warrior. But another brave challenged her lover for her hand and he won. The maiden was so distraught she climbed the rocky ledge and jumped to her death rather than marry the brave."

"Well, that's a gloomy story."

Gavin laughed. "You're right. Let's dig into this food and find something less depressing to talk about."

Gavin had bought all their favorites from the Grab 'n' Go Deli, and they dug in. She thought about the first time they'd come up here— when Gavin first told her he loved her. Laurel smiled wistfully at the memory. She'd fought her feelings for him hard. But despite all her reservations about love, when it came to Gavin she'd been as helpless as she was now.

After they finished eating, he leaned back against a rock. She settled in the V of his legs, and they watched the sun sink lower still, swaths of gold and orange sweeping the horizon.

"Remember the first time we came up here?" he asked.

"I was just thinking about that."

"I was so nervous."

"You were? I couldn't tell."

"I'd never told anyone I loved them before—at least, no one outside my family."

She folded her arms over his. "It was the nicest thing I'd ever heard."

"I never would've believed I could fall even deeper . . . but I have," he whispered the last in her ear.

Laurel tilted her face up to him. "You say the sweetest things."

Their gazes held for a long moment. His eyes still mesmerized her. And they were so serious just now she could only wait to hear what was on his mind.

"It seems like I've been in love with you forever. I can't imagine my life without you, Laurel. You're everything I want, everything I need . . . and nothing would make me happier than to spend every day with you for the rest of my life."

He reached around for something, and when his hand reappeared it held a pale-blush jewelry box. He flicked it open and a solitaire diamond flashed against the black velvet.

She sat up, gasping, her gaze locked on the beautiful ring. Her heart raced. She was excited—that was why. They'd talked about getting engaged after Laurel graduated.

But it seemed the thought of being married one day and the reality of being married *now* were two entirely different things. Fear buzzed inside like a dozen angry bees.

"Laurel?" He gave a shaky laugh. "You're kind of freaking me out here."

"No, no, I'm just . . . overwhelmed." She pushed her hair off her face. He was still holding that ring.

This wasn't unexpected. She should be thoroughly delighted. But every time she thought about marriage, panic followed. Her mom's words sprang up in her mind. *"They always leave, Laurel. You're gonna get hurt."* The thought of Gavin leaving her the way Dad left Mom made her stomach twist hard.

"What's going on?"

"I just . . . I didn't expect this today, that's all." Her smile trembled on her lips. "I'm surprised."

Gavin let out a humorless laugh. "This is hardly sudden. We've been dating nine years." He stared out at the sunset that had seemed so beautiful just minutes ago. "Sometimes it's like you don't trust me or something. Or don't trust *us*. I don't know."

"It's not that." She was going to mess this up. Maybe she already had. What was wrong with her? She loved him so much. She set her hand on his arm. "I'm sorry, Gavin. Can we just rewind and do this over? I want to marry you. Of course I do."

He looked away. "That's not the feeling I'm

getting. You don't think we're going to make it for the long haul."

The rebuff made her go cold inside. Maybe it was *he* who thought that. "Well, you dropped out of my life once before, so forgive me if I have a few trust issues."

"Dropped out of your life? You broke up with me!"

"I just beat you to the punch."

"I was never going to break up with you, Laurel. How many times do I have to say that? I *love* you."

His intense tone, the desperate look in his eyes, melted her into a puddle. All the fight drained out of her. She shouldn't have brought up that stupid breakup again. Everything she wanted was right in front of her, and she was going to let it slip through her fingers. He'd said all those lovely things, and she turned it into a fight.

Her eyes stung with tears. She covered her face. "What is wrong with me?" She tried to swallow down the tears. But she couldn't hold them back.

A long moment later Gavin gathered her into his arms.

She pressed into him, wrapping her arms firmly around him, as if she could keep him forever if she only held on tightly enough.

"There's nothing wrong with you, baby. You're just scared. Love is scary sometimes. But I won't let you down. I promise."

Could she make herself believe that? She wanted to so badly. Maybe he could believe it enough for the both of them.

He held her until her tears subsided, then he dried her face with the tail of his shirt, gazing at her with such affection she thought she might break down in tears again. What had she ever done to deserve this man? "I ruined your proposal." She bit her wobbling lip.

He swiped at the stray tear. "You didn't ruin anything, Short Stuff. The offer's still good whenever you're ready."

"I'm ready now."

"You don't have to say—"

She put her fingers over his lips. "I'm ready now. I love you so much, Gavin. I'm sorry if I get all weird sometimes."

"I love you, weirdness and all." He placed a soft kiss on her lips.

Her heart gave a tug at his tender gesture. "Can I—can I see the ring again?"

He chuckled. And dropped one arm long enough to locate the jewelry box and hand it to her.

She opened it up again and gazed down at the beautiful solitaire. "Will you put it on me?"

His eyes grew intense. "Are you sure that's what you want?"

"Positive."

He removed the ring from the box and slid it

onto her finger. She watched it twinkle in the last rays of sunlight. "It's so beautiful, Gavin."

"You're beautiful." He tipped her chin up and gave her another kiss. But this one lasted so long, they later found themselves hiking down the mountain in the dark.

Twenty-Eight

Gavin lifted a sleeping Emma carefully from the car seat and headed toward the house. Once they were inside, Sunny's entire backside wagged with glee at the sight of them.

"Put her in the master," Laurel said quietly. "That way we can assemble the bed in her room."

"Good idea." He headed upstairs.

After the phone call from Patty, it had been a quiet ride back to Riverbend. Gavin spent the time digesting the fact that Patty might not take Emma after all. And thinking about what Laurel had said—that she wouldn't let the girl go to foster care—and what that would mean for Emma. For him.

Sadly, he also spent a great deal of time picking apart Laurel's comment about closure. His stomach twisted hard every time he thought about that. Maybe that wasn't what he wanted.

Just as he laid Emma on the bed, a text came in. Thankfully the toddler settled in for a longer nap. He pushed some pillows around her and closed the door on his way out.

The text was from Wes. *Did you get a chance to check on the drywallers today?*

Gavin winced. He shouldn't have shirked his

275

duty today. Wes was holding down a full-time job and couldn't swing by the site at a moment's notice like he could.

No, I didn't get over there yet. Got some things going on here. I'll try and stop by tonight. PS: Not looking good with Emma's aunt.

Sorry, man. No worries. I can check on it tonight.

Gavin should step up. He was the boss. But his time with Laurel and Emma was winding to a close, and that somehow left him feeling desperate. *Thanks.*

He pocketed his phone and went outside to retrieve the bed. Laurel was there, struggling to lift the large, awkward box from the truck.

"Here, I got it." He took the package from her and headed back into the house, Sunny underfoot the whole way.

"Want some coffee?" Laurel asked once they were back inside. "The sun really took it out of me."

"Love some. Thanks." He headed up the steps and into the nursery where he set the box down and surveyed the tight space. The crib would have to go first.

His phone vibrated with a call, and he checked the screen before accepting it. "Hey, Avery, what's up?"

"I just heard about Patty. She's not going to take Emma?"

"Wow, that was fast even for our family." He headed back out to his truck for his tools.

"I just got off the phone with Wes. What's going to happen to Emma now?"

"She hasn't given her final answer yet." He went on to explain Patty's extenuating circumstances. "She's going to let us know by Friday."

"What a terrible set of circumstances. Why can't *something* work in Emma's favor?"

He opened the truck toolbox and grabbed his screwdriver and utility knife. "I know. But maybe they'll decide to take her after all."

"Poor kiddo's had enough change. But if they don't decide to raise her . . . jeez, Gav. Would you really be able to just hand her over to strangers?"

He headed back into the house. He hadn't planned to bring up Laurel, but maybe it would ease Avery's worry to know there was a plan B. "If Patty bails, I think Laurel's planning to take her."

He was back in the nursery by the time his sister answered. "She'd be staying in Riverbend?"

"She'd take Emma back to Asheville."

"Okay, good."

The relief in her tone set him off. "No, that's not good. Emma needs familiarity right now. Packing her up and taking her to a whole new place—a city of all things—isn't exactly ideal, Avery. Plus there's the orchard. This place meant a lot to the Claytons, you know. The thought of seeing it all go to seed at this point—"

Laurel stood in the doorway, holding two mugs of coffee. That wall he'd been chiseling at for days was back in place. She set one of cups on the dresser and left.

Great. He palmed the back of his neck. Avery was talking about selling the orchard. "Listen, sorry to cut you off, but I have to go. I'm in the middle of something."

"Oh. All right. I'll be praying all this gets sorted out."

"Thanks." He said good-bye, tapped Disconnect, then left the room. He found Laurel in the kitchen, taking produce from the fridge.

Best to just dive right in. "I think it's great that you'd take Emma if Patty ends up backing out."

"Didn't sound like it."

"I know." Recalling the tone he'd taken on the phone, he winced. "I was reacting to Avery's attitude. I was upset with her, not you. I think it's incredibly generous that you'd be willing to raise her."

She spared him a look as she turned on the faucet and began washing cucumbers.

"I don't think I could stand to see her shuffled off to strangers. When you said that in the car, about taking her . . . I can't tell you how relieved I felt. But I also think . . . maybe I was a little upset because you'd be taking her away from me.

I guess I've grown more attached to her than I realized." Gavin shifted in place. She was so hard to read sometimes. "Are we okay, Laurel?"

After a beat she arched a brow at him. A playful light gleamed in her eyes. "Since when do you spill your guts, Robinson?"

He breathed a laugh. "Guess I've learned a thing or two along the way. Better late than never."

"You just don't want to get stuck sorting all those nuts and bolts in that box upstairs."

"You know I hate that part." He blinked his eyes at her, all innocence.

She heaved an exaggerated sigh. "Fine. I'll be up in a minute."

"That crib will have to go first." Laurel leaned against the frame of the nursery's doorway, cradling her coffee between two hands. Her hair had dried into tousled brown waves, and she looked comfy in a pair of leggings and a white T-shirt that now slid to the side, baring one sexy shoulder. And there was that spot in the cradle of her neck that he used to—

Gavin tore his gaze away. *Not your wife anymore.* He cleared his throat and turned back to the task at hand. "Crib will have to come apart— it's not fitting through that door."

"May as well get to it before she wakes up." Laurel pulled off the bedding.

Gavin removed the mattress and leaned it against the wall. "What do you think we should do with it?"

"Speaking of not waking her up . . ." Laurel closed the door. "Does the church still collect baby things for families in need?"

"Yeah, let's donate it. Mike and Mallory would've liked that." He began taking apart the crib with the screw gun. Of course, if Mike and Mallory were here, they would've kept the crib for the next child. They'd planned to have a few.

"I hope Emma takes to the toddler bed," she said when it got quiet again. "She's already had so much change."

"But she can't keep sleeping in her crib. She might fall and get hurt."

"I know, I just . . . You're right. When she wakes from her nap, we'll tell her we have a surprise and show her the bed. Let her play in it, maybe read some books to her there so she can get used to the idea."

"The new Minnie Mouse bedding you picked out will help."

"Yeah, that might be what saves the day."

When his phone vibrated, Gavin stopped to check the screen.

Mom. *Avery told me Patty is waffling. That poor baby. Praying it all works out for the best.*

He replied. *Thanks, Mom.*

Will Laurel be staying till you hear from her again?

He pressed his lips together as he texted back *Yes* and tapped the Send button with more force than necessary. As he pocketed his phone it vibrated with a call. His mom. He rejected the call and texted her instead. *Sorry. In the middle of something. Can I call you back later?*

Of course. I'm worried about you.

"Avery again?" Laurel's tone was laced with sarcasm.

"Mom. She heard about Aunt Patty's situation."

Laurel gave a mirthless smile. "The family grapevine is still alive and well, I see."

"You have no idea."

He replied to his mom. *I'm fine. Talk later.*

Before he pocketed his phone another text came in. This one from Cooper. *Hey, can I drop by in a bit?*

Gavin huffed. *Sure,* he replied. Then just because he was feeling a little facetious he added, *Just come on in when you get here. I'm upstairs in the nursery.* He wouldn't give Cooper the option of avoiding Laurel. If his family was going to be on his case, why make it easy for them?

Okay, Cooper replied.

Thirty minutes later the crib was unassembled and in the bed of his truck. Laurel sat pretzel-style on the carpet, sorting hardware while Gavin stacked the new bed frame parts by piece.

"Hopefully Emma will sleep a little longer," he said.

"My job here is almost done anyway."

"Oh no you don't. You still have to read me the directions."

"Since when do you use directions?"

"Since the Great Entertainment Center Disaster of 2018."

"I told you to read the instructions."

He'd had to take the whole thing apart and start over. It was a little humbling for a big-city contractor. "Never let it be said I don't learn from my mistakes."

"All right. The nuts and bolts are all sorted." She read off the first instruction.

On his knees Gavin moved the large frame into place. "Gonna need your help holding this."

"Here." She handed him the hardware and held the frame in place while he connected the pieces. "How's your new build coming together?"

"Good. It's being drywalled as we speak."

"Don't you need to go over and check on things?"

"It's a capable crew. Wes is heading over there tonight. Maybe I'll go over tomorrow."

She gave him a surprised look. "Maybe?"

Yeah, he used to be a bit of a workaholic. But losing his son and wife had a way of bringing everything into perspective. "Campground needs mowing. That's a full day's work all by itself."

"Yeah, but this company you've started—that's your dream. That's what you've been gunning for all these years."

She wasn't exaggerating. He'd worked his way up from the bottom, laser focused on his goal. Sure, he thought he'd be starting the business in Asheville, not Riverbend. But things change.

"I trust Wes to check their work. He knows what he's doing."

Gavin tried to scrape up some of that excitement he'd been feeling about his new build, his new business. But he couldn't seem to find it at the moment. Besides, his part-time job at the campground was all that kept him from having to move back home. And as small as that camper was, it beat living with his parents at the ripe, old age of thirty-four.

They continued piecing together the frame, Laurel handing him the hardware and holding the boards, and Gavin connecting them. They worked well together. They always had.

Until they hadn't.

"Time for the big one." Laurel grabbed the headboard and leaned over his shoulder to grab the frame. Her sweet scent teased his senses. Her long hair brushed the side of his neck.

He dropped the washer. It fell to the carpet somewhere near his knees.

"I got it. It's under your—" She tapped his knee.

He moved aside, best he could while supporting the pieces.

"Here." She handed him the washer and resumed her position. That gorgeous mane of hair hung over her shoulders, and her lashes swept down over her cheeks, her gaze fixed on the lined-up holes.

There was so much to admire about Laurel. She was smart. She was diligent and focused. She never gave up on her goals. And yet, she'd always had time for him. And once Jesse had been born she was a wonderful mother, always putting him first, despite the fact that her own mom hadn't exactly been the warm, nurturing type.

He hadn't been so good with his priorities. He put his dream, his work above his family. They'd argued about it often. He'd told himself—and her—that he was doing it for them, but that wasn't entirely true. Why couldn't he have seen the truth then, while there was still time to salvage his marriage?

"What?" Inches away, Laurel gazed up at him, a hint of confusion in her eyes.

He couldn't quite bring himself to tear his gaze away. "What?"

"You're looking at me like . . ."

How had he forgotten those caramel spokes in her eyes? They were downright mesmerizing. "Like . . . ?"

The door opened. Cooper appeared in full uniform. "Oh. Sorry."

The headboard started to fall.

Gavin and Laurel both caught it before it hit the floor. Their gazes locked. Her chin was up, shoulders square. Nothing like the arrival of a Robinson to set her defenses back in place.

Gavin cleared his throat. "Hey, Bro."

"Hi, guys. What are you up to?"

Besides gawking at his ex-wife? "Toddler bed." Gavin stood and leaned the headboard against the wall. "Emma climbed from her crib this morning."

"Where is the little bug? Katie made cookies for her, asked me to bring them by."

Laurel leaned back on her haunches. "She's down for her nap, but she should be waking up any minute now."

A cry sounded from down the hall.

"Wow," Cooper said. "That is some uncanny timing you've got going on."

"I'll get her." Laurel jumped up and dashed from the room, no doubt happy to escape.

Gavin couldn't blame her. He set his hands on his hips and kept his voice low. "What's up? Come to warn me off Laurel?"

Coop's brows shot up. "Whoa. Defensive much? I came bearing gifts, remember?"

"I've heard from the entire Robinson brigade on the matter so I already got the message loud and clear."

"I'm not your enemy, man."

"I know; you're just concerned. But I could do without all the daily checkups and second-guessing and—"

"Knock it off—I haven't done any of that."

Gavin stared at Cooper. Okay, maybe he had a point. Probably wasn't fair to put him in the same basket as the rest of the family.

Outside the doorway footsteps retreated down the stairs, and the sound of Laurel's chatter grew fainter as she went.

Gavin released a slow breath. "Sorry. Guess I shouldn't be taking it out on you."

Cooper regarded him silently, his expression inscrutable. No doubt the poker face served him well in law enforcement. "What happens between you and Laurel is none of my business."

Gavin threw his hands up. "Finally."

"On the other hand, you know they're just trying to look out for you."

"I'm a grown man. I can take care of myself."

"Sure. But we watched you go through a pretty rough spot. No one wants to see you back in that place—"

Gavin narrowed his eyes.

"Right. Not here to defend them. But I am here for you, if you need to talk. And you have to admit, this is a pretty sticky situation you got going on here—living with your ex-wife and all."

Gavin growled.

"That wasn't a warning, just an observation. You know, I'm in law enforcement, right? Being objective is part of my job. And I can see where things could get a little . . . confusing."

Gavin recalled the sight Cooper had walked in on moments ago. How could he blame his brother just for stating what was obvious? He was confused. He was having feelings for his ex-wife again. Maybe he'd never even stopped.

Crap.

Cooper grabbed the headboard. "Want some help? I got a few minutes."

Now that Emma was awake, probably best to get this done ASAP. Besides, he didn't need another excuse to get close to Laurel. "Fine. But you have to be in charge of the directions."

"Like I'd pass up a chance to tell you what to do." Cooper positioned the piece while Gavin bolted it together. "So is it?"

"Is it what?"

Cooper lined up the next piece. "Confusing."

Gavin pressed his lips together as he connected the boards. He'd noticed the way the colors blended in her eyes, the way her back arched, the way her hips flared gently. He'd remembered how a kiss to her neck provoked a husky laugh, and the way she felt curled up to his side after they'd made love.

"You could say that." He'd given Laurel a lot

287

of head space the past week. It was frightening just how quickly that had happened.

"Do you think it's messing with her too?"

Gavin thought back over the recent days. She'd lowered that wall at times. She'd shown him mercy and compassion. But that was something kind humans did for each other. He'd been grieving their son, and she offered comfort.

He scowled. Just the sort of thing a woman might do when she was ready for *closure*. That word stuck in his brain like a fly in a spiderweb. "I don't think so. I kind of tested the waters—said something about this situation bringing about something good between us." Gavin pushed a washer onto the bolt.

"And?"

Gavin cut him a look. "And she used the word *closure*."

"Oh."

"Who can blame her?" He was single-handedly responsible for their child's death. He could hardly forgive himself. How could he expect her to forgive him?

"I don't know, though . . ." Cooper placed the next piece, adjusting his position for a better hold. "The way she was staring at you when I walked in here . . ."

As much as Gavin might want to believe Laurel still felt something for him, there were too many factors pointing the other direction. He needed to be realistic. They weren't married. They weren't a family. This wasn't his second chance—he hardly deserved one. When would he get that through his thick skull?

"She's dating some guy back home. And a woman doesn't throw out a word like *closure* when she's interested in rekindling a romance. Anyway, any confusion I'm feeling about her at this point is probably just an old habit, right?" He needed to change the scenery. Get back on the dating app and turn his thoughts somewhere else.

Gavin slid a bolt into the hole, shaking his head. "I just need to forget Laurel. Get my head on straight."

"Well . . . it'll be over soon, one way or another, right?"

Gavin's stomach went leaden at the thought. "Right."

Twenty-Nine

On Thursday evening they were still waiting to hear from Patty, and Laurel was getting impatient. She dished out a scoop of vanilla bean ice cream and set the bowl on Emma's high chair. "Here you go, angel."

"Ice cream!" Emma fisted her small spoon and went to work.

Gavin joined Laurel at the island, shoving a bowl the size of the moon her way.

"Really?" she asked even as she began scooping.

"It's my favorite."

She already knew that—it's why she'd picked it up at the grocery store today. "Vanilla isn't even a flavor, you know."

"Not all of us need cookie chunks in our ice cream. Some of us prefer the simpler things in life."

She laughed. "Simpler? I seem to recall—"

The doorbell rang.

Sunny shot toward the foyer, tail swiping a wide path.

"Who could that be?" Laurel asked.

"I'll get it."

Probably one of the Robinsons, come to make sure Laurel hadn't gotten her claws back in him. Although, to be fair, Cooper had been perfectly nice the other day—he'd even tracked her down in the backyard to say good-bye. She wasn't sure what to make of that.

She grabbed a cereal bowl, added a couple of scoops, then put the ice cream container back in the freezer.

"Laurel," Gavin called from the living room. "Can you come here a minute?"

Emma was content with her ice cream, so Laurel headed into the next room.

She knew Darius Walker from the meeting they'd had regarding the will. Tonight he wore a crisp white shirt, unbuttoned at the collar, with a pair of carefully creased khakis.

Sunny sniffed his brown, lace-up oxfords.

"Hi, Darius." Laurel put out her hand to shake his even while her stomach twisted. She couldn't imagine that anything good would bring an attorney to her doorstep at eight in the evening.

"Sorry to bother you all so late."

"No problem," Gavin said. "Have a seat. Can I get you something to drink? Tea? Water?"

"Or ice cream?" Laurel asked. "We were just dishing out dessert."

"Oh, no thank you, ma'am. I'm eager to get home to my wife, but I wanted to stop by and deliver the news in person."

At his tentative tone Gavin and Laurel changed glances.

"I got word today that Mallory's mother and her husband are pursuing general guardianship."

Laurel froze in the seat. Her thoughts spun a million miles per hour, tangling up, never making it to her tongue.

"But she didn't even come to Mallory's funeral." Gavin's voice was hard.

"I know that. I realized this would come as a surprise and not necessarily a good one."

"That can't happen," Laurel said. "This is not what Mallory would've wanted."

"Laurel's right," Gavin said. "She wasn't close to her mother."

"They weren't even on speaking terms. Darcy's never even met Emma." Her voice escalated.

Gavin set a hand on her arm.

Right. The girl was within hearing distance. But Laurel's heart threatened to burst from her chest, and her lungs seemed to have forgotten their purpose. She jumped to her feet and paced the room.

"I didn't realize that," Darius said. "And I know this is hard to hear, but the woman has filed a petition, and the court will be hearing it in two weeks. She's a blood relative, and if no one else steps up, she'll likely be preferred over foster care."

"She was not a good mother," Laurel said firmly but quietly. "She ran Mallory down— she was verbally abusive, and she all but aban-

293

doned Mallory the second she graduated high school."

"I hate to hear that. I understand your reservations. But according to the petition, she's happily married now and living a respectable life in Chicago. They have the means to support a child."

"She's always had the means," Laurel said. "That doesn't make her a fit mother. Wait, you said 'general guardianship'?"

"That means she's asking for guardianship of Emma and the estate. The court will consider her situation via a guardian ad litem. But I did a little background work myself. Darcy's new husband seems to be well respected in Chicago's medical community—he's a podiatrist. And Darcy does volunteer work for several charities. Those things will reflect well on them."

Laurel let that piece of news settle for a few seconds, her hopes plummeting deeper like an anchor in the water.

"Laurel . . ." Gavin paused a beat, his posture suggesting he was treading carefully. "Don't get upset—I'm just asking—but is it possible Darcy's changed in the years since Mallory saw her last? Maybe her new husband's been a positive influence?"

"One week ago," Laurel said through gritted teeth, "her daughter had a funeral, and she chose not to attend. She didn't care to be here for Emma then—hasn't bothered to even *meet* her two-year-old grandchild—and now she wants to raise her? Seriously?"

"All fair points," Darius said. "I don't know what inevitably transpired between Mallory and her mother to drive such a deep wedge, but I do know she didn't name her mother as Emma's guardian. And I also know the court will do what they think is best for Emma."

"What if Patty agrees to take her?" Laurel asked. He'd explained this before, but it seemed irrelevant at the time. "She's supposed to let us know tomorrow."

"If Patty wants to raise Emma, she'll need to file a petition. The court will look into both parties, and all that will matter is what's in the child's best interest."

Laurel crossed her arms. "There's no doubt in my mind which woman that is."

"Patty has an ongoing relationship with Emma so that will certainly work in her favor."

If she chose to accept the challenge. And that was a big *if.* Laurel pressed her fingertips to her temple. Everything Mallory had ever said about her mother swam in Laurel's mind. The time she'd called her daughter a moron for bringing home a C in algebra. The time she'd barely missed curfew, and Darcy called her a whore. The woman had a trigger temper and regularly took out her bad moods on Mallory. All th phone calls Laurel had gotten from her distressed friend . . .

The thought of Emma suffering the woman's brutal tongue made Laurel want to snap up the child and run.

"I'm sorry to drop this on you two so late in the evening, but I felt you should know. I'd hoped it might be good news, but clearly that isn't the case. I should let you get on with your evening." Darius stood. "Please keep me apprised of the situation."

Gavin stood and shook his hand. "Thank you for coming by, Darius. We do appreciate it."

Laurel dredged up a smile for the man. "We'll let you know what Patty says."

"You all try and have a good evening."

When Gavin shut the door behind the man, he turned to Laurel, his brow crinkled. "This just seems to get worse and worse."

Laurel glanced at Emma. Her sweet cherub cheeks were now covered in vanilla ice cream. She set her spoon aside, picked up the bowl, and gave it a lick. "That woman is not getting Emma. Not if I have anything to say about it."

Thirty

Gavin strained to pull the mesh fencing tight to the new wooden post. Once in place, he secured it to the pole and gave it a wiggle. Sturdy enough. The deer fence Mike had put in wasn't optimum, but it did the job.

A peal of laughter sounded from across the orchard where Laurel was inspecting the trellis. Emma scampered nearby, trying to catch Sunny's tail.

He and Laurel had been working as a team for more than a week now. It took him back to those early days, back to that English project that had first paired them up. It didn't take him long to figure out what a great partner she made—in school, and later on in life. He'd been the one to ruin that.

Gavin's phone buzzed in his pocket, and he checked the screen. Wes. "Hey, buddy, what's up?"

"Hey. Just checking to see if you got my message the other day."

Gavin winced. "Yeah, I did. Sorry. Things have been a little hairy here between the harvest and campground and all."

"Yeah, no problem. I went ahead and called

the drywall crew. They'll be out tomorrow to fix those seams upstairs."

"Great. Thanks, bud. Appreciate you stepping in."

"That's what I'm here for. Have you had a chance to confirm the painters?"

He squeezed the back of his neck. What was wrong with him? He was letting his partner down even as their business was starting to thrive. "No, I haven't. Sorry I dropped the ball."

"No worries. I might as well save you the effort. The Johnsons changed their mind on the paint colors, so I can pass that information along while I'm at it."

"That'd be great. Thanks." The phone bleeped an incoming call and he checked the screen.

Patty.

"Listen, I gotta run. Got a call coming in." Gavin made a beeline for Laurel as they quickly wrapped up the conversation, then he accepted Patty's call.

"Hi, Patty, how's it going?" As he approached Laurel, he caught her eye.

She dropped everything and moved his way.

"Hi, Gavin. Hope it isn't too early to call."

"Not at all. We've been out in the orchard an hour already."

"Right, right. You all are so good to keep up the work there. Mallory would've appreciated that."

Emma was entertaining Sunny a good distance

away. "I'm putting you on Speaker, Patty. Laurel's right here."

The women exchanged greetings.

"Listen," Patty said. "This has been so painful for me, and you two have been very patient. I'm going to get right to the point—Robert and I have decided we can't do it. This is just something we don't feel we can take on. I hope you understand."

Gavin locked eyes with Laurel, seeing the same veil of distress come down over her features.

In the distance Emma's laughter carried across the field.

"I want you to know"—Patty's voice quavered with unshed tears—"this is just breaking my heart. It really is."

Laurel cleared her throat. "We understand this was a big ask, Patty."

"I so wish I could just . . ."

Gavin fought through the disappointment. Laurel had said she'd step in if Patty stepped aside. But had she really meant it, or had she just said it in the heat of the moment? Either way, there was no point keeping Patty on the hook. "We understand. We appreciate you taking the time to consider it."

They'd already decided if Patty turned down the guardianship, they wouldn't mention Darcy's petition. It wouldn't be fair to Patty and her fiancé—or even Emma—to force them into something they didn't want.

"Please," Patty said. "Is there some way I can stay in touch with her? I still want to be her aunt—I'd love to have her down for visits and come see her at the holidays. Is that even possible?"

Laurel met his gaze. "I think that can be arranged. We'll keep you updated, okay?"

"Please do. I don't want to lose track of her. And again, I'm so sorry this has fallen on the two of you. Mallory and Mike would be so grateful for the way y'all have stepped in."

"Thank you, Patty," Gavin said. "That means a lot to us."

They said their good-byes, then Gavin disconnected the call.

Laurel hugged herself as she watched Emma chasing Sunny around a tree. The girl took a tumble, and the dog doubled back to check on her. Emma got back up and snatched at Sunny's tail. The dog gave a joyful bark.

"Well," Gavin said. "I guess that's that."

"I guess so." It was all sinking in. Patty was out of the picture. Laurel was going to raise Emma. As she watched the girl scamper through the grass, her heart swelled a size or two.

She's mine now.

The thought quickened her heart. She hated

that Emma wouldn't have a father figure. Single women raised children all the time, of course, but growing up without a dad had left a hole in her heart. And she also disliked the thought of taking Emma from her home—but it couldn't be helped. Her job was in Asheville and the long commute would keep her away from Emma far too many hours of the day.

She'd need to find a good day care. She'd need to pack up Emma's things and move them, set up a nursery in her guest room. Put her spare bedroom suite in storage or sell it.

Sunny gave a cheerful bark.

Wait.

Her apartment didn't allow pets. And there was no way she could separate Emma from that dog. She'd have to move, and she still had three months left on her lease. Her stomach bottomed out. Well, there was nothing to be done about that. Maybe she could get out of her lease. Either way, she'd need to find a new place and soon.

"Are you going to do it?" Gavin asked.

It wouldn't be easy—none of it. But there was a beautiful little girl who needed somebody, and there was no way Laurel would abandon her. She would do Mike and Mallory proud. Resolve threaded through her innermost parts. "I'm going to do it."

His gaze sharpened on hers, no doubt taking in her set shoulders, her raised chin, and the determination that filled her so thoroughly it must be leaking out through her pores.

"Are you sure this is what you want?"

"I've never been so sure of anything in my life."

His lashes lowered briefly, his facial muscles relaxing. He nodded slowly, something coming over his expression. Flickering in his eyes. Something that looked an awful lot like admiration. "All right, then, Jenkins. Let's give Darius a call."

As it turned out, the attorney was in court, so Laurel left a message on his voice mail. Then she did a little homework. She put in a few calls to the day-care centers on her side of town. A coworker recommended a place nearby, and they were supposed to call her back.

She also found an affordable apartment that allowed pets and had an immediate opening.

A while later Laurel grabbed the baby monitor and moved it down the row, closer to where Gavin worked on the trellis.

"When are you planning to head back home?" he asked.

"As soon as I can arrange everything, I guess."

"Maybe you could leave Sunny here for the week. That way Emma would go to a place she's familiar with. It would give you a little time to settle things with the new apartment."

"That's a good idea. You wouldn't mind?"

"Of course not. You'll be back to work on Monday."

"I guess so."

"I can bring Sunny down next weekend and help you move to the new apartment."

Laurel reeled. She was taking a child who'd just lost her parents to a new city, a new home. Laurel and Sunny would be the only familiar things in her life.

She paused in her task, her hands slowly dropping to her sides. "How am I going to tell Emma what's happening? That I'm moving her away? Am I doing the right thing, Gav?"

"There's no doubt in my mind. Think of the alternatives. There's no route that would leave Emma here in her home. And she's so much better off with you than Darcy."

Laurel expelled a long breath. "You're right. I know you are. This is just going to be so hard on her. I don't know how to prepare her for that."

"You don't need to have a heavy conversation with her. We can just tell her you're going to your place. She likes it there. You can always come back here for the weekends for a while— till the place sells."

Till the place sells. It was all sinking in. She was leaving Riverbend. Leaving the orchard.

Leaving Gavin.

Her heart stuttered at the thought. Her gaze

drifted around the beautiful property the Claytons had so lovingly tended. Somehow over the past week, it had started to feel like her own purpose. Her own home. And the thought of letting it go made her achy inside.

She gave her head a shake. That was absurd. "Who's going to buy this place? Do you think they'll keep the orchard?"

He lifted a shoulder. "That's out of our control."

"And what about harvest? Who's going to handle all this while I'm in Asheville? We can't just let it go to ruin."

"Don't worry, I'll figure it out."

Laurel sighed. "Before I go I'll show you how to test the apples. And we can come back on weekends. The Fuji make up most of the orchard, and getting them in might be a challenge."

"I can handle it."

"I know you have your business to tend to."

He waved her away. "The harvest will be my priority. We need this place looking as good as possible on paper. We'll get a good price on it—you'll need the equity for Emma."

"I'm not worried about that." She earned a decent wage—and if she got that promotion, she'd really be set.

"You could always put the money away—for college or whatever."

"Yeah, I'll definitely do that."

A flash of royal blue caught her eye. Darius

strode around the side of the house, heading toward the backyard. He lifted a hand in greeting.

Laurel waved back. "Darius is here."

Gavin grabbed the nursery monitor, and the two of them joined the attorney on the patio.

"Sorry to interrupt your work."

Gavin shook his hand. "Time for a break anyway."

"And Emma's down for her nap, so your timing's perfect. Can I get you something to drink?"

"I actually just had lunch at the deli. I got your message, Laurel. I thought it might be easier to stop by and have the conversation in person."

That didn't sound good. She gestured toward one of the patio chairs. "Of course. Have a seat."

Once they were settled, Darius began. "First of all, Laurel, I was delighted to hear you've decided to petition for guardianship."

"It's the right thing to do. I love that girl, and I can't turn my back on her."

"I have a lot of respect for you for that, I want you to know that."

Laurel traded glances with Gavin. "But?"

Darius leaned forward, placing his elbows on his knees. "But I'm afraid it's not quite as simple as that. There's still Darcy's petition to consider. The court will want to hear this out."

Laurel's chest tightened. "But . . . the Claytons named me as Emma's guardian. They wanted me to raise Emma, not Darcy."

"That's true. But they'll want to hear from any petitioner. And remember, the Claytons actually named the two of you: Gavin and Laurel Robinson. Their choice was to leave their daughter in the care of a married couple. You're not that couple anymore. You're a single woman now and—"

"Single women raise children—adopt children even—all the time."

"That's true. Nothing wrong with that at all. But wanting a married couple to raise a child is a different thing than wanting one-half of that couple to take on that task."

Gavin leaned forward, his jaw twitching. "That's ridiculous. Mike and Mallory would've wanted Laurel to raise her over Darcy, hands down. No doubt in my mind."

"All that matters now is what's in the child's best interest: Darcy or Laurel."

"Laurel is in her best interest!"

"I have to agree with you there, Gavin. But at this point, I'm afraid it'll be up to the courts to determine that."

Laurel's stomach turned. She sagged against the chair back. She'd thought this was settled. How could Darcy's petition still matter?

"You have a lot going for you, Laurel," Darius said. "The court will appreciate that you have an ongoing relationship with Emma. I assume you're gainfully employed?"

"Of course."

"She's a horticulturist for the Biltmore. She's about to be promoted to manager of the Walled Garden. It's a prestigious position."

"That's good. We'll petition the court for general guardianship. I can put together a case and present it at the hearing. Laurel, we'll need to set up an appointment for you to come down to my office and go over a few things."

"Anything you need." Laurel remembered to breathe. "What are my chances here, Darius? What do you think will happen?"

He gave her a wan smile. "I wish I could give you an answer. I already mentioned a couple of the factors working in your favor. And there's always the possibility the Gordons will drop their petition once they discover you're petitioning. But if they don't . . . they have some selling points too. Darcy is Emma's grandmother, and she seems to be in a stable marriage. It's going to be up to the clerk to make the call."

Gavin pinned the attorney with an unwavering look. "We'll do whatever we have to do to make sure this goes the right way."

"Absolutely."

Sounds of stirring came from the baby monitor, then Emma began talking to her animal friends. Laurel stood, feeling as if she'd left her stomach back in the chair. "I should go get her."

Darius rose. "Don't forget, I'm on your side.

Call my office and set up an appointment with Shelley. I'll work you in this week, and we'll get that petition filed. We'll get all our ducks in a row for that hearing."

"I will." Laurel shook his hand. "Thank you, Darius. I appreciate it."

"Of course. We'll do everything we can. Y'all try and have a good day now."

Thirty-One

"How can this be happening?" Laurel plopped down at the end of the sofa, turning slightly to face Gavin at the other end.

They hadn't had a chance to talk about Darius's revelation. Gavin had been called away to a campground emergency, and Laurel spent the rest of the day taking care of Emma and finishing the repairs to the trellis.

"It's just not right," Gavin said.

At Gavin's feet Sunny heaved a sigh and set her head on her paws.

Laurel concurred. What a long, long day. Her emotions had gone on a very unpleasant roller-coaster ride, and now her stomach twisted with the dramatic ups and downs. "I don't know how they could even consider Darcy. But Darius seemed to think she has a chance. More than a chance. He almost seemed like he thought it was a fifty-fifty thing, didn't he?"

"Kind of made it sound that way. Unless they end up dropping out . . ."

"I'm not holding my breath. That woman cannot get Emma. I have stories about her that would make your stomach turn." She was getting sick just thinking about the way Darcy had made

Mallory feel about herself. Emma was so young. Laurel couldn't bear the thought of the child being raised to believe she was nothing.

Gavin ran a hand over his jaw. "Maybe we can talk to Darcy about this. Maybe we can convince her you're Emma's best option."

The woman was so stubborn. She'd never relented on a single act of "discipline" even if she later found out Mallory was innocent. "You don't know her. She's spiteful—and she was never my biggest fan. She'll hang on all the harder when she finds out how badly I want Emma."

"What does she want with her anyway? Is she just trying to get her hands on the estate? Even with the sale of the house and orchard, there isn't that much money to be had."

"I don't think it's the money. She's got plenty. She cares about appearances. That's the only reason she sent Mallory to a private school, took her to Asheville for haircuts, and bought her designer clothes. Taking in her orphaned grandchild will make her seem like a saint."

Gavin's face fell. "I never met her."

"She's a real piece of work. The scary thing is, she's a whole different person outside her house. Everyone at Hopewell Academy loved her. She headed up committees and showed up for all the field trips." Being a little older and wiser now, Laurel recognized the pattern. "She's a sociopath, Gavin. I'm no psychologist, but she has all the behaviors. Mallory was convinced of it. She had no empathy—never apologized once to Mallory—and it was always all about Darcy. She's manipulative but she can be so darned charming when she wants to be—it's scary."

A sociopath could end up raising Emma.

The oxygen evaporated from the room. Laurel jumped to her feet and paced the room. All those times she'd seen Darcy snow a room full of parents flashed in her mind. And now she had a husband at her side—a respected member of the Chicago community—and she was Emma's *grandmother.*

The guardian ad litem would fall for her charm, and Emma would be caught up in the same sticky web Mallory had had to deal with. Having her mother leave after graduation had actually turned into a blessing. It had allowed Mallory to grow as a person—to see herself through someone else's eyes other than her narcissistic mother.

Laurel's gaze collided with the family photo on the mantel—Mike, Mallory, and Emma at the child's second birthday party. Emma had a glob of icing on her finger and held it out to Mallory, who was laughing. Mike peered at the camera. They seemed so happy. So much hope. So much promise.

Laurel could not let this happen.

Gavin watched Laurel wear a hole in the living room rug. He understood. He felt sick after

311

hearing her description of Darcy. No wonder Mallory had cut ties with the woman. She hadn't wanted that toxicity in her life or marriage. The last thing she would've wanted was her own child being raised by the woman.

If Darcy really was as manipulative and charming as Laurel described, it was entirely possible Darcy would end up with guardianship.

And seeing Laurel so upset elevated his anxiety to a whole new level. He wanted to protect her from this. He'd already caused her so much grief—more than any woman should have to bear. He wished he could spare her the agony of losing another child. Wished he could spare Emma the plight of being raised by a sociopath.

Maybe he could.

Darius's words floated to the front of this mind. *"The Claytons actually named the two of you."* Maybe they weren't a married couple any longer—but there was no reason they couldn't be. Was there?

Sure, there were obstacles. They lived in different towns. Also, there was that canyon of hurt and hostility looming between them. But they'd overcome that these past two weeks for Emma's sake. Couldn't they work through the rest of it for the good of an orphaned child they both loved?

His pulse raced with the idea, excitement warring with fear. Getting caught up with Laurel again was a risk. From their first connection he'd completely lost his heart to her. Even when he'd been busy building his career, neglecting her, she'd been everything to him. She was his kryptonite. There had never been anyone else for him. After losing her it had taken everything he had just to get back on his feet.

Even still, he didn't feel worthy of her. He'd let her down, let his son down.

But maybe this time he could be there in the way she deserved—and certainly in the way Emma deserved. Maybe this was his second chance to prove he could be that kind of man.

Laurel chewed her lip as she paced. Everything about her posture and movements were familiar. She stopped nearby and met his gaze, agony embedded in her expression. "Help me think. There has to be something we can do."

Gavin swallowed hard, his heart thrashing about his rib cage. "What if we got married?"

Laurel did a double take. "What did you say?"

Too late to back out now. "Okay, hear me out. Mike and Mallory left Emma to us, right? If we were still an *us,* it would be an open-and-shut case. The court wouldn't even hear Darcy's petition, right? We'd be appointed Emma's guardians automatically."

She gave her head a shake. "You can't be serious."

He stood, the *knowing* feeling pushing him forward. "I know it sounds extreme. I do. But you just told me how awful Darcy is, what kind of damage she did to Mallory. She would've laid down her life rather than see the same thing happen to Emma."

"I get that but—"

"If we lose Emma at the hearing, she will be *gone*. Do you understand that? She'll be lost to us forever."

"Well, I can't marry you, Gavin!"

He flinched at her acerbic tone. Okay, he probably had that coming. He'd put Laurel through a lot. But the thing was, he could do it this time—be a good husband and father.

If she would only give him a chance.

They could come together and do what was best for Emma. He knew without a doubt it was exactly what Mike and Mallory would've wanted. It was right there in their will.

Laurel was pacing again, except her shoulders were stiff now, her brows pulled tight, those two little furrows dividing them.

God, give me the words. "I'm sorry. I didn't mean to upset you. But I think we have to at least consider it as an option."

Laurel speared him with a glance. "It's a terrible option."

He flinched. Okay, then. He'd tried. Somehow that didn't make him feel any better.

He should set aside his disappointment and focus on the more important task at hand—taking care of Emma. "All right, then. I'm open to suggestions. All I know is we can't let her go to Darcy. We can both agree on that point."

At least they agreed on something. He sat back down, his legs trembling as the adrenaline wore off. He palmed the back of his neck and found it hot to the touch. Stupid. He'd forgotten what it felt like to put his heart on the line only to have it stomped on.

"Don't even live in the same town," Laurel muttered.

Gavin lowered his hand, his gaze sharpening on her. Was marriage still on the table then? "I'd be willing to move to Asheville. You could still take that promotion. You've earned it. You deserve it."

She scowled at him.

Okay, still angry. He'd be quiet now.

"How could we even be sure we'd get guardianship?"

He gave her a wary look. Opened his mouth. Closed it again. "Is that a rhetorical question?"

"No, it's not a rhetorical question! There's no point in discussing this any further if it's not a viable solution."

"Okay, right. Well, that would be a good question for Darius, I guess." Should he suggest calling the attorney right now?

She whipped out her phone and tapped the screen a couple of times, then went to stand in front of the picture window. Beyond the glass, darkness had fallen and the mountains were mere silhouettes against the night sky.

"Hi, Darius, how are you?" Laurel said. "That's good. I'm sorry to call so late . . . Thank you. Listen, I was calling because I have a hypothetical question to run by you . . . Okay, let's say Gavin and I were to—to get remarried. Would we automatically get guardianship of Emma?"

Gavin's breath froze in his lungs. He listened intently, but all was quiet on Laurel's end while Darius apparently gave an answer he couldn't hear. The silence went on. The length of the attorney's response indicated the matter might not be as simple as Gavin had assumed.

"I see," Laurel said. "No, not at this time . . . Right . . . I appreciate that . . . Yes . . . Thank you . . . I do appreciate your taking my call so late . . . Okay, sounds great. Good night." Laurel tapped the screen and pocketed her phone. She crossed her arms, still staring into the darkness.

When Gavin could take it no longer he asked, "Well? What did he say?"

Her reflection in the window gave nothing away. But her rigid posture announced she was still on guard—with him anyway. She'd sounded perfectly fine with Darius. But then the attorney hadn't robbed her of a son, divorced her, then asked for a second chance.

"It would probably work," Laurel said finally.

She didn't sound angry anymore—that was

good, wasn't it? Maybe they could have a calm discussion about this. "Probably?"

She hitched a shoulder. "There's a good chance Darcy would drop her petition once she finds out we're petitioning together since Mike and Mallory named us in the will."

"So if we were to get remarried . . . he thinks we'd be declared Emma's guardians?"

"There would still be a guardian ad litem and a hearing—that's standard."

"Does Darcy know we got divorced?"

"How would she? She hadn't spoken with Mallory, and she's been gone from this community for years."

Though all Laurel's pacing had made him dizzy, the resolute stillness now unsettled him. What was she thinking?

He stood and moved toward her, needing to read the emotions on her face. "I meant what I said. I could move to Asheville. I'd figure something out with the business. Maybe Wes would want to take the reins." How quickly his career ambitions faded in the light of Emma's need.

Then he thought of Connor—the guy Laurel had been texting. It would kill Gavin to have his ring on her finger and know her heart belonged to another. But they had to get it all on the table if they were going to make this work. "What about that guy you're seeing?"

"Connor? We've only had one date. He's

not even a factor here." Those guarded eyes sharpened on him. "But what about you? Is there someone you haven't told me about?"

"There's no one."

She shook her head. "This is crazy. We can't get married because of a child. This won't work. Our marriage didn't work before."

"It would be different this time." But would it? With Emma being their main priority and not each other? The thought caught in his mind.

"How do you know that? How do you know it wouldn't just be one huge mistake?"

"This is what Mike and Mallory wanted."

"But what about *us?*"

"I don't know. I guess we'd need to be clear on, ah, the terms of the marriage."

She gave him a flinty look. "We'd be marrying for the distinct purpose of raising Emma together. The terms would be exactly the same as they've been the past two weeks."

His heart took the express elevator to basement level. Separate beds. Separate lives. Basically a marriage in name only. It wasn't at all what he'd had in mind. Didn't sound as if she even held out hope for more—and only now could he admit to himself that he must've. "So we'd just keep living together, just like this."

"Just like this." Her cheeks flushed even as her chin notched higher. "That's all I could offer you."

This time he made good use of the rug, long slow strides eating up the distance. Live together. Raise Emma together. Sleep down the hall from one another.

He stopped in front of the mantel, where Mike stared back at him from a photo. Upon seeing the family so alive, so happy, Gavin scrubbed his face with his hand. He was so selfish. His friend had his life snuffed out in a moment, had been stolen from his baby girl, along with his wife, leaving his child *orphaned.* And all Gavin could think about was himself.

God, help me. This is crazy, isn't it? I don't know what to do. Show me what's right.

His head was about to explode. But what other choice did he have? Let Laurel take Emma off to Asheville? Hope the guardian ad litem would see through Darcy's false charm? Lose Emma for good?

He closed the distance between them, not taking his eyes from her. He stopped when he was a step away. "I can't leave her to that woman, and I don't think you can either."

"If we did this—I'd move back here. This is Emma's home and community, and she's more important than any job could ever be. It's what we wanted for her all along. I would stay home and take care of her and tend the orchard—and you would rake in the big bucks."

He dredged up a smile.

"But this is too big a decision to make impulsively."

He nodded slowly. "You're right. We should sleep on it." He had his own reservations. He just didn't see another solution.

"Agreed." After a long beat she smirked. "You know, if we go through with this, your family will think you're nuts."

They would, actually. But he'd deal with them later.

"Maybe you are." Her expression sobered. "Maybe we both are. But I know one thing: I'm nuts about that little girl, and I'm not giving her up."

Thirty-Two

After a long engagement, Gavin and Laurel married in a simple ceremony in Riverbend Gap. Mallory and Mike, also engaged, were their sole attendants. The newlyweds took a short honeymoon to the Outer Banks.

After the honeymoon Laurel moved into Gavin's Asheville apartment and continued her position as assistant manager at the nursery.

One month into the marriage, she discovered she was pregnant. And even though it was unexpected, the thought of a baby made her happy. She revealed the news to Gavin over a quiet dinner in their apartment.

"I'm pregnant," she blurted as he pushed his plate back.

He stared at her for a long moment before he smoothed her hair from her face. "Babe . . . Are you feeling okay?"

"Just a little fatigued sometimes."

"I thought you were dragging a bit." He stared into her eyes, his gaze growing intense.

Please be okay with this. Please don't be mad.

Finally he gave a slow nod, and his lips turned up at the corners. "All right then. I guess we're going to be parents."

Laurel studied his face, attempting to see beyond the joyful expression to any resentment he might be burying. "You're not mad?"

He leaned forward and set the gentlest of kisses on her lips. "How could I be mad, Jenkins? You're carrying our baby."

The coming weeks were full of work and laughter and newlywed excitement. On weekends they stayed up too late watching movies, soaking in the hot tub, and making love in their queen-size bed. He often set his hand on her growing stomach, dreamed with her about their future, and got in mock arguments about ridiculous baby names.

But slowly, small issues creeped up. Gavin seemed to expect her to handle all the home-related chores even though she worked outside the home too. He didn't cook at all and she wasn't much of one either, so they ate takeout until they grew tired of it. The division of chores was a sore point with Laurel, but something prevented her from complaining. Instead she took the inequity with the grace of a martyr.

"You have to talk to him, Laurel," Mallory had said one day when they were visiting in Riverbend on a weekend. "It's not fair for him to put all the chores on you."

"I don't really mind. He does work more hours than I do."

"You do mind. And he can't fix it unless he knows something's wrong."

"It's how he was raised—his mom did all the household chores and his dad took care of the exterior stuff." Besides, she shouldn't complain. She had a safe, warm home and all the food she could eat.

"You live in an apartment—there is no exterior stuff!"

"I'm kind of enjoying cooking now anyway— I've started growing my own herbs and experimenting with them."

But Mallory was right. Laurel needed to say something. So she began dropping hints. And when Gavin didn't pick up on those hints, she grew more frustrated. She should be more direct, but the thought of conflict filled her with fear.

Everything else was great. Gavin took such good care of her in other ways: bringing flowers home regularly, drawing her a bath after a long day, telling her how beautiful she was and how much he loved her. She shouldn't make waves.

As spring bled into summer and the days grew longer, his work hours increased. He got a promotion and suddenly most nights there was nobody to cook for. Most nights Laurel made do with cereal suppers. She got off at five, and Gavin didn't come home till dark, around nine o'clock— she had plenty of time for laundry and grocery shopping now.

Each night the hours between supper and his return stretched ahead like a runway. And when he finally did come home, he was too exhausted to join her in the hot tub or draw her a bath. He wanted a shower and bed.

Laurel tried to tell herself he was just tired. That he was as goal focused as she was and trying to make a path for himself at Burgundy Construction. But those excuses felt empty during the long evening hours. She felt so *alone.*

None of her college friends lived in Asheville anymore, and being the boss at work hadn't endeared her to her coworkers who were mostly high schoolers anyway.

It would get better in the fall when the days grew shorter again.

But as September eased by, Gavin continued coming home around nine even though it was dark much earlier. Paperwork at the office, he'd said.

Was there a woman at work? He'd mentioned a couple of female coworkers, but Laurel had yet to meet anyone from the office.

So one night she surprised him with supper. He was alone in the office and, just as he'd said, doing paperwork at his desk. He welcomed her with a beaming smile, but as soon as they'd consumed the roast beef sandwiches, she could tell he was eager to get back to work. So she left.

She tried bringing him supper a few more times

but eventually she stopped. She must be lacking in some way. Did he find her boring now? Was he falling out of love with her? He still sent flowers and said she was beautiful. Still professed his love and enjoyed the little kicks coming from her womb.

It would get better after the baby arrived.

Late in the fall Jesse Lee Robinson was born in the middle of the night after a twelve-hour labor, and it was love at first sight for Laurel. Gavin, too, seemed spellbound by that little red, wrinkled face and cap of dark-brown hair.

He took a week of paternity leave, then went right back to his daily grind.

If there'd been any worry in Laurel's heart that she'd take after her own mother in the parenting department, that notion quickly faded. She couldn't get enough of her son. Couldn't possibly kiss him, cuddle him, and stare at him enough.

Jesse's early months passed too quickly. Laurel went back to work after maternity leave. It wasn't easy leaving her baby, but the small home day care was clean and safe, and the middle-aged woman who ran it was kind and nurturing.

Laurel adored the newborn stage, and she finally had something wonderful to fill those lonely evening and weekend hours. So she powered through. She still felt abandoned, but not enough to cause trouble. Every now and then

325

she complained to Mallory, but she suspected her friend had tired of her grumbling.

One night, after a long day at work—she'd been promoted to manager—and a grueling evening with a teething baby, Laurel carefully laid Jesse in his crib. It was her third attempt to put him down for the night. The poor guy's gums were inflamed with two new teeth. She was just easing away from the crib when the front door slammed.

Jesse stirred in the crib and let out a wail.

Her blood pressure shot up ten notches. "Seriously?" she called down the hall before she returned to the crib to pick up Jesse.

Gavin appeared in the darkened doorway. "What's wrong?"

"You woke him up," she said over the wailing, suddenly aware that she was still wearing her work clothes since she hadn't been able to shower.

"Sorry . . ." Surprise was embedded in his tone. He dropped a kiss on the squalling child's forehead. "Want me to take him?"

"No, he's teething." These days he wanted only her when he was upset. Who could blame him? His dad was rarely home. She swept past Gavin and went back to the living room where she could at least watch TV while she bounced her poor baby.

Gavin followed her, passing their new leather sectional and heading into the kitchen. "Bad day?"

She pressed her lips together. Jesse had been teething for two weeks. Hadn't her husband even noticed?

"Are there any leftovers? I'm starving."

Laurel stormed toward the kitchen. "Are you kidding me? I've been bouncing our child on my hip since I got home."

He straightened from the fridge.

"You might know that if you were ever *here*. But you're not here. You're at work. *All the time.* If it's dark out you're doing paperwork, and you never even make it home before nine anymore. Why should I cook for someone who's not even here? Huh? So you can come home and heat up leftovers before you fall into bed?"

The light spilled over his lax facial muscles, his gaping mouth.

A long beat passed. Her heart thudded in her chest like a jackhammer. What had she done? But it was too late to back down now. And besides, she was just getting started.

"Where is this coming from?" he asked finally.

Her muscles quivered. "It came from months of being alone, Gavin! I didn't get married to feel so *alone*. You put a ring on my finger and then you just . . . you just abandoned me." The words ripped right from her heart. Everything she'd been feeling, months of being ignored, her deepest fear, encapsulated in that one simple phrase.

And it left her vulnerable. Terrified.

"Babe . . ." He closed the fridge door and approached her. "You know I'm doing this for us, don't you? You wanted out of this apartment. We're saving for a house where we can spread out a little. Where you can start a garden—that's what you wanted. All these hours get me one step closer to that promotion."

Her spine lengthened even as her stomach sank to the floor. Hadn't he heard what she'd just said? She needed *him,* not a house.

He reached out to her.

She flinched away.

His brows creased. "Laurel . . ."

She'd finally gotten up the courage to confront him. Okay, maybe the words had gushed out like a geyser. But she'd held out her vulnerable heart in her hands—and he didn't seem to care. He only made excuses.

Adrenaline pulsed through her body. "I'm going to rock him to sleep." The words came out like gravel. She turned and headed toward the nursery before the sting behind her eyes materialized as tears.

Thirty-Three

Laurel's legs trembled as she headed toward the playground with Gavin and Emma, their feet swishing through the long grass. The sun hadn't yet peeked over the mountains to dry the morning dew, and a chill hung in the late-September air.

The park was all theirs, and as they neared the equipment Emma quickened her steps. "Go play!"

"Yes, angel, you go play," Laurel said. "Be careful."

By silent agreement she and Gavin headed toward one of the benches facing the playground. It had been a long night filled with tossing and turning and little sleep. Gavin's proposal had hung like a dark cloud over her bed. She was glad they'd agreed to sleep on it.

Emma had awakened them both at dawn, but their busy morning hadn't been conducive to life-altering conversations. The park had been Gavin's suggestion.

Laurel sank onto the wooden bench and Gavin did the same. The tops of the mountains were just coming alive with a kaleidoscope of autumn colors. Soon the vibrant hues of red, yellow, and orange would sweep down the mountains into the valley, ushering in a brilliant fall display.

"So . . ." Gavin stretched his legs in front of him. "What's on your mind today?"

A laugh bubbled from her throat. He'd always been good at breaking the tension. And there'd been enough tension between them this morning to disrupt cell tower signals.

"Listen," he continued, "I'm just going to get right to the point because I don't know how long Emma's going to occupy herself. I spent all night weighing the pros and cons. You probably did too. I know all this was my idea, but after considering it all night—I don't think we should get married."

Her breath spilled out. He was absolutely right about that—even though the thought of staying in Riverbend held plenty of appeal. "I'm glad you said that. I agree with you. No offense."

"None taken."

They shared an awkward laugh.

"Look, Waurel," Emma called from where she bent over the rubber swing, feet lifted from the wood chips. "I swing."

"Good job, Emma." She glanced at Gavin. "Marriage is hard enough when the couple prioritizes each other. If we got married for Emma's sake, she would be our priority."

"And while she's definitely worthy of being a priority, a marriage based solely around her wouldn't be healthy."

"For any of us."

He gave a slow smile. "We've done some growing and maturing while we've been apart."

"Seems so. But we still haven't solved the problem. I can't let Darcy get guardianship."

"I had another idea last night—or rather early this morning. Bear with me, I'm functioning on very little sleep."

"Lay it on me."

He scuffled the toe of his shoe in the dirt. "What would've happened if Mike and Mallory died with a child when we were still married?"

She hitched a shoulder. "We would've gotten guardianship."

"And then, what? After we divorced . . ."

"We would've had to come up with a custody arrangement I guess."

"Exactly. Why couldn't we do that now?"

She blinked at him. "You're proposing we petition for joint guardianship?"

"Why not? She'd get to stay in her home, in a community of people who love her, and we'd share the responsibility of raising her."

"That's . . . far from ideal."

"Darcy is far from ideal. Families do this all the time. You could petition for guardianship of the estate. You could live there with Emma, manage the orchard—who better to do it?"

"That's not fair to you."

"I don't care about the money. We can't sell

331

the place—Emma deserves to stay in her home, and the orchard keeps it sustainable. This is a workable plan. She spends half the time with you, half with me."

"In a camper?"

"I'll be looking for something else now that the business is taking off—I just haven't had time. This way, Emma could be our main priority. She'd have a mother and father figure. You could even take your promotion and commute if you wanted. I know you could do this on your own, but I can be your partner in this. I can even help with the orchard. You can count on me to carry my end. Let me be there for her."

She weighed his words. She believed him. She hadn't discounted his idea of marriage because she didn't believe he'd be a better partner this time around. He'd been there for Emma and, indirectly, for Laurel. "Would the clerk really see that as a better option than Darcy and her husband?"

"I put a call into Darius this morning. He thinks it's a reasonable solution. The guardian ad litem would weigh in, of course, once she meets with us."

"But surely an intact home would be preferable to a split one."

"But the will names us—both of us. They trusted us with their daughter. The court won't take that lightly."

"And Darcy has no relationship with Emma."

"Plus, she'd be removing her from her home and all the people who love her—assuming she doesn't do us all a favor and drop the petition."

Laurel absorbed all of that. He made some good points. And while she'd come to the conclusion that a marriage based on Emma's care wouldn't work, this arrangement was different because Emma could be their priority. However, it would still involve a certain amount of teamwork.

She watched the girl climb up the small slide while she weighed the pros and cons. She and Gavin had come a long way. For two weeks they'd put the child first, and she believed they could go on doing so as long as things didn't get personal between them. As long as old hurts didn't flare up.

No doubt the arrangement would be better for Emma than anything she could have with Darcy. In short, it would solve the problem—as long as the clerk granted their petition.

She loved the idea of making the home, the orchard, hers. It was the kind of home she'd always dreamed of. And the notion that she could use her skills to maintain her own security held lots of appeal.

She stared at Gavin. Those soft blue eyes were trained on her. He was quiet, waiting. But beneath the patient façade was an energy that implied nervous anticipation. "What do you think? A plausible option or sleep deprivation?"

"It's plausible. There would be a lot of details to work out. But we could probably pull it off if we stayed objective. Viewed this as a business arrangement between two adults."

"We can at least work on being friends, can't we? I mean, even business goes more smoothly, more pleasantly when there's a friendly relationship between colleagues."

"Friendship is based on trust and respect, and those things are earned."

He shifted his weight around in the seat. "I believe we can handle a friendship at this point. Don't you?"

"Sharing a child will mean making decisions together for years. Spending time together. We'll never be free of that commitment, not even after Emma's an adult. There'll always be birthdays and holidays, graduations and weddings—and grandchildren. If we won guardianship, if we're committed to Emma, our lives will be bonded in a way that can never be completely severed." Fear dripped through her veins, steady and relentless. Letting Gavin in her life again was a risk. But she was even more afraid of what would happen to Emma if Darcy won guardianship.

"I realize that. I spent hours mulling this over last night. But we'll communicate better this time around. Look at you—you express yourself quite well these days. You've grown in other ways and so have I. That's a good thing." His gaze sharpened on hers. "We can do this, Laurel. We should do this, for Emma's sake."

She wasn't entirely sure it would be that easy. Especially when, deep down, she longed for more than friendship. But maintaining reasonable expectations would keep the situation from spinning out of control. Keep her heart from getting trampled on again.

"All right. This sounds like a viable solution, and if Darius thinks it betters our chances, I'm on board."

He beamed at her. "Really?"

It was time to verbalize something that would've shocked her only weeks ago. But the truth had been growing in her heart over the past few days. "One other thing . . . I don't want to commute to the Biltmore. I want to stay home with Emma. Run Harvest Moon full-time."

His mouth went slack. "Are you sure, Laurel? That's a big sacrifice. You don't have to make that decision right now. You should take some time and think about it."

"I don't need to. I don't want to leave her with a sitter all day. She's been through enough. She needs stability and continuity, and I'm going to be there for her when she needs me."

"If you're sure that's what you want. I can help with the bills until the orchard is self-sustaining."

It warmed her heart that he'd offer. "Thanks, but I still have that big nest egg from the sale of our house."

"You do?"

"Every dime. It's time I put it to good use. Now, what about our families?"

He shrugged. "They might not like it, but this is our decision. Eventually they'll get on board. They'll be a great support system for Emma."

She took in his steady gaze and fixed expression. "You're going to have a time of it with your family."

"Leave them to me."

She was glad she wasn't him. Telling her mom wouldn't be the easiest either, but that would be nothing compared to facing the Robinsons.

He studied her for a long minute, his face softening. Some of the starch left his shoulders. "We have a deal then?"

She tore her gaze away and homed in on the little girl now climbing atop the frog-shaped spring rider. Laurel was about to commit the rest of her life to this child. But watching Emma giggle as she rocked back and forth, Laurel couldn't bring herself to regret it. What could be more important than giving this child the parents she deserved? The parents Mike and Mallory had wanted her to have? Laurel would leave her hurt and disappointment in the past. Emma was all that mattered.

"All right," she said. "We have a deal."

. . .

Gavin turned into Cooper and Katie's driveway, still feeling as though someone had filled his head with helium. He was just relieved there was hope of keeping Emma from Darcy's influence. Nothing more. Even the thought of telling his family couldn't bring him down today.

Sure, the "business arrangement" talk had been a little off-putting. But they'd made huge strides in just the past two weeks. Imagine what kind of ground they could cover over months? Years? Something inside squirmed at the thought.

But he pushed those feelings away as he shut off his engine and exited the vehicle. Laurel was headed to her mom's to announce the news. He'd wanted to handle that task together, but as Darius had pointed out thirty minutes ago, time was of the essence. With the hearing in just thirteen days, they should lay the groundwork as quickly as possible—and that meant getting their families on board.

Speaking of which . . .

He knocked on Cooper's door and shifted his feet as he waited, practically buzzing with energy.

A moment later the door opened. "Hey, what brings you by today?" Cooper opened the screen door and ushered Gavin inside.

He stepped into the cozy living room, replete with stuffed sofas, throw pillows, and blooming plants. College GameDay blared from the large screen TV. "Where's Katie?"

"She rode her bike to the diner to have breakfast with Avery. Have a seat. Want some coffee?"

Last thing he needed was caffeine. "Nah, that's all right." He took the sofa while Cooper lowered himself into the eyesore next to it. "I can't believe she let you keep that ugly thing."

"It's comfortable." Cooper grabbed the remote and lowered the volume. "I assume you didn't come by just to watch college football or insult my man chair."

"I'm here for a favor, actually. But before I get to that . . . I have some big news."

Cooper waited him out.

"Laurel and I are petitioning for shared guardianship of Emma."

His brother's expression went unchanged. Not a single muscle so much as twitched. Son of a gun had a poker face like a CIA agent.

Still, Gavin knew what he was thinking. "Aren't you going to say anything?" His tone came out a little combative.

"I'm processing."

"Well, process this: it's going to happen no matter what you or anyone else says."

"What exactly would that look like—shared guardianship?"

"Just like you'd think. Laurel stays in Riverbend and we share custody."

338

"That's a big commitment."

"Her sociopathic grandmother is going after guardianship, and we can't let that happen. Joint custody would comply with the terms of the will—both Laurel and I would be raising Emma."

"I see."

"Do you?"

Cooper regarded him for a long, drawn-out minute. Finally he leaned forward, planting his elbows on his knees. "Listen, that's really great what you guys want to do for Emma. I admire your dedication. But just go with me here. This arrangement would tangle you guys up like last year's Christmas lights. For years. What if you develop feelings for Laurel again? To be honest, you already seem a little—"

"I'm doing this for Emma." And yes, he wanted to be there for Laurel in a way he hadn't before. Was that so wrong?

"What was that favor you mentioned?"

Gavin shifted on the couch. "I could use some help with the family. I'm going to tell them today, and I could use a little support."

"Are you sure this is what you want?"

"I haven't been so sure about anything in a long time." Gavin meant those words down to his marrow. He could feel Mike's approval from beyond the grave like a warm embrace. His daughter would have everything she needed.

Cooper regarded him for a long moment.

"Fine. If you're sure about this, I'll back you up."

The sound of an approaching engine had Cooper tweaking the curtain aside.

"Who's that?" Gavin asked.

"Mom's here."

"Good. I need to talk to her too."

"Great." Cooper's voice was laced with sarcasm. He got up and went to the door.

"Don't worry, I'm not breaking the news here. Better to tell the family all at once."

"Hey, Mom," Cooper said a minute later as he ushered her in and gave her a hug. "What brings you by today?"

"I brought some of those mums Katie was admiring at the nursery last week. I set them on the porch. Where is she?"

"At the diner with Avery."

Mom spotted Gavin. "How lucky am I to catch both my boys at the same time?"

When she approached, Gavin gave her a hug.

"What are you two doing on this beautiful Saturday?" She glanced at the TV. "Not wasting it on televised sports, I hope. Oh, the Tar Heels are already down by seven. Good grief, this is going to be a stressful season."

"Can I get you some coffee, Mom?"

"No thanks. I just came by to drop off the plants." She lowered herself next to Gavin, gaze fixed on the screen. "I need to get the chili going in the Crock-Pot. Oh, come on, hold on to the ball for heaven's sake."

Gavin supposed now was as good a time as any to make his request. "Say, Mom, I was wondering if I might bring Emma with me tonight—and also Laurel."

Her head whipped around. *"Laurel?"*

"Yes, Mother, Laurel. My ex-wife. The woman I've been raising a child with the past two weeks."

Mom frowned. "I know who you—why would you want to bring her to our family supper? Wouldn't that be a little awkward?"

"Come on, Mom," Cooper said. "Don't you think it's high time we put our sticks down and played nice?"

"Don't make light of what she did to your brother."

"She's not responsible for the demise of our marriage, or for what I went through afterward. It's time you accepted that. We've managed to smooth things out between us, and I'd like to see the family do the same."

"Isn't she supposed to be leaving this weekend?"

"Mom. You've gotta drop this grudge. You of all people know marriage is complicated. What happened back then was terrible, but it's between Laurel and me."

Cooper chimed in. "Plus, you always say

everybody's welcome at the Robinson table."

Mom nailed him with a look. "Aren't you help-ful."

"He's right, you do say that."

Mom pursed her lips together. Studied Gavin for a full ten seconds. "Fine. Bring her along."

"And you'll be on your best behavior?"

"When have I ever been rude to anyone we've welcomed into our home?"

Well, there was a first time for everything. But rather than pushing his luck, Gavin gave her the sweet smile that always did her in. "I love you, Ma. You're the best mother in the world."

She swatted the back of his head. "Oh, you. You're gonna be the death of me yet."

Thirty-Four

"Maybe you should do this alone." Laurel's heart bucked as she stared through the windshield at the familiar farmhouse, set back off the river on several acres of wooded land. Avery's blue Jeep was already in the drive along with Cooper's truck. Now that she and Gavin had arrived, everyone was present and accounted for.

"I know it might be uncomfortable," Gavin said. "But Mom promised to be nice."

Laurel huffed. "What about everyone else?"

"Has anyone said something to you since you've been back?"

"Not at all—they've just treated me like I have a raging case of leprosy. This is a bad idea."

"If all goes well, we'll be raising a child together, Laurel. We can't put this off. They'll have to get used to the idea, and that'll start today. I won't leave your side, and I won't let them be mean to you. I promise."

She stared into his clear blue eyes. He had his faults, of course, but he'd never been dishonest. Her mind flashed back to their early relationship in high school—he'd been quite adept at standing up for her when others thought she was beneath him.

She shifted her gaze to the house once again and drew a deep, steadying breath. Once upon a time she'd loved coming here. It had taken her a while to drop her guard with the family, but she eventually let the Robinsons in. It was impossible not to. Gavin loved her and that was enough for them. They were so welcoming and loving.

After the separation, she'd missed them terribly—especially Lisa, who was more affectionate than her own mom. Laurel's current feelings of abandonment didn't really make sense. After all, that was what happened after a divorce. But that hadn't made the rejection hurt any less.

"Ready?" he asked.

She let out a sigh. "I guess so."

She exited the vehicle while Gavin carefully removed a sleeping Emma from her car seat. The toddler draped over his shoulder like a rag doll—the girl could sleep through a tornado.

Spine straight, Laurel followed Gavin across the grassy lawn toward the back of the house. She had to admit, it was a perfect day for a picnic, the temperature in the midseventies, the sun shining against a blue backdrop. The smell of grilling burgers wafted her way, making her stomach rumble. Sounds of chatter and laughter floated through the air. The siblings were probably playing cornhole while Jeff finished up at the grill. Lisa would be scurrying around with the table settings and side dishes.

Side dishes. Laurel was showing up empty-handed. Too late now. They rounded the corner of the house and came upon the very scene she'd envisioned.

There were two newcomers in the assembled group. The tall guy with the athletic build and dark-blond hair must be Avery's boyfriend, Wes. And the beautiful, petite blonde with the pink top, white shorts, and trendy sandals would be Katie, Cooper's new wife—and Gavin's ex-girlfriend. No wonder he'd been attracted to her.

When Laurel pulled her gaze away, it collided with Lisa's.

The woman offered a plastic smile. "Oh, hello, kids. Look who fell asleep on the way here. Do you want to put her down in the house, honey?"

"That's okay," Gavin said. "I'll just put her here on the chaise."

By now, of course, everyone was looking Laurel's way. She fought the urge to turn and run. It was obvious by their lack of surprise that Lisa had forewarned them.

"Hey, Laurel," Cooper called from his spot by the cornhole board.

"Hi, Cooper."

"Come help me out." He tossed the sandbag. "I could use a better partner."

"Hey, I'm having a bad day." Avery sent Laurel a reluctant smile. "Hi, Laurel."

"The burgers are ready," Lisa said before

Laurel could respond. "Come eat while it's still hot."

Lisa had added a seat to the end of the table. Where should she sit?

A hand on the small of her back nudged her forward. "Come on. Let me introduce you to Wes and Katie."

Thirty minutes later the burgers were gone, but the conversation continued. Laurel had forgotten how easily the chatter and teasing flowed in this family. At the beginning of the meal, Lisa, Jeff, and the siblings had made a point of speaking to her, each of them so carefully cordial. Cooper and Katie were especially gracious.

But during the past ten minutes Laurel had gladly retreated into her shell and become an observer. Except for a curious glance or two her way, she was almost able to pretend she was watching the gathering on TV.

She observed Katie, who added so naturally to the banter, fitting in perfectly with the Robinson clan. She seemed positive and cheerful, always offering words of encouragement or playfully teasing. It was difficult to dislike her, and somehow that made it even harder to accept that last summer Gavin had been dating her. Laurel could see why though—not only was Katie beautiful but she seemed so open, so uncomplicated.

So unlike Laurel.

The sting of jealousy made her squirm. She couldn't develop feelings for Gavin again. Talk about complicated. But why else would she be feeling jealous of Katie?

The reminder of their upcoming announcement made the food in her stomach churn. She and Gavin hadn't discussed how he would broach the subject, but surely he would do it soon. She almost wished Emma would wake up so she'd have a distraction. She glanced at the sleeping child, but Emma didn't so much as stir.

At least her conversation with her mother had gone well. Mom's marriage seemed to have softened her up on the subject of men. And realizing Laurel would now move back to River-bend helped Mom overcome her bitterness toward Gavin. A grandchild only sweetened the deal. Maybe Laurel and her mom could even work toward a closer relationship now that she was coming home to stay.

A clinking sound quieted the group. But it was Wes who'd demanded everyone's attention.

The group went silent as every head turned his way.

"Wow," he said. "If I'd known that would work, I would've done it a long time ago."

The family chuckled.

Wes flashed a grin. "Avery and I have an announcement to make." He gazed adoringly at

347

her on the bench beside him. "Last night I asked her to marry me—"

"And I said *yes!*" Avery whipped out her hand and waggled her fingers, flashing the solitaire diamond.

The table broke out in pandemonium. Congratulations and well-wishes flowed like water over Walker Falls.

Laurel's own wishes were swallowed up by the exuberant response. Even if her and Avery's relationship was now strained, Laurel was glad she'd found someone special. After all the other woman had been through, she deserved a nice guy like Wes. And since Gavin had chosen him as a business partner, she had to assume that's exactly what he was.

Gavin made eye contact with her and lifted his shoulders. He hadn't known the announcement was coming.

Laurel hated to steal Avery and Wes's thunder, but she and Gavin still had to tell the family. She returned his shrug. It was what it was.

Gavin waited until the excitement died down. Until the group was finished fishing for a date, weighing the pros and cons of personal vows, and discussing how many attendants might be involved.

He waited until Lisa stood and began clearing the table. "Wait, Mom. Can you sit down for a second? I have something I need to say."

His mom sank back onto the bench, a frown creasing her forehead.

Everyone stared at Gavin now. He gave Avery and Wes a pained look. "I'm really sorry to do this today, guys. I'd wait till next week, but I feel you should know."

"What's up, son?" Jeff asked.

Lisa gave a strained smile. "You have us worried."

"No need for concern. I have good news—at least that's the way I see it." He glanced at Laurel.

Her heart shuddered in the anxious pause.

"Laurel and I are petitioning for joint guardianship of Emma."

The table went quiet. Even the squirrels seemed to stop nattering. Laurel gathered the courage to glance around the table. Then she wished she hadn't.

Lisa's mouth hung open. Jeff's lips pressed together. Avery frowned. Wes looked at her for direction.

Only Cooper was unsurprised. His lips turned up. "Wow. That's big news."

"Yes," Katie blurted. "How wonderful."

The disparity of reactions between the two announcements was impossible to ignore. Laurel's throat thickened. They would react this way. Had she really expected anything different?

Gavin leaned his elbows on the table. "I know

this is a surprise, but Mallory's mom petitioned for guardianship, and we think this would be best for Emma. I really hope you guys can get on board."

Lisa leaned forward. "You don't have to do this, Gavin."

"*Mom* . . . we're not doing it because we have to. This is what we want."

She aimed a laser-focused look his way. "Can we talk in private please?"

"There's nothing you can you say that will change my mind about this, Mom."

"But I don't know if you've—"

Jeff set his hand on Lisa's, then offered Gavin and Laurel a gracious smile. "We're surprised, of course. But you have our full support."

"Thank you, Jeff," Gavin said. "We appreciate it. And again, Avery and Wes, sorry to horn in on your big announcement. But since the hearing is in a couple weeks there's really no time to—"

"A couple weeks?" Lisa said.

"Honey . . ."

"Have you thought this through?"

"This is a huge decision."

"It's a lifelong commitment."

"Lisa, honey, sit down."

"For heaven's sake, what are they thinking?"

Questions and comments poured in too quickly to respond.

Laurel exchanged a helpless glance with Gavin.

Gavin shot Cooper a *Help!* look.

Cooper popped up from the bench. "Hey, everybody, Katie and I are expecting a baby."

Thirty minutes later, the pandemonium had settled. The family still seemed a little shell-shocked as they cleared the table. Emma rested on Laurel's shoulder, still groggy from her nap.

"Ready to go?" Gavin asked Laurel after the last dish was carried inside.

"Yes."

Mom appeared at his side. "Gavin, could I have a word please?"

"We were just leaving."

"Please. It'll just take a minute."

He pressed his lips together.

"I'll take Emma to the car," Laurel said. "Thank you for having me, Lisa."

"You're welcome." Mom ran her hand through the child's curls. "Bye, honey. I'll see you soon."

For a moment Gavin watched Laurel walk away, then he turned back to his mom. "Go ahead, Ma. Have your say."

"Honey . . . I just think you're rushing into something you're going to regret. I know Emma needs a home, and you must feel so burdened for the child. But trying to raise a child with your ex-wife—is that a good idea?"

"People do it all the time."

"But so much has happened between the two of

you. Have you forgotten what a mess you were when she kicked you out of your home? When she filed for divorce? Because I haven't. I haven't forgotten one bit." Mom's eyes glazed over, and she blinked back tears.

His heart softened. "Maybe it's time you do, Mom. I wasn't the best husband, you know. I worked obscene hours and she was lonely. Then I was responsible for our son's death."

She started to speak.

He held his hand up. "And somehow she doesn't hate me for that. I have an opportunity here to do the right thing by Emma—and yes, by Laurel too. We both want to honor our friends, and that means making sure Emma is loved and safe. Mallory's mom will provide neither of those things. I love that kid, Ma, and I really need you to get behind this, 'cause it's going to happen."

A tear slipped down her cheek. She dashed it away. "Oh, honey. You know I'll always support you."

"I need you to forgive Laurel. I need you to accept her. She'll be coming around from time to time, and Emma doesn't need to be picking up on your resentment. Think you can do that?"

She sniffled. Shuffled her feet. "Yes, I can do that. For you, I can do it. I'm sorry. I know Laurel's been through a lot too. Someone hurts one of my kids, and I just turn all Mama Bear on them. I'll do better."

He turned his lips up. Then he pulled his mom into an embrace and held her for a long moment. "There's the mom I know and love." He kissed her on the cheek, gave her one last smile, and left.

Thirty-Five

Gavin darted through the Asheville rush-hour traffic as he sped toward home. His work was finished in time for Christmas weekend, but he still had one more errand to run before Laurel, Jesse, and he could head toward Riverbend Gap and their families.

He'd had his nose down for the past five months on this project—his biggest to date. His boss was impressed with his work, and Gavin anticipated another promotion soon.

Minutes later he turned into the upscale neighborhood and slowed when he reached their long driveway. A feeling of pride washed over him as he gazed at the contemporary Craftsman home he'd contracted himself. He and Laurel designed it together, from the clean, flat rooflines and large, sleek windows, all the way to the rich, warm colors of the cedar siding and stonework. And they'd nailed it.

He parked his work truck, leaving room to get his Denali from the garage and back it up to the trailer in the drive. But first he needed to run inside and let Laurel know what was going on. He braced himself for her reaction.

She'd been distant lately. All these hours he

worked hadn't helped. But once winter came things would slow down, and he could spend more time at home with her and Jesse. It occurred that he'd had the same thought each year of their marriage. But somehow when winter rolled around, it was just as hard to find time for family as it had been through the spring and summer.

He was determined to provide well for them. To make something of himself. Be a better example than he'd had in his deadbeat, alcoholic father. If he could just get this promotion he could relax a little. Enjoy the fruit of his labors.

Besides, Laurel didn't really complain about his work hours. She was busy working at the Biltmore now and was good at balancing work and home. But Jesse was already three, and Gavin had missed too much of his childhood. He'd do better after he earned that promotion. He'd make the most of these early years before they were gone altogether.

He entered the house through the garage door and found Laurel in the kitchen, putting a delicious-looking pie into a container, Jesse at her side. "Hi, guys. Smells great in here."

"Oh, good, you're on time."

"Daddy!" Jesse ran to him, his dimple showing. He wore his favorite tee—the one featuring excavation vehicles. He knew them all by name.

Gavin swept his son into his arms. "Hey, buddy. You ready to go to Nana and Poppy's house?"

"I played with Sarah today."

"You did? Was she nice?"

"She took my juice and spilled it."

Laurel topped the pie keeper with the lid. "But she said she was sorry, and now we should forgive her, right?"

"I told her it was okay."

"Good boy," Gavin said.

"We'll be ready to leave in thirty minutes," Laurel said.

"About that . . . I have one last errand I need to run, but we can do it on the way."

Laurel's lips pursed.

"The trailer's already loaded; I just have to hitch it up to the Denali. I'll drop it at the site and then we'll be on our way."

"Seriously?"

"I'm sorry, hon, but the project's been running behind schedule. They're working tomorrow to catch up, and they'll need that concrete."

"The site is in the opposite direction. We'll be late."

She had a point there. "Okay, what if I hitch up the work truck and run it over there now? I'll be back before you're finished getting ready."

"I only said thirty minutes because I thought you'd be here to keep Jesse occupied. He's been 'helping' me pack all day. Haven't you, sweetheart?"

"I helped Mommy pack. We're bringing Blue

Bear and Bugs Bunny 'cause I have to show Nana."

"Sounds good, pal." Gavin ruffled the boy's hair and addressed Laurel. "Listen, I'll take him with me. There's a backhoe at the site today. Wanna come check it out, bud?"

Jesse's brown eyes lit. "Can I, Mommy?"

Her shoulders lowered a fraction. "Of course."

"Can I sit in it?" Jesse asked Gavin. "Will you take me for a ride?"

"No time for a ride today, but you can definitely sit in it."

Laurel frowned at Gavin. "And you won't tour the jobsite? I told my mom we'd be there for supper at seven, and you know how she gets when we're late."

"Just going to drop the trailer, I promise."

"Put a jacket on him."

"Yes, ma'am." Gavin grabbed a jacket from the hall closet and helped Jesse put it on.

That hadn't gone so bad. He wished his relationship with Laurel was more like it used to be—more warm, more open. They had their moments, of course. But more often it seemed like Laurel was a million miles away, living on a deserted island with Jesse. But in the past few years they'd managed to build their dream home, and they had everything they could possibly need. He was home every night—that was more than he could've said about his dad.

On the way out to the truck, Jesse rambled on about the kids at preschool. Gavin didn't really know who any of them were.

Jesse stopped talking and stared expectantly at Gavin.

"Oh. Uh, what did Mrs., uh . . . ?"

"Carmichael, Daddy." He rolled his eyes, looking so much like Laurel in that moment.

Gavin couldn't help but smile. "Right, what did Mrs. Carmichael say?"

"She gave him a red card. Donovan already had *two* red cards this week. He didn't get to go outside today."

"Too bad for him, huh?"

"Too bad! I played with Oliver instead."

Once they reached his work truck, Gavin buckled him into his car seat. "Well, wait'll you tell your friends you got to sit in a backhoe today."

"Yeah!"

Gavin ruffled his hair, then closed the door and got in on the driver's side. He pulled the truck from the driveway, then backed it back in, positioning it carefully in front of the trailer. When he was finished he said, "Be right back, Jess."

He rounded the truck and found the trailer's coupler poised nicely over the ball, so he unlatched the coupler and lowered the trailer until the hitch was fully seated. He should really use a sway bar—the trailer was loaded with cement

359

bags so it was heavy enough to require one. Plus he'd be driving on the freeway. But the sway bar was currently attached to the other trailer, and he'd only be on the highway for ten minutes. Besides, he really didn't have time to spare—it would be a long, silent ride to Riverbend if he was late returning.

He finished hitching the trailer and got back in the truck. "Ready to go, bud?"

"Can I drive the backhoe, Daddy?"

"Remember what I said?" Gavin carefully pulled from the drive. "We only have time to sit in it today. You can tell Papaw all about it."

He turned left and headed toward the highway. The site was twelve minutes away—without pulling a trailer. Plus a couple of minutes for the backhoe. That would be pushing it.

When he reached the highway, he drove up the ramp and accelerated. Traffic was fairly heavy, but it was flowing well at least. He got up to sixty—really shouldn't go any faster—keeping his eyes on the clock as Jesse chattered away in the back seat.

Gavin was looking forward to going home for the holiday weekend. He'd had to work over Thanksgiving weekend, so they'd only gone to Riverbend for the day, much to his mom's dismay.

Since Christmas fell on a Sunday this year and the project was almost back on schedule, he was taking the whole weekend off. It would be good to see Avery—she was doing her residency in Pennsylvania and hadn't made it home for Thanksgiving.

A semi passed on his left, and the gust of wind pushed the trailer to the right, tugging at the truck. Gavin lifted his foot from the accelerator. The trailer fishtailed the other direction. He clenched the steering wheel. Tried to correct. But it was already out of his control. A terrible sense of doom filled him just before his world turned upside down.

When Gavin awakened hours later, the last thing he remembered was the tilt of the truck. The world rolling. If Jesse had cried out in those final seconds, he couldn't remember it. Maybe that was for the best.

Later, he would wish he could forget all the hours that came afterward . . .

When he realized the horrifying cost of his recklessness.

When he had to face his wife.

When he had to somehow keep breathing with the burden of their son's death pressing down on him like a boulder.

But he couldn't forget any of it. Instead, reality sank deeper with each passing second, dragging him down with it. Gavin had walked away with hardly a scratch. But inside he was dead—just like his son.

Thirty-Six

Laurel felt oddly serene as she drove past the "Welcome to Riverbend Gap" sign. She'd driven to Asheville this morning and told Diane what was transpiring. Laurel didn't want to resign yet in case the worst happened and they lost Emma, but she needed to be honest with her boss.

Diane had been more than understanding. "We'd be very sorry to lose you, Laurel. But I can't say I'm surprised you'd be willing to give up your job for your friends' child. You've been nothing but loyal to this place for six years, and I can only imagine you'd be just as loyal to your friends. It's a wonderful thing you're trying to do for that little girl. We can extend your leave another two weeks. Let me know how the hearing goes. Selfishly, I hope to have you back."

Laurel beamed. "I'll keep you looped in. Thank you, Diane."

The possibility of giving up her dream position should be agonizing. But dreams could shift and morph over time. Sometimes new dreams were born. And somewhere along the way, that's what must've happened to her. Because she wanted Emma more than she wanted anything else.

She drove down Main Street, observing the

hikers who ambled through town with their spindly walking sticks and lumpy backpacks, searching for a hot meal. She passed the Trailhead Bar and Grill and Owen's Nursery where she'd worked so many summers. Once through town, she pressed the accelerator. She was eager to get home to Emma. Anticipated Sunny's enthusiastic greeting. And the ripening orchard that awaited her.

The scenery had changed in the three days since she and Gavin sat in the park and made their life-altering decision. Autumn colors were already trickling down the mountains. Fall was in the air. And her entire life had done a one-eighty. Instead of feeling whiplashed, she just felt . . . content.

Only thoughts of her relationship with Gavin unsettled her. As always, when she thought of their new arrangement, fear bubbled up inside. Resolutely, she pushed the feeling back down. She would manage her expectations. She wouldn't be seeking his time or attention or love or counting on him for emotional support. She would expect nothing but his partnership in Emma's care, and then she wouldn't wind up disappointed and heartbroken. Her mother had been so right about that.

As she pulled in to the drive she pushed away her apprehension and determined to dwell on the positive. She would have a beautiful child to raise. A charming home to care for. A lovely orchard to run. The thoughts brought a smile to her face.

Gavin had moved back to his camper yesterday, but he'd come over this morning to watch Emma while she drove to Asheville. Laurel turned into her driveway. Gavin's truck was still there. She'd half expected him to take Emma to his work site today. She opened the front door to Sunny's welcome. The dog's tags jangled wildly, and her entire backside wagged back and forth as if she hadn't seen Laurel for months.

Her gaze caught on Gavin, lounging in the recliner, a sleeping Emma stretched across his chest. Her head was nestled in the cradle of his neck, and his hand rested on her back.

Laurel's heart squeezed tight. And in that moment a sinking realization hit her, filling her stomach with lead.

She was not over her ex-husband.

She wanted to deny the thought. But revisiting the past couple of weeks . . .

With a trembling hand she shut the door, then gave Sunny some affection so she'd settle down. And also to stall for time. These feelings were unwelcome. She and Gavin had already agreed that getting married wasn't a good idea. Especially since he didn't seem to return her feelings.

What was she doing? What was she getting herself into?

When she'd stalled as long as she could, she joined Gavin in the living room, noting that the space was clear of toys for once. Also the wood floor had been swept—there were even vacuum lines on the area rug.

"How'd it go?" he asked.

Laurel sank onto the couch, feeling the weight of this morning's task—if not her new revelation—slide off her shoulders. "It went well. Diane was very gracious. She even extended my leave for two weeks."

"That's great. Did she mention the promotion?"

"She didn't say so outright, but she did insinuate that it's in the works."

"Aw, Laurel. I'd hate for you to give that up."

"All that matters now is that the hearing goes our way." She dropped her gaze to Emma's sweet little face. "Did she have any accidents while I was gone?"

"She actually went to the potty twice."

Laurel hiked her eyebrows. "Progress."

"I was so proud of her. I will admit—I bribed her with movie time."

"Of course you did."

"She's on a *Monsters, Inc.* kick. She loves that part at the beginning where the monster falls down."

Laurel smiled. "What else did you do?"

"We played all morning, had lunch, and she conked out during the movie. She's really good at those magnet blocks. Maybe she'll be an architect."

"I was thinking librarian. Have you noticed how she puts her books back on her shelf just so?"

"That's true." He dropped a kiss to the top of Emma's head. "She's very careful with her books. I made you a sandwich, and the soup's still simmering on the stove—it's Mom's chili."

They'd saved the funeral dish for fall weather. Laurel was surprised he'd gone to so much trouble for lunch. "Sounds great. I'm hungry. Thank you. Want me to take her up to bed?"

He glanced down at the child's sleeping form, his face softening. "Nah. I think I'll just hold her awhile."

Later that afternoon, Gavin traipsed through the orchard behind Laurel. It was a beautiful fall day, with temperatures in the midseventies.

Up the aisle Sunny ran around a tree with her blue ball, Emma on her heels laughing hysterically.

Laurel stopped beside a tree loaded with reddish apples. "Know what kind this is?"

"Red Delicious?"

"Not a bad guess. It's a Cameo."

He inspected the skin. "Never heard of it."

"It's relatively new. And unlike most modern varieties, which are derived from long breeding programs, it developed by accident. A chance seedling was found in a Red Delicious orchard—so that's where it's thought to have come from. The flavor is fairly bland, kind of like a pear. But it's crisper than a Red Delicious."

"Are they ripe yet?"

Laurel lifted the apple and gave a twist. "That's what we're going to find out." She set it in her bag.

Sunny gave a happy bark.

Emma stopped chasing the dog in circles, wavered on her feet a moment, then plopped on her bottom in the grass.

Gavin and Laurel laughed.

"Are you dizzy, angel?" Laurel asked.

"Emma fall down!"

"Are you okay?"

"I fine." She popped back to her feet.

Gavin's phone vibrated and he checked the screen. "I missed a call from Wes."

"Go ahead and call him back. I have to gather more samples."

Gavin hit the Redial button.

Seconds later Wes answered. "Hey, did you see what went up for sale today?"

"No."

"A repurposed house in Mulberry Hollow. It's across the street and down the road from Avery's clinic. It used to be a dentist's office, but they're moving into a different building."

"The brick Craftsman next to the outfitters' shop?"

"That's the one." Wes named the asking price. "I was thinking we should take a look. What do you think?"

"That's a little more than we talked about. But it would be a great spot for the business. Maybe they'll come down a bit."

"That's what I was thinking. Want me to call the Realtor and set up an appointment?"

"Sure. Also, I could really use your help at the work site. The painters are coming Saturday. And I need to mow the campground."

"Okay, no problem."

Gavin had really been negligent lately on the project. "Sorry I haven't been involved as much as I'd like lately. I appreciate your picking up the slack."

"That's what partners are for. You've had a lot going on."

"Congrats again on your engagement. I'm happy for you both."

"Thanks. A lot going on in the family right now."

"Good things, though." Gavin watched as Laurel held Emma up and showed her the proper way to pick an apple. Emma took a bite, making Laurel laugh. "Once this hearing is over things should settle back down."

"Hey, Avery's calling. I'll set up an appointment and text it to you."

They said good-bye and Gavin disconnected the call.

Laurel approached him, phone to her ear, a frown etched between her brows.

What's wrong? he mouthed.

She stopped in front of him. "Okay. Yeah, we'll be right there. Thank you." She tapped the screen and pocketed her phone. "That was Darius. He asked if we could swing by his office this afternoon."

"What for?"

"I don't know. But I don't have a good feeling about this."

"Thank you for coming by," Darius said.

Gavin's stomach churned as the attorney gestured them to the two empty chairs and sat in the one behind his mahogany desk. They'd first settled Emma in the office's corner, which was dominated by a child-size table-and-chair set and various toys.

"Has something happened?" Laurel asked.

"I'm afraid so. As you know, I notified the Gordons about your petition through their attorney in the hopes they'd see the futility of their own petition."

"I take it that didn't happen," Gavin said.

"It didn't. I'm sorry to say they're going forward with this."

Laurel leaned in. "But you said it was unlikely

the clerk would grant them guardianship, given that the will named us her guardians."

"I did say that. And the Gordons still have an uphill battle. But they've apparently fired their previous attorney, and Willis Groveland has agreed to take on their case."

"Who's that?" Laurel asked.

"Only the best family attorney in the state."

Gavin's gaze shot to Emma, quietly reading to herself. Laurel had put her hair in pigtails this afternoon, and her wispy bangs drew attention to her big blue eyes. The thought of handing this innocent child over to Darcy turned his stomach.

Laurel cleared her throat. "But we're still the ones named in the will."

"And that will definitely work in your favor. You've done everything for her you can possibly do. She's obviously adjusting well, all things considered."

There was something Darius wasn't saying. "But . . ."

"But . . . you're not blood relatives. Darcy Gordon is her grandma, and she has a seemingly stable life, and—as I mentioned—the best family attorney she could ask for. And Emma would live in one home with the Gordons while with you she'd be going back and forth. Maybe you'd be better off with someone who specializes in guardianship cases."

"But you know us," Gavin said. "And you

knew Mike and Mallory. No one could possibly represent us better than you."

"I agree," Laurel said. "We couldn't ask for a better attorney."

"I appreciate your faith in me. I know this is a frustrating situation. I'll do my very best to build a winning case for you. To that end, we need to think about who you can bring to court as witnesses. We can go over that in detail later." He gave them a wan smile. "And a few prayers wouldn't hurt either."

Gavin slipped carefully from Emma's bed and gazed down at her in the glow of the night-light. It had taken seven books, but she'd finally fallen asleep. She looked so small and helpless in her big-girl bed, surrounded by all her furry friends.

He slipped from the room, eased the door closed, then made his way downstairs. He and Laurel had been quiet since they'd left Darius's office. If they lost guardianship, the consequences would be far-reaching: not only would they lose Emma, but Laurel would return to Asheville.

The thought of losing them both made his nerves jangle. To say nothing of that sweet kid being raised by a sociopathic woman.

He growled as he entered the kitchen. It just wasn't right. This whole thing sucked rotten eggs and made him feel so helpless.

Laurel was on the back patio in front of the firepit table, which was now glowing with a nice, low fire. He'd step outside and chat a minute before going home.

He headed toward the French doors, but a *ding* stopped him before he opened it. Laurel had left her phone on the table. He snatched it up, unable to keep from seeing a text notification on the screen from Connor.

Are you coming home this weekend? There's a terrific new Mexican restaurant over on—

Gavin scowled at the abbreviated message, then whipped open the door and stepped out onto the patio. He walked over to Laurel and handed her the phone. "You have a message." Practically vibrating with tension, he dropped into the Adirondack chair next to hers while Laurel checked her phone.

He had no right to feel jealous. But that didn't stop the emotion from crashing into him like a tsunami. What was it going to be like having Laurel back in his life? Watching her date other men? Get serious? Get married? This wasn't good. He didn't need to complicate an already complicated situation by falling for Laurel again.

But the gnawing in his gut told him it was already too late for that.

He took a breath. Two. The adrenaline surge slowed. His pulse returned to normal range. He closed his eyes in a long blink, then stared into the fire's flickering flames. "Sorry if I snapped. I guess I'm just irritable tonight."

It was quiet for a long moment. "You're afraid."

He gazed at her. And darn it, she was right. His breath left on a long exhale. "Scared to death. I looked up that attorney."

"Me too. If it helps any, so am I. But we have to stick together, Gavin. Especially now."

"You're right." His gaze sharpened on her. She still looked the same as when they'd last been married, but her face had matured in some indefinable way. Her features had softened a bit. And that wasn't the only thing that was different about her. "You've changed. You're more vocal than you used to be."

Her chin notched up. "So?"

He smiled at her automatic defense. "It's a good change, Laurel. You have the right to speak your mind, and I need to hear whatever you have to say."

Her posture relaxed as she gazed into the fire. "You've changed a bit yourself, Robinson."

"How do you mean?"

"Well, for starters, you learned how to do the dishes."

She wasn't wrong. "Touché." He really had been a lame husband. Why was it so easy to see that now? "I'm sorry I didn't do my part before. I worked too much. Told myself I was doing it for our family, but that wasn't true, not really. I was just selfish."

Her lips parted in surprise. "Thank you. I appreciate that. I know I wasn't perfect either. As you implied, my communication skills left some room for improvement."

He stared at her until she met his gaze. "I wasn't very good on that front either." His lips curled into a smile. "Look at us . . . communicating like mature adults."

She pulled her sweater tighter and snuggled into the chair. "Better late than never, I guess."

Thirty-Seven

Laurel could hardly believe how easily it had happened: she, Gavin, and Emma settled into a new daily routine. Each morning Gavin stopped by the house to have breakfast with Emma. When he left, Laurel and Emma spent the mornings playing and tidying up the house, getting groceries, and running errands. While Emma took her afternoon nap, Laurel tested apples and attended to orchard business. They'd harvested the last of the apples yesterday. She'd also reserved booths in a few area festivals, including Trail Days. The extra income couldn't hurt.

In the back of her mind she wondered if she'd even be here to work the festivals. But she wouldn't allow herself to go there.

The routine helped everything feel normal. In the afternoons when Emma awakened from her nap, the two of them went for a walk or to the playground. The trees were changing in the valley, turning beautiful shades of red, gold, and orange. After their outing they would return home to start supper.

Last week Emma had her first play-therapy session with the psychologist Avery had recommended. Gavin and Laurel had also met with the woman to discuss best practices for handling grief in small children. All in all, it had been helpful, and if all went well with the hearing, they planned to continue the counseling as long as was needed.

Gavin stopped over about five thirty each evening. He always complimented Laurel on the meal, and they reviewed their days. Afterward they cleaned up together, usually with Emma's "help."

The guardian ad litem had come over one afternoon just after Emma woke from her nap. The thirtysomething woman was kind and thorough. She'd quizzed Laurel and Gavin about their routines. She watched them interact with Emma and went with Gavin to check out his place. And by the time it was over, they felt good about the way it had gone.

They'd gathered the documents Darius had requested, and Darius had called two witnesses to testify on their behalf: Avery and Paul Clayton, who was flying in for the hearing. Having another grandparent testify on their behalf was the strongest witness they could have. They were officially prepared for the hearing. Now, all they could do was wait until tomorrow when their cases would be presented, and the clerk would determine Emma's future.

As they had every night, on the eve of the hearing Gavin stopped by for supper. When it was bedtime Laurel gave Emma a bath, and Gavin put her to bed.

Laurel settled outside by the firepit, a spot she'd come to enjoy in the evenings. The nights were turning chilly, and the sweetness of the apples and earthy scent of fall hung in the air.

She'd brought the nursery monitor outside, and as had become her habit, she turned it on and caught the black-and-white image of Emma and Gavin, snuggled up with a book and a dozen of her furry friends. Laurel probably shouldn't eavesdrop, but he was so sweet with her, she couldn't seem to help it. Even though it definitely wasn't helping those growing feelings.

Gavin's voice carried through the speaker. He was reading *Alexander and the Terrible, Horrible, No Good, Very Bad Day*—one of Emma's longer books. Laurel smiled as he omitted entire paragraphs in the reading.

When he was finished with the book, Emma fished another from the pile. "This one next."

"*Goodnight Moon.* Okay, but this is the last one, and then it's time to go to sleep."

"Mama read."

Gavin stilled on the monitor's screen.

Laurel's breath stuttered. Her heart pulsed as she awaited his response.

"Did Mama read this one to you?"

"Yeah." Emma opened the book, then turned another page. "Mama 'n' Dada not coming home."

379

A chill swept over Laurel, raising gooseflesh on her arms. She pressed a hand to her chest.

"That's right, Emma Bear." Gavin's voice was gravelly. "And I am so sorry about that. Your mama and dada loved you very much."

Emma looked up at Gavin. "Sad."

"I know you're sad, sweetheart. I'm sad too. But you're going to be okay. Laurel and I love you so much. We'll never . . ." A moment of silence ticked out. He wrapped his arms around her. "We'll never stop loving you, honey."

Emma snuggled into his arms. A moment later she held out the book. "Read book."

Gavin cleared his throat and a moment later he began reading.

Laurel turned off the monitor and dashed away a tear. Her throat was so tight she could hardly swallow. The child was coming to understand what had happened to her parents, and it was bittersweet. A necessary thing, but so hard. And so sad. She stared up into the starry heavens.

Oh, Mallory. You would be so proud of her. She's an amazing child. And if you have any pull up there, please tell God we need His help tomorrow. We love her so much.

She couldn't bear the thought of losing Emma just when the child was starting to understand what had happened. Surely a clerk would see that.

Minutes had passed by the time Laurel gathered

herself. Gavin had had plenty of time to finish the book and tuck Emma in one last time.

Sure enough, a few minutes later he appeared, easing through the doorway. "She's down for the night." He joined her, dropping into the chair, only inches away.

"I wish you'd tucked her in tonight," Gavin said. "She asked about Mike and Mallory."

Time to own up. "I actually heard everything. I had the monitor on."

"Oh." He ran a hand over his face. "She broke my heart. This is so unfair. I hate this for her. I was so afraid of messing it up. Did I say the wrong things?"

Laurel set her hand over his fist, curled on the armrest. "You handled it beautifully, Gavin."

He turned his head. "Really?"

"You were amazing."

His weight sagged into the chair. "She's really figuring it out. It was all I could do to hold it together up there."

"But you did. And you let her talk and process her emotions. Meanwhile, I was down here crying my eyes out."

He gave her a sad smile as he turned his hand over and laced their fingers together. "We have got to win tomorrow. We've got to prove to that clerk that we're what's best for her. They can't just rip her from her home and everything she knows."

"Keep the faith, Gavin." Under the guise of turning on the monitor again, Laurel eased her hand from his. She set it on the table, her fingers trembling with want. But she clenched her hands in her lap instead.

Gavin leaned his head against the chairback, staring into the orange flames. His thoughts were heavy tonight. Everything would be decided tomorrow. There was so much on the line, and the outcome was completely out of his control.

They'd done all they could to prepare for the hearing—including plenty of prayers. But the question that had plagued them since their last meeting with Darius weighed on him like a boulder.

In the light of day he'd pushed it away. Sometimes a little denial was easier than facing reality. But now, on the eve of the day that could change the course of their lives, he couldn't deny he had feelings for Laurel.

Darkness had fallen around them, making it easier to ask the question somehow—though his heart still jackhammered against his ribs. If the clerk placed Emma with the Gordons tomorrow, not only would he lose Emma—he'd lose Laurel as well. And he was just starting to realize how devastating that would feel. Having her back in his life . . . those old feelings had resurfaced. He wished they'd agreed to that wedding—but it wouldn't have worked if his feelings were unrequited. He would've been miserable.

His sigh was loud in the quiet evening. "I hate all this waiting."

"I know. Me too. But it'll be over soon."

One way or another. The fire crackled in the silence. Sparks drifted into the darkening sky.

Laurel's chair squeaked as she shifted. "Did you know Mallory always thought we'd get back together?"

"She did?"

"I used to get so mad at her for saying that. But she seemed so sure of it." Laurel toyed with the frayed edge of the blanket. "I think that's why she and Mike never changed their will."

Huh. Gavin let that sink in. Had Mallory known something Gavin didn't? As Laurel's best friend she'd been privy to Laurel's thoughts and feelings. Did his ex-wife still have feelings for him? Sometimes over the past couple of weeks he'd caught her staring at him with something akin to affection in her eyes. But every time he casually touched her, she discouraged his efforts. Case in point—he glanced down at their separated hands.

But who could blame her?

His chest tightened as he considered his next words. "Do you think . . . ? Could you ever forgive me for what I did, Laurel?"

383

A lonely owl hooted somewhere in the distance. A log shifted on the fire, shooting a cluster of sparks into the night sky.

"For what you did?"

He closed his eyes, wishing he didn't have to say it out loud. "I killed our son, Laurel. That's what I did. And I'm so sorry. I have no right to ask your forgiveness when I can't even seem to forgive myself."

"*Gavin . . .*" She waited until he turned his head.

Her face softened in the golden glow of the fire. Her eyes sparkled with tears. "It was an accident. I forgave you for that a long time ago."

The words were a balm to his soul. But he thought back to the day she'd shown up here. Her animosity toward him had been pretty obvious. "You don't have to say that. I know it's not true. When you got here you were plenty angry."

"You're right; I was angry. But not about that. You loved Jesse as much as I did. You would've traded your own life for his. I know that."

He gave his head a shake. "Then what? Why were you so angry?"

"Gavin . . . you left me."

"You told me to go!"

"Not then. Before that—you withdrew from me. You disappeared inside yourself and left me all alone. I grieved our son *alone*. You wouldn't talk to me, you wouldn't comfort me or let me comfort you. You abandoned me when I needed you most!"

"I didn't deserve you after what I'd done."

Their gazes locked. He could still feel the burden of remorse. The weight of guilt. But now, taking in her pain-ravaged face, he could feel her pain too. She hadn't deserved to suffer alone. She hadn't deserved to be shut out. To be left alone in her grief.

"I've learned a few things since then," she said. "I have abandonment issues from the way my dad disappeared. So when you shut me out like that, it felt like rejection. Abandonment. I was sure you were going to leave me so . . . I left first. Or I told you to leave. That way it was *my* choice— not something being done to me."

Gavin stared at her, absorbing this revelation. All this time he'd been wrong about what had happened between them.

An image flashed in his mind. A day, weeks after the accident, he'd come home from work, entered the house like a zombie. He'd been working as late as possible, trying to stay busy so he didn't have to think. Trying to avoid Laurel so he didn't have to face what he'd done to her. And he'd been dealing with insomnia, so he'd begun sleeping on the couch.

But when he came home on this night he'd gone up to their bedroom. He just needed a glimpse of her, sleeping peacefully. Needed to see her without that awful blank expression she'd worn since the accident.

The loud hum of the furnace was the only sound in the house as he passed the closed nursery door and stopped at the master bedroom. He quietly pushed open the door.

The moonlight filtered through the sheers, highlighting Laurel's form on the bed. She lay in the fetal position, her body quaking with sobs. The kind that were so hard and wrenching they made hardly a sound.

He'd done this to her. To his wife, the woman he loved more than any other. It was too much. Anxiety clawed at his insides, raking him raw. He couldn't handle her raw grief on top of his own pain and guilt. He turned, fled down the steps and out the door.

He blinked and her face sharpened in his vision. A vise tightened around his heart at the pain his rejection had caused her. "I'm sorry I didn't comfort you, support you. I left you and you didn't deserve that. I felt so guilty. I was drowning in my own pain. I have so many regrets, and it's too late to fix them. But I'm so sorry I hurt you, Laurel."

She reached out and brushed tears from his cheek. "I forgive you."

Another tear fell. Then another. Now that the dam was open, he couldn't seem to stop the flood.

"You need to stop punishing yourself, Gav."

He sniffed. "I'm not."

"Really? You took nothing from our marriage but your truck. And a job at the campground? What's that all about?"

"It was just a stopgap. I'm starting a new business."

"And you're practically letting Wes run it." She palmed his face and pinned him with a look. "You deserve good things, Gavin."

Did he? It seemed impossible to believe. And maybe, just maybe, that's why he'd been shirking his duties lately. He didn't feel deserving of good things. He swallowed against the boulder in his throat. He shook his head.

She tightened her grip on his face. "Yes, you do. I have regrets, too, you know. I didn't have to kick you out. I could've dragged you to counseling instead—heaven knows we both needed it. You, out to prove you were better than your dad; me, just waiting for you to abandon me like mine did. I realize now you were working so hard to provide the stability I didn't have as a child. You were trying to give me a life where I didn't have to worry about money."

"I wanted to give you that so badly. But you needed *me*. I see that now."

"We should've fought harder, but we were both wounded and lost. We did the best we could, and it wasn't enough."

He gazed at her beautiful face, seeing her as she was, as flawed as he. And yet he loved her with the kind of love that peered past those things to the beautiful heart beneath them. That love still reverberated throughout his body, all the way down to his bones.

He wanted to tell her this. But there was enough on the line tomorrow without adding to her burden. Besides, she might have granted him forgiveness, but that wasn't the same as giving him her trust. Or her love.

And he hadn't earned the right to ask for either.

Thirty-Eight

By the time Laurel, flanked by Gavin and Darius, settled into a chair, her nerves were screaming. At the table next to them, Darcy and her husband were seated with their lawyer. The older woman had aged well—hair still the same shade of dark blonde, makeup applied with precision. A demure blue suitcoat adorned her carefully maintained shape. Her husband was attractive for his age and equally well groomed. They looked like Barbie and Ken, Middle-Age Edition.

Their attorney was an attractive man in his midsixties. A crisp black suit adorned his still-athletic frame, and he sported a full head of gray hair, a pair of trendy glasses, and a mouthful of white teeth.

Emma's grandfather had flown in this morning and now occupied the bench behind Gavin and Laurel with their other witness, Avery. Darius had met with them all beforehand to review the proceedings and tell them what to expect on the stand.

Emma was at home with Laurel's mom. She'd offered to come, but it was more important that Emma was in the care of someone familiar.

Gavin put his hand over Laurel's, and only then did she realize she'd been tapping her fingers on the table.

"We're prepared," he whispered. "We've got this."

The clerk took the judge's stand. He was a sixtysomething man who was bald but for a few whisps of white hair. He wore a tired navy-blue suit and thick-framed glasses straight from the seventies. This was it. The next hour would determine Emma's entire future. Did the clerk realize the power he wielded?

A shuffle sounded at the back of the room. Laurel blinked in surprise as Lisa and Jeff filed through the door, followed by Cooper, Katie, and Wes. She hadn't known the Robinsons were coming. They made eye contact with Laurel and Gavin, each offering a smile or a nod. Lisa slipped Laurel a wink before she slid down the row behind Avery and Paul.

Huh. Maybe the woman was coming around.

Laurel hadn't realized how much familiar faces would put her at ease. Plus having a supportive family network would surely reflect positively on their case.

The rows behind the Gordons were empty. Had they brought no witnesses? The thought buoyed her spirits.

The hearing had already begun, and Laurel was daydreaming through it. She jerked her attention forward in time to hear Darcy's attorney calling her to the stand.

Fifteen minutes later Mr. Groveland had finished questioning Darcy. The woman still perched on the witness stand, clenching a tissue in her fist. She'd come across as a loving mother and grandmother as well as a pillar of the Chicago community. Laurel's stomach turned at the massive discrepancy between perception and reality.

Hopefully Darius's cross-examination would clear that up.

"Mrs. Gordon," Darius said. "First of all, let me say I'm sorry for the loss of your daughter."

"Thank you."

"I was wondering if you could tell me, when was the last time you saw your daughter?"

A thoughtful expression came over her face. "Well . . . let's see. I'm not quite sure. As I mentioned, Glenn and I live in Chicago now. There was quite a bit of ground between Mallory and me."

"Would you say it had been weeks? Months? Years?"

"Well, it probably would've been years. She's been so busy with her young family, and I've been quite occupied with my charity work."

"Did you talk with her on the phone then? FaceTime with her regularly?"

She tucked her hair behind her ear. "My

daughter and I had some differences of opinion, Mr. Walker." She turned to address the clerk. "I loved her dearly, but she was not an easy woman, nor a forgiving one. I admit I made my own mistakes with Mallory. I indulged her. And I'm afraid I'll have a whole lifetime to regret it."

Laurel clenched her teeth. Mallory was the least spoiled person she'd ever known.

"So would you say you and your daughter were estranged at the time of her death?"

"I'd say that was a fair assessment. But not because I wanted to be."

"And when did you last see your granddaughter, Emma?"

She pursed her red lips. "Unfortunately, Emma and I have yet to meet. That was also my daughter's choice. She was angry with me, and sadly, withholding my granddaughter from me was her way of retaliating."

"Your daughter passed away"—Darius consulted his notes—"four weeks ago, is that correct?"

Darcy dabbed at the corner of her eye with the tissue. "Yes, sir, that's right."

"Did you get to see Emma when you came in for the funeral then?"

Darcy blinked. "Well . . . no."

"And why is that?"

"Why, I—I wasn't feeling well at all. I was overwrought with grief, as you can imagine.

Given the circumstances, it simply would've been too painful."

"You suggested that your daughter was the only thing standing between you and Emma, is that correct?"

"Yes, absolutely."

"And yet at her funeral, your daughter gone, you would've been able to see Emma. Is that right?"

"Well, I . . . I just assumed they wouldn't take her there." She cut a glance at Laurel and Gavin. "Wouldn't expose her to such a traumatic event."

"And in the four weeks since your daughter's passing, how many times have you reached out to Emma?"

"I was busy filing a petition for guardianship, Mr. Walker."

"So none?"

She pursed her lips. "No."

Darius smiled. "Thank you, Mrs. Gordon. That's all the questions I have."

Laurel tried to contain her excitement. Darius had revealed some critical information. She could only pray that the woman's lack of regard for Emma was obvious.

Darcy's husband was called to the stand next, and Mr. Groveland took him through much the same line of questioning he'd taken with Darcy. His answers made the two of them sound like Couple of the Year. Darcy would stay home with the child as she'd already taken early retirement, and they planned to enroll the child at an elite private school—they'd even brought brochures for the clerk.

By the time Mr. Gordon took his seat, he'd spent half an hour regaling the clerk with details of the wonderful life the Gordons would provide Emma. Except for Darius's cross-examination, Laurel would've almost believed it herself.

Darius asked Glenn to clarify a couple of points and then, at last, it was time for Darius to present Laurel and Gavin's interest. "I'd like to call Paul Clayton to the stand." They'd decided to start with their best foot forward—Paul being Emma's other grandparent.

He proceeded to answer Darius's question about his and Judy's close relationship with Emma and the older couple's unfortunate health situation that preempted them from petitioning for guardianship. Darius saved the best question for last. "Where guardianship of your granddaughter is concerned, what do you think is in Emma's best interest?"

Paul glanced at Gavin and Laurel. "No doubt in my mind, Gavin and Laurel are the right people for the job. They're very close to Emma and they love her. My son and his wife knew what was best for their daughter—and they handpicked the Robinsons. They made the very best plan for their child."

When Darius returned to his seat, the Gordons' attorney took over. "Mr. Clayton, I'm so sorry for your loss. Can you tell me, do you know my clients, Mr. and Mrs. Gordon, at all?"

"No, sir."

"Had you even seen them before today?"

"No, I hadn't."

He gave a thoughtful nod. "Then how can you be certain the Robinsons are the right people to raise Emma?"

"They—that's what my son and daughter-in-law wanted."

"Thank you. That will be all."

Avery was next. Darius called her to the stand, and she was sworn in. Darius proceeded to pepper her with questions that explored her professional relationship with Emma and her familial relationship with Gavin. Avery came across as professional, objective, and confident that Gavin and Laurel would be the best guardians for Emma. And she made sure it was clear that Emma had the love and support of the entire Robinson clan.

Opposing counsel asked Avery the same two questions he'd asked Paul.

All right, you've made your point. Laurel gritted her teeth. She hoped the clerk wouldn't forget the most important detail of all: Darcy and her husband had no relationship with Emma.

Gavin was called next. They'd decided to

save Laurel for last since she had the closest relationship with Emma. Darius asked Gavin to describe his relationship with Mike, Mallory, and Emma, and explain how he and Laurel planned to care for Emma in the future. He painted a glowing picture of what her life would look like.

When Darius was finished, surprisingly, Mr. Groveland had no questions for Gavin.

Laurel traded smiles with her ex-husband as he returned to his seat. He'd done well, and she was optimistic about how the hearing was going.

"I'd like to call Laurel Robinson to the stand," Darius said.

Darius's poised expression buoyed her confidence as she stood on shaky legs and made her way to the stand where she was sworn in.

"Ms. Robinson," Darius said, "you and Mr. Robinson were named guardians in the will of the deceased. Can you tell us about your relationship with the couple?"

"Mallory and I had been best friends since elementary school. She was as close to me as a sister—even when we lived in Asheville, we kept in close contact. When she and Mike married, we became couple-friends. We were very close."

"So you and Emma had a relationship as well?"

"Of course. I was at the hospital when she was born. I saw her every month at least. When Mallory and Mike took an anniversary trip recently, I came to stay with Emma for two nights. I know her routines and what her favorite movie is and which stuffed animal she can't sleep without."

Darius gave her an encouraging smile. "Can you tell me how you and Mr. Robinson plan to care for Emma? Support her?"

"Well, as Gavin mentioned, we feel it's best to keep her routine as normal as possible. I'll continue to stay home with her and run Harvest Moon—the apple orchard Mike and Mallory started." She glanced at the clerk. "I'm a horticulturist by trade. As for the trauma she's been through, we're seeking help for her. She's already begun play therapy with a well-respected psychologist in Asheville. Gavin and I have also been consulting with her. We'll continue to make Emma's care our number-one priority."

"As you know, a shared guardianship would be an unusual situation. Can you tell me why you feel this arrangement would be in Emma's best interest?"

"Of course. Either one of us would be happy to be Emma's sole guardian. But we feel it would be ideal for Emma to have both mother and father figures in her life. Gavin and I work well together. We're on friendly terms. This past month, we've come together and given Emma a stable, nurturing environment. We've kept to her routines, and we'll continue to do so."

"Very good. To sum things up, can you tell

us why you feel you and Mr. Robinson are best suited to be Emma's guardians?"

"First of all, we love her very much, and we have an ongoing relationship with her. She knows us and she loves us too. We're willing and able to put her first. But also, Mallory and Mike obviously felt that way too—that's why they asked us to be her guardians in the first place. In the event that some tragedy took them both, they wanted *us* to raise their daughter, and we don't take that responsibility lightly."

Darius gave her a nod. "Thank you, Ms. Robinson."

Laurel expelled a silent breath.

"I have some questions for the witness." Mr. Groveland rose from his seat and aimed a smile Laurel's way. "I'm sorry for the loss of your friends, Ms. Robinson."

That anchorman smile, if not his position as opposing counsel, put her on guard. "Thank you."

"Could you tell the court how long you and Mr. Robinson were married?"

"Five years."

"And how long have you been divorced?"

"Three years."

"And how often have you met up with Mr. Robinson since the divorce?"

Laurel blinked.

Darius's chair scraped as he stood. "Your Honor, I don't see how this is relevant."

The clerk pushed his glasses into place. "I'll allow it."

"How often have you been in contact with your ex-husband since the divorce."

Laurel swallowed. "We haven't been in contact."

Mr. Groveland's forehead furrowed. "I'm sorry, I just thought—you made it seem as if you were still friends."

Darius stood. "Your Honor, does Mr. Groveland have a question for my client?"

"I apologize. Let me rephrase. Ms. Robinson, if you had no contact with Mr. Robinson after your divorce, can you tell me how you came to be such good friends?"

Laurel's eyes locked on Gavin's face. She needed words. "Um, I hadn't seen my ex-husband in three years. When we heard what happened to Mike and Mallory we immediately came to care for Emma. We've worked well together."

"So after a bitter divorce and three years of radio silence, the two of you now want to raise a child together?"

"It wasn't—yes, but . . ."

"Maybe you'll even magically fall in love again."

Darius stood. "Is there a question there, Your Honor?"

"Withdrawn. No further questions, Your Honor."

"Mr. Walker?" the clerk said.

"No further witnesses, Your Honor."

Wait. This couldn't end here. The momentum had shifted. The case had taken a turn in the Gordons' favor, and it was all her fault. Because of her feeble answers, she and Gavin had come across as the typical embittered exes who'd quibble over who got Emma for Christmas.

But Mr. Groveland was already seating himself behind his table, and closing arguments were about to commence.

"Ms. Robinson," the clerk said. "You may resume your seat."

She stood and dismounted the stand, her legs quaking beneath her. Gavin stared at the table, and for the first time since the hearing had started, a frown creased Darius's brows.

Laurel took her seat, her mind spinning as the closing statements began. Had she blown it? Had she ruined their chances for guardianship? She'd given such lame responses. She could now think of a hundred things she could've added. But she'd been caught off guard and she failed Emma, and now the child would likely be raised by that awful woman. An arrow of terror struck her heart, its poison shooting through her veins in a millisecond.

Laurel was going to lose Emma.

And she was going to lose Gavin too.

". . . Emma deserves more than to be raised in

what would obviously be a loveless arrangement between two acrimoniously divorced people. Mrs. Gordon is not only the child's grandmother, but she clearly offers a warm, loving environment in which to raise Emma. Thank you, Your Honor." Mr. Groveland took his seat.

Darius stood and began his closing statement.

Laurel tried to focus on his recap, but her heartbeat reverberated in her skull, and she struggled to draw breath. She couldn't let this happen. She had to do something, and fast.

"Your Honor?" she blurted.

Darius stopped midsentence and jerked his head her way.

Gavin stiffened in his seat.

"I'm sorry to interrupt." She stood and addressed the clerk. "Is—is it too late to make a statement?"

The clerk tilted his head. "Certainly not. Go ahead, Ms. Robinson."

"Thank you." A hush fell over the courtroom. Fear sucked the moisture from her mouth. The heat of every gaze in the room converged like a laser on the back of her head. But that didn't matter. All that mattered was that she set the record straight.

"I—I realize that after a divorce and long period apart, it might seem unlikely that my relationship with Gavin is friendly and warm or conducive to co-parenting a child." Her voice trembled. She took a breath, looking directly into the clerk's eyes. "But the truth is . . . we would do anything for Emma. We love her that much. I wish I could just give you a little glimpse of how we care for her day to day. How Gavin reads her as many books as it takes till she falls asleep. How we talk to her about her mom and dad to help her understand what happened. And how we remind her daily of how much her mommy and daddy loved her." She blinked against the sting of tears. "I wish Emma was old enough to make this decision for herself, because if she were . . . she'd choose Gavin and me."

The room was so quiet she could hear the hum of the air-conditioning. The tick of a wall clock. The buzzing of the fluorescent lights.

She glanced down at Gavin. Tears had gathered in his eyes. Her feelings for him welled inside, a flood of feelings she'd happily drown in.

Unable to face him for this next part, she pulled her gaze away. Adrenaline coursed through her body, making her stomach turn. Bringing to the surface her most deeply rooted fear. She was about to face it head-on, because the alternative—losing Emma and Gavin—was intolerable.

She cleared her throat, pulled herself erect, and dug deep for courage. "I can promise you there's no acrimony between us. And I disagree with Mr. Groveland on yet another point: I will not magically fall in love with my ex-husband."

A quiet murmur rose.

In her peripheral vision Gavin lowered his head.

Laurel waited. One shaky breath. Then two. "The truth is, Your Honor, I never *stopped* loving him."

The murmurs grew louder, but she was only aware of Gavin, rising slowly to his feet beside her. A weighted silence pierced the courtroom.

"The same is true for me, Your Honor."

Her breath escaped in a puff of disbelief. Through her blurry vision, she met his teary gaze.

He took her hand, brought it to his lips, and brushed her knuckles with a soft kiss. His warm blue eyes expressed even more than the gesture ever could. "I was afraid to tell you. Afraid you didn't feel the same."

"I do. I love you so much."

"I love you too." He brushed her lips with a soft kiss.

"Your Honor," Mr. Groveland said. "This grandstanding is offensive to the court. May we please get on with this hearing?"

Gavin continued as if the opposing counsel hadn't spoken at all. "Marry me, Laurel. Give me another chance and I'll prove I can love you better this time. I want to raise Emma with you. I want us to be a real family."

A buoyant feeling filled her from the tips of her toes to the top of her head. The reservation she'd felt at his first proposal was absent this time. She was ready to trust him this time in a way she hadn't before. She beamed. "Yes. I want all that too."

"Your Honor!" Mr. Groveland bellowed.

"Mr. Groveland, if you can't appreciate rekindled love perhaps it's time to hang up your hat. I, for one, am a big fan. Is there anything else you'd like to say, Ms. Robinson?"

Laurel tore her gaze from Gavin's. "Oh, uh, no, Your Honor. Thank you."

She and Gavin took their seats and he clamped his hand around hers.

"Mr. Walker, the floor is yours again. You may proceed with your closing statement."

Darius quirked a grin. "I don't believe I could give a more eloquent closing than the one already provided, Your Honor. So if it pleases the court, I'll turn the floor over for your decision."

"Very well then."

Please God. Please God. They were the only words her brain could formulate.

"Guardianship cases are always difficult." The clerk shoved his glasses onto the bridge of his nose. "There are two petitions here, and all involved seem to care about the child. It's my job to decide which of these situations would better serve her, and it's a duty I don't take lightly. I can only hope that all gathered in this courtroom want the same thing: a safe and loving home for Emma. And in this case, I believe Emma's interests would best be served as a ward of Mr. and Ms. Robinson, so I hereby grant them general guardianship."

Laurel clutched her chest. *Thank You, God!*

Gavin grabbed her around the shoulders and pulled her close. "Thank God."

The clerk continued. "I presume the two of you will now be sharing one household?"

"Yes, Your Honor," Gavin said with a wide smile.

"Very well," the clerk continued. "I also think a relationship between the child and maternal grandmother would be in the ward's best interest. And so, I hereby grant the Gordons visitation rights on the last Saturday of each month. Court is adjourned." He rapped his gavel.

The gavel had no sooner dropped than the entire Robinson clan descended upon them. Gavin couldn't have been more thrilled. But after a good five minutes of celebration, there was only one thing he wanted: a moment alone with Laurel. With the woman who—if he hadn't dreamed it all up—had just agreed to marry him in front of a courtroom full of people.

He took Laurel's hand and pulled her from the throng. She followed him down the hallway, where he took the first turn.

"Where are we going?" Laurel asked.

"Someplace my nosy family won't find us."

"Gavin." Her chuckle contradicted her chiding tone.

"Hurry. Mom'll be hot on our heels."

At the end of the hall he made an abrupt turn into a quiet alcove, put Laurel's back to the wall, then peeked around the corner. "Coast is clear."

She gave him a wry grin. "What are you doing?"

"Getting you alone, that's what I'm doing." He homed in on her beautiful eyes. The shutters were gone—he could see all the way to her heart now. His own heart bucked in his chest. "You said some things in there."

"So did you."

He searched her eyes, loving the warmth radiating from them. "I meant every word. I never stopped loving you, Laurel. And I promise not to let you down this time."

She framed his face. "I love you, Gavin. We won't let each other down."

A smile still on his lips, he brushed her mouth with his. The kiss quickly escalated. He pulled her close. She threaded her fingers into his hair. And when she made a little mewling sound, he nudged her lips open for more.

She surrendered to his kiss, returning his passion with equal fervor. He couldn't get enough of this woman. He would never be so careless with her again. His head was filled with helium, his blood with fire. He left her mouth only long enough to drop a trail of kisses down her jaw and along her neck.

"Gavin," someone called from a distant galaxy.

He made his way back to her mouth, hungry for more.

"Laurel?" another voice called.

"Go away," he murmured against her mouth. When her lips parted in a smile he took full advantage and delighted in her needy gasp. She tasted so good. He would never stop kissing her.

"Gavin . . ." Laurel whispered.

"Shhh." He nibbled at her lips.

She chuckled. "Gavin . . . they're coming."

Sure enough, footsteps were growing louder. Voices too.

"Where'd they run off to?"

"Just text him."

"I already did. He's not answering."

Breathless, Gavin set his forehead against hers. "I'm gonna kill 'em."

Laurel leaned back, smoothed his hair down, then straightened his tie. "Be nice. They're just happy for us."

When she stepped away, he caught her around the waist and pulled her back against him. "If they're really happy for us they'll offer to baby-sit for our honeymoon, which will last about a decade because that's how long it'll take to get my fill of you."

Her eyes flared with heat—and there was that look that used to knock him right off his feet. He pulled her closer.

"Behave, Robinson."

His family—every last one of 'em—rounded the corner and came up short at the sight of them.

"Oh, there you are," Mom said.

Reluctantly, Gavin let Laurel go.

"We thought we'd go out to celebrate." Avery arched a brow. "But looks like you got a head start."

Gavin scowled. "Which you interrupted, by the way."

Laurel elbowed him. "We'd love to go. How about the Trailhead? We can swing by the house and pick up Emma and my mom on the way."

"Wonderful idea!" Mom said.

Jeff tugged Mom's hand. "We'll go now and grab a table."

The group headed back the way they'd come.

"See you there," Laurel called, then grabbed Gavin's hand. "Come on, grumpy. Let's go tell Emma we're her forever family."

The words caught him by the heart. *Emma.* She was really theirs. They were going to raise that sweet little girl. They were going to be a real family.

Gavin returned her smile. "Well . . . when you put it like that."

Epilogue

Laurel slipped inside the back of the Robinsons' house, the music fading as the door closed behind her. She carried the empty glasses to the sink and paused to watch the shindig going on in the backyard.

A small crowd had gathered for Avery and Wes's wedding reception: family, close friends, Avery's staff from the clinic. Speaking of which, on the makeshift dance floor, Lucy, Avery's doctor in residence, was getting down with her boyfriend, Rick Rodriguez.

A little distance away the newlywed couple was finding their own groove. Avery was beautiful in her sophisticated white gown, her veil long gone. She and Wes made a gorgeous couple. They'd come through a lot to be together, and Laurel was so happy they'd found their way to each other.

Not far away, Cooper danced more reservedly with a very pregnant Katie. Her blue bridesmaid dress fit like a glove, outlining her generous baby bump—a boy. The two of them had eyes only for each other. They fit together like two puzzle pieces.

That little wave of jealousy she used to feel toward the woman had faded months ago in the wake of Gavin's extravagant love. The way he held Laurel, the way he looked at her, the way he loved her every day soothed her insecurity.

Her gaze drifted across the floor to where her husband, holding Emma in his arms, was dancing like a fool. Emma laughed at his antics, and Laurel found herself smiling too. Two days after the hearing they'd remarried in an intimate ceremony, surrounded by family. It had been a beautiful day.

The past seven months had been an adjustment, but their little family was running along pretty smoothly. Emma had made great strides. She progressed with her potty training and was sleeping through the night again. She still mentioned her mom and dad often, and each time Laurel and Gavin took the opportunity to remind her of her parents' love. To reminisce about Mike and Mallory, to keep their memory alive for Emma.

In December Paul and Judy had moved into a senior living community in Riverbend. The initial months were difficult as Judy adjusted to her new surroundings. But she was doing better now, and the two of them spent time with Emma frequently.

In January Laurel and Gavin had started the adoption process—they were on track to become her legal parents by July. In April they'd gone to visit Patty and her new husband in Florida.

Emma had enjoyed playing in the sand and riding in her aunt's sailboat.

Laurel's mom had resumed her role as nana in a way that surprised Laurel. She and Brad were regular visitors in their home these days.

Darcy had yet to pursue her visitation rights.

Laurel was enjoying her work in the orchard. Each season brought its own rewards, and tending the land that Mallory had treasured was a labor of love.

Gavin was leaning into his new business, and it was well off the ground. He'd officially quit his position at the campground. They'd bought a renovated house near town from which they ran Robinson Construction. They had one custom home completed, one in process, and another on the drawing board. Most importantly, Gavin seemed happy to have returned to his calling.

On the dance floor her husband lowered Emma in a deep dip. When he raised her up again, she laughed. Laurel loved watching them together.

She and Gavin had grown so close since that hearing in the fall. Closer than they'd ever been before. They formed the kind of bond only two wounded survivors could enjoy. Her eyes stung as she focused on the man she had never stopped loving.

Thank You, God. Sometimes she couldn't believe the way He'd brought them through the fire and out the other side, happier and healthier than they'd ever been before.

The patio door opened, and the boisterous music flooded inside.

Laurel blinked back tears as Lisa entered, carrying an armload of empty cups. Speaking of relationships that had come a long way . . .

"It's getting crazy out there!" Lisa said. "I can see why you beat a hasty retreat."

"Guess I needed a quiet moment."

"Well, a moment's all you'll get. I was asked to come find you." Lisa set the dishes in the sink. "Your dancing partner wants you back."

"My feet are killing me."

Lisa gave her a sideways hug. "Told you to go with the flats. I hear the happy couple's leaving soon, so you'd better go claim one last dance. Jeff's already getting the sparklers ready—I get a terrible feeling every time a Robinson man mixes matches and fireworks."

"Oh boy."

"Those boys better behave tonight!"

Laurel laughed as she slipped out the door. "I'll pass the word along."

She made her way through the milling crowd, and just as she stepped onto the dance floor, the song segued into a slow melody. Laurel stepped up to her family and put her arms around her husband and Emma, who looked adorable in a wispy silver princess dress.

Gavin's eyes softened as they fell on Laurel. "There you are. I've been looking all over for you."

"I was in the house. Your mom sent me out."

"Gabin dancing with me."

"I saw him dip you all the way to the floor."

"He won't drop me."

"No, he'd never do that."

Cooper tapped Gavin on the shoulder. "My turn. Come on, little bug. You haven't danced with me all night."

She held out her arms. "Dance with Cooper!"

Gavin handed the girl over. "She might fall asleep on you. It's way past her bedtime."

"Not a chance."

"Don't drop me," Emma told Cooper, then started giggling as he spun around like a top gone mad.

Laurel turned her attention to her husband and settled into his arms. He was so handsome tonight in his navy-blue suit and silver tie. He'd recently gotten his hair trimmed, and his face was so clean-shaven she wanted to kiss his jaw just to feel the smooth skin against her lips.

"Better stop that, Jenkins."

"Stop what?"

"Staring at me like that. A man's only got so much willpower, and that dress alone is about to drive me mad."

She batted her lashes. "This little ol' thing?"

He pulled her closer, growling in her ear. "You're a minx. And I'm going to make you pay later."

"Promise?"

His warning chuckle sent a shiver down her arms. Emma was spending the night with Cooper and Katie again—the kid was in love with Scout, the puppy they'd adopted from the pound a few months ago.

Gavin held Laurel tightly as the chorus swelled around them. Laurel closed her eyes and just took it all in. The masculine smell of him. The strength of his arms wrapped around her. The whisper of his breath against her temples.

Sometimes she marveled that they were back together again. That they were so happy. She opened her eyes, gazing up at the dark sky, and thought of Mike and Mallory. Laurel hoped they could see them right now.

"What's on your mind, Mrs. Robinson?" Gavin asked suggestively.

She chuckled. "Not what you think."

He drew away and their gazes tangled together, his growing more serious. "What is it? Something wrong?"

"I was just thinking about Mike and Mallory. Us, and how we're together again . . ."

His lips turned up at the corners. "Kinda crazy, huh?"

"Yeah, it's pretty crazy."

"Crazy good." He caught her chin and swept her lips with his.

The gentle touch turned into a sweeping kiss. In the wake of his efforts Laurel forgot everything around her. All she could think of was this man. This marriage. She was overwhelmed by the blessings in her life. Overwhelmed by the love of this amazing man.

He pulled away, their hot breaths mingling between them. The music faded to an end.

Just then a firework exploded. Then another. Brilliant blooms of red and white filled the sky.

"Oh, good grief." Lisa called over the sudden hush on the lawn, "What have you guys done? Jeff! You know what happened last time!"

Gavin chuckled as he turned Laurel to face away from him, wrapped his arms around her waist, and set his head on top of hers to watch the display. Another *boom* sounded and a green bloom burst over the night sky.

"Exactly what did happen last time?" Laurel asked.

"Well, it involved Jeff, Cooper, me, a bottle rocket, and a trip to the ER." He shrugged. "You know us."

"What have I gotten myself into?"

"Too late now." He squeezed her and pressed a kiss to that ticklish spot in the cradle of her neck.

She lifted her shoulder and chuckled. "Stop that."

"You know what that husky laugh of yours does to me. How about we sneak out of here while everyone's distracted. Get started on that project we talked about."

Laurel curved her lips into a smile. They were officially ready to expand their family. "What about Emma?"

"I already gave her overnight bag to Coop. We'll stop and tell her good-bye on the way out. Come on." He grabbed her hand and led her around the outskirts toward Cooper and Emma. Once there, they gave the girl kisses and told her they'd see her tomorrow.

Cooper gave Laurel a wink as Gavin dragged her away at a fast clip.

"Wait," she said. "What about Avery and Wes—we're supposed to see them off with sparklers?"

"You see the happy couple anywhere? That was just a ruse."

She glanced over her shoulder at the group—no bride and groom in sight. "They snuck out of their own reception?"

He just laughed and pulled her toward his truck where he opened the passenger door and helped her inside. When she was settled he pressed a kiss on her lips, his blue eyes sparkling down at her. "Now you know exactly what you've gotten yourself into."

Acknowledgments

Bringing a book to market takes a lot of effort from many different people. I'm so incredibly blessed to partner with the fabulous team at HarperCollins Christian Fiction, led by publisher Amanda Bostic: Patrick Aprea, Kimberly Carlton, Caitlin Halstead, Jodi Hughes, Margaret Kercher, Becky Monds, Kerri Potts, Nekasha Pratt, Anna Sudberry, Savannah Summers, Taylor Ward, LaChelle Washington, and Laura Wheeler.

Not to mention all the wonderful sales reps and amazing people in the rights department—special shout-out to Robert Downs!

Thanks especially to my editor Kimberly Carlton. Your incredible insight and inspiration help me take the story deeper, and for that I am so grateful! Thanks also to my line editor, Julee Schwarzburg, whose attention to detail makes me look like a better writer than I really am.

I was blessed with a lot of assistance on the legalities of guardianship. Reader Daphne Woodall was nothing short of a research assistant as she tracked down the help I needed. Bless you, Daphne! Yancy Washington, Clerk of Superior Court in Granville County, North Carolina, was an enormous help. Terri Lawson, Assistant Clerk of Superior Court in Catawba County, North Carolina, provided additional information. I'm so grateful for their help! It's critical for an author to have all the details straight, even when she decides to take artistic license in an area or two—as I did with this story.

Author Colleen Coble is my first reader and sister of my heart. Thank you, friend! This writing journey has been ever so much more fun because of you.

I'm grateful to my agent, Karen Solem, who's able to somehow make sense of the legal garble of contracts and, even more amazing, help me understand it.

To my husband, Kevin, who has supported my dreams in every way possible—I'm so grateful! To all our kiddos: Chad, Trevor and Babette, and Justin and Hannah, who have favored us with two beautiful granddaughters. Every stage of parenthood has been a grand adventure, and I look forward to all the wonderful memories we have yet to make!

A hearty thank-you to all the booksellers who make room on their shelves for my books—I'm deeply indebted! And to all the book bloggers and reviewers, whose passion for fiction is contagious—thank you!

Lastly, thank you, friends, for letting me share this story with you! I wouldn't be doing this without you. Your notes, posts, and reviews keep me going on the days when writing doesn't flow so easily. I appreciate your support more than you know.

I enjoy connecting with friends on my Facebook page: www.facebook.com/authordenisehunter. Please pop over and say hello. Visit my website at www.DeniseHunterBooks.com or just drop me a note at Deniseahunter@comcast.net. I'd love to hear from you!

Discussion Questions

1. Who was your favorite character in *Harvest Moon* and why?

2. How were you feeling initially as Laurel and Gavin were forced to care for Emma together? Have you ever been stuck with a person who hurt you? How did you handle it?

3. Discuss why Laurel and Gavin each felt compelled to be there for Emma. How did their past wounds affect this decision?

4. How did you feel about having a glimpse into Laurel and Gavin's former relationship via flashbacks? What light did that shed on their present-day story?

5. Discuss how the death of their son tore Laurel and Gavin apart. What might they have done differently to save their marriage? What aspects of their past kept this from happening?

6. After the divorce, Gavin settled for a job at a campground even though he was capable

of more. Even after starting his own business he faltered a bit. Why do you think that might be? Have you ever settled for less than what you were capable of? Why do you think that is?

7. At one point Laurel admits to herself that she needs to end her relationship with Gavin because she can't bear waiting for the other shoe to drop. Discuss why Laurel had such difficulty trusting Gavin throughout their relationship. At what point do you think she finally laid that aside?

8. Throughout the Riverbend Romance series, Gavin has dealt with guilt over the death of his son. How was Emma's presence and Laurel's reappearance in his life healing for him?

9. How did you feel about the role of the Robinson family in this story? Did you understand their unfavorable feelings toward Laurel, or were you impatient to see them give up their grudge?

10. Name some ways in which Laurel has changed since her marriage and divorce. How has Gavin changed? Do you think they're now capable of having a healthy marriage?

About the Author

Denise Hunter is the internationally published, bestselling author of more than forty books, three of which have been adapted into original Hallmark Channel movies. She has won the Holt Medallion Award, the Reader's Choice Award, the Carol Award, the Foreword Book of the Year Award, and is a RITA finalist. When Denise isn't orchestrating love lives on the written page, she enjoys traveling with her family, drinking chai lattes, and playing drums. Denise makes her home in Indiana, where she and her husband raised three boys and are now enjoying an empty nest and two beautiful granddaughters.

DeniseHunterBooks.com
Facebook: @AuthorDeniseHunter
Twitter: @DeniseAHunter
Instagram: @deniseahunter

Center Point Large Print
600 Brooks Road / PO Box 1
Thorndike, ME 04986-0001 USA

(207) 568-3717

US & Canada:
1 800 929-9108
www.centerpointlargeprint.com